Distorted Perceptions

Paula Puddephatt

Published by Paula Puddephatt, 2020.

This is a work of fiction. Similarities to real people, places, or events are entirely coincidental.

DISTORTED PERCEPTIONS

First edition. April 10, 2020.

Copyright © 2020 Paula Puddephatt.

ISBN: 979-8215417478

Written by Paula Puddephatt.

Introduction

Distorted Perceptions, in its original form, was a novel which I began at the age of eighteen. I wrote it, on and off, in extremely difficult circumstances, until finally forced to give up, when I became severely depressed, at twenty-six. I'd almost completed my first draft, at the time.

For many subsequent years, I worked on other writing projects, and was prolific as a poet, but *Distorted Perceptions* has never left my heart.

I started to write it again in recent years, but from scratch, since I could only find parts of the original outline, which had pages missing, and none of my previous manuscripts or notes. Anything that is worded as it was before, would literally have to be some part of the novel that I remembered, having read it over so many times. The opening paragraph is, I believe, close to the original.

I retained most of the original plot, although for many parts, had to go by memory alone for the details. I changed a few aspects, which in itself, presented issues. Still more alterations occurred, as I wrote - some of which were major. I did try to stay as true as I could to what I felt, in my heart, my eighteen- to twenty-six-year-old self would have intended, since I do see it as her story, first and foremost. However, the ending changed drastically.

There are strong autobiographical elements, but it is by no means an autobiography or memoir, and should not be read as such. However, I have used the novel as therapy, and it has helped me to work through many of the painful events in my own life.

The novel doesn't fit neatly into any genre or category. This is perhaps appropriate, as I have never fitted in, either.

The story is dedicated to all who have believed in and supported me. You know who you are.

Chapter One

I first met Kev Tanner in September 1983, at my brother, Danny's, twenty-first. I was seventeen, at the time. My eldest brother, Matthew, was twenty-five, and my sisters, Catherine and Sarah, aged nineteen and fourteen, respectively.

I was helping my mother and younger sister to prepare for the party, which had mainly involved rearranging the furniture, in order to create a "dance floor" in our living room, and identifying valuable items, which would need to be moved to comparative safety.

We were currently in the, thankfully decent-sized, kitchen, sorting out the food and drink. The dining room table, covered with a russet table cloth, had been temporarily moved there. That table held the food, and the smaller, Formica breakfast table, the drinks: primarily cans, of both the alcoholic, and soft drink, varieties.

Sarah looked the most like our mother: tall and slender, with glossy, raven-black hair which, in my sister's case, was almost waist-length. I'd never strongly resembled Mum, or any of my siblings. My red hair came from Dad's side. In truth, I'd always felt like the ugly sister, compared to both Catherine and Sarah.

Mum had, incredibly, agreed to go to her sister's for the evening, trusting us to "behave like responsible adults", and not smash the place up in her absence. As *if*, right?

Not that I particularly cared. I wasn't exactly in the mood for partying. And it made me feel physically sick, each time I thought about the reason why - each time I remembered.

"And you say Fiona definitely *has* this banner, Sarah?"

"Yes, Mum. I told you that before."

"So, where *is* she?"

"I'm sure she'll be here soon. I think Tracy's dad is bringing them both."

"Well, I hope they're here before Daniel. It might not be a surprise party as such, but it would still be nice to have the 'Happy Birthday' banner up before he and Hannah arrive. I know I should have made more food. Look at all these cans of beer. It's a disaster waiting to happen: a lot of young people, getting drunk, without any decent food inside them."

I looked at the plates, piled high with sandwiches, quiche, and sausage rolls. Only *Mum* would worry that she should have "made more food" - but I knew better than to point this out. It wasn't *about* the food.

"I'm sure everyone will be sensible," said Sarah, "and it *is* Danny's twenty-first. We couldn't *not* have alcohol."

"Of course, *you* won't be drinking anything alcoholic, Sarah. Technically, Lucy shouldn't either, since you're both underage, but I'm not totally naive, and really, you youngsters are beyond me. However, I do draw the line at fourteen-year-olds drinking. It's not happening under this roof."

Yeah, right. I couldn't imagine Sarah drinking, even when she finally did reach eighteen. She was a complete angel, bless her - didn't take after either Cath or myself, that was for sure.

"Mum," I said, endeavouring to control my temper, "won't Sylvia be expecting you?"

"Not for another hour or so. I told her I had to help the two of you - well, and Catherine too, except that she isn't here yet. I don't know what's keeping her."

"Probably flirting with some guy," I suggested.

"She can't always get off work on time," said Sarah, her tone defensive. She always saw the best in everyone, and I loved her for that.

"And please remember to *be surprised* when Daniel and Hannah announce their engagement," said Mum.

"Yeah, biggest surprise of all-time. Seriously, Hannah Jackson is just about the most boring person I've ever met. Nice enough, but totally, mind-numbingly boring." I visualised Hannah, with her long, light brown hair, wearing that awful beige cardigan of hers. "I mean, remember that girl Danny used to go out with, Melanie someone or other? His taste has certainly changed."

Sarah frowned. "Well, I'm thrilled for them both. They seem really happy. I don't know why you're always so mean about Hannah, Lucy. I think she's lovely."

"You just like everyone."

"No, I don't. Anyway, what's wrong with liking people?"

"Nothing, if they're *worth* liking."

"All right, girls - that's enough. Lucy, Sarah's right. Hannah's a polite, sweet-natured girl. Believe me - I, for one, am delighted that she and your brother are getting married. She's certainly a much better influence than girls like that Melanie, and I'm relieved Daniel's finally settling down. You know, you still haven't confirmed whether James will be coming." That was my mother for you. The woman didn't know when to shut up.

I finally lost it. "I don't give a damn about James McIntyre, and whether he comes or not. He chucked me, okay? Satisfied? So, you won't be getting any more marriage announcements tonight. Now, I'm going to my room, and if you need any more help, you'll have to wait for Catherine to show up, if she can be bothered. And *don't* tell me not to slam the door. I am *not* a kid."

And yes, I slammed it.

***

She gave me five minutes, before tapping on the bedroom door.

"Come in, Sarah."

It had to be my sister, as Mum would simply have barged in. Sarah had the decency to knock, even though we shared a room, and she was effectively knocking on her own bedroom door.

"I knew something was wrong." Sarah sat down next to me, on my bed. "You've been quiet for weeks. Are you sure James meant to finish with you? You've had rows before."

"Well, I thought I might have misunderstood, to begin with, but he hasn't been returning my calls. Then, I saw him in town, with a group of his mates from work, and he blanked me, so I don't know what to think, but it's not looking good. Just do one thing for me, okay? Don't be nice to me. I'll bloody cry, and I'm sick of crying."

Sarah looked so confused, that I felt guilty for making the one request of her, with which she couldn't possibly comply. "I love you, Lucy. I'm here for you."

Well, that finished me off, naturally. I broke down completely, and allowed my fourteen-year-old sister to hold me, and gently stroke my hair. "It's okay. It's okay to cry. I think you're wonderful. If James McIntyre really doesn't love you, he must be crazy. You're better off without him."

"I'm not, though. I love him so much. I've always loved him - since we were kids. I won't ever get over him, Sarah - not ever. I don't care what anyone says. I'll love him until I die, and I won't even try to get over him, because I can't."

"I know, Luce. I know you love him. You're all right. Everything's going to be fine."

I didn't contradict her, because it hurt to get the words out, and I was beginning to lose my voice, anyway. I just sobbed in her arms, like a baby.

"Is he seeing anyone else?" asked Sarah, at length.

"I don't know." I'd calmed down, by this point, but all the crying had left me feeling shattered. "I don't think so."

"Then there's hope."

"You really think so?"

"Yes, I do."

I smiled at her, weakly. I wanted to believe her. I wanted to so badly that, for one insane moment, I actually almost did.

The front door opened and slammed. Catherine talked briefly to Mum, before heading upstairs. The last thing I needed right then was to deal with my elder sister, but there was no avoiding it.

"Congratulate me, then. I've just achieved what clearly neither of you could manage."

In those days, Catherine had shoulder-length, blonde-from-a-bottle, permed hair, and wore ridiculous quantities of jewellery - an eclectic mix of gold, silver, and fashion jewellery.

"Congratulations. What's this one's name, or did you not catch it?"

"Oh, very funny, Lucy. For your information, I persuaded Mum to leave for her sister's."

"'Bye, girls! Have fun!"

"We will, Mum! You, too!" called Catherine.

Following which, the front door duly slammed. As simple as that.

"See?" said Catherine. "Now, what would you do without me?"

"Well, we've actually done quite a bit without you," I pointed out. "As in, pretty much everything really. Apart from, admittedly, getting rid of our mother. Credit where due, but you've not exactly done much, in the grand scheme of things, have you?"

"We *do* appreciate your help though, Cath," added Sarah.

"Thanks. At least *someone* appreciates my invaluable contribution around here, Lucy Ryman." She studied me for a moment. "You've been crying again. No prizes for guessing who *that's* over."

"Don't have a go at Lucy. She's really upset. You can be completely insensitive at times." Somehow, Sarah's extreme understatement about Catherine's being "insensitive at times" annoyed me almost more than my elder sister's "insensitivity", which was certainly to be expected.

"I wouldn't expect *you* to understand, Catherine," I said. "It's not as if you've ever cared much about any of the guys you so readily get off with. I still have to work with Amy Clark, after you decided it would be a bit of fun to screw her fiance."

"Oh, get real. It does take two, you know, and Rupert wasn't exactly complaining. Anyway, their little engagement is back on, isn't it?"

"I believe so, yes."

"All's well, then. What's the big deal?"

"I'm not even *answering* that," I told her.

"Don't, then. The subject's boring anyway, if you ask me. It's ridiculous to get engaged so young, and it's not as if Amy's even pregnant. I thought Danny and Hannah were bad, but at least they waited until they were *just about* in their twenties."

"I don't know. That's kind of cynical," said Sarah, playing with a strand of her hair. "How about romance?"

"Romance is dead," I told her. "Interesting, that. I think there's finally something I agree with Catherine about."

"Well, it's a pity you don't listen to me more. You might actually learn something."

"I doubt it - nothing I want to know, anyway."

"Whatever. Sarah, can I borrow your mascara?" It wasn't really a question, as she'd grabbed it already.

"Sure," replied Sarah, even though her response was irrelevant.

"It's not exactly as if he's moping around over you, is it?" Catherine stood in front of the full-length mirror, expertly applying Sarah's mascara, even though there was no real point, as my elder sister would inevitably redo all of her make-up, after changing into whatever she planned to wear later.

For my part, I wasn't bothering with any of that. The navy trousers and cream silk blouse, which I'd been wearing all day at work, would be fine. So what if I stank of sweat? A quick squirt of perfume should fix that and, if it didn't, too bad.

Sarah looked distressed. "Catherine, please don't. I don't think it's even true."

"What do you mean?" I had a horrible, slightly sick feeling, at the back of my throat, and felt momentarily dizzy. I'd barely registered Catherine's words at first, but Sarah's reaction had forced me to do so. "Will one of you tell me what the hell you're talking about?"

"Lucy, it's probably not even true. You told me that, as far as you know, James isn't seeing anyone else. I'm sure, if he was, he'd have told you," reasoned Sarah.

"I can't believe you haven't heard about James and Erica by now. It's all over town," said Catherine. "Everyone knows."

"Erica who?"

"Erica Lee."

"Catherine, she's a lesbian," I pointed out, exasperated, but also relieved. It was just Cath, talking out of her backside. Erica Lee had been living with our cousin, Tara, until roughly six months ago.

"Ever heard of bisexuality?"

"Yeah, right - whatever you say. Anyway, she's *way* too old for James. She must *be* about thirty. It's ridiculous."

"Twenty-seven, but yes, I see your point," said Catherine. "There *is* an age gap."

"I don't think James would go out with a twenty-seven-year-old, either," said Sarah. "Anyway, he's in love with Lucy."

"Yeah, so much so that he's basically finished with her," remarked Catherine. "And it really *is* all over town - about him and Erica."

"*Is* it, Sarah?" I asked, trying to keep my voice neutral. Some chance. My heart was thudding, and I was on the verge of tears again - seemingly my usual state, these days.

"No, I don't think so. I'm sure Catherine was exaggerating." Sarah was fiddling more than usual with her hair, as she generally did when nervous.

"But you heard it too, didn't you?" I pressed, even though I wasn't sure why. I didn't want confirmation that this rumour, true or false, had been "all over town", and that I, like the complete idiot I clearly was, had been the last to know. And I didn't want to bully Sarah over this either, and make her feel bad. It was hardly *her* fault. Yet, I couldn't seem to stop myself. Couldn't let this go. "Who told you, Sarah?"

"Tracy."

"Tracy? Where the hell would she hear something like that? Kids in your year can't be that interested in James and Erica, surely?"

"Her sister, I think."

"Tracy's *sister*? And where did she...? No, on second thoughts, I don't think we need to go there. I get the picture." My mind was racing, and I knew I couldn't leave this - do nothing at all. "Listen, I need to talk to Matt about something. I'm going to see if I can catch him."

"Matt?" Sarah looked confused. "I don't know if he'll be home from work yet, but in any case, he's going to be here later. You can talk to him then."

"He isn't coming over until pretty late. I really need to ask him something, and I'd rather not do it over the phone. It will only take fifteen minutes, to walk over there. I might be able to catch Charlotte, too." Charlotte, my best friend, who would also be at the party.

But I caught Sarah's eye, and she understood. Our eldest brother, Matthew, and his partner, Clare, lived very close to the McIntyres, and Charlotte and her mother were next-door neighbours to the McIntyre family. I probably *would* drop in on both Matthew and Charlotte, whilst in the vicinity.

My glare, in Catherine's direction, dared her to say a word, and for once, she kept her mouth shut.

Chapter Two

The McIntyres' back garden was directly opposite to Matt and Clare's, and a tarmac alleyway led to both gardens, effectively making them more or less neighbours, despite the fact that technically Matt and Clare lived in Newton Lane, and the McIntyres, Greenfield Road.

I knew this neighbourhood well, because our family had lived in Matt's current home, which my father still owned, until I was nine years old, when we'd moved to our somewhat larger house. Ironically, Dad himself had moved out, within a couple of months. He lived, at present, in a two bedroom flat, with his ridiculously young girlfriend, and their two kids.

I tapped on the back door, which was duly opened by ten-year-old Rachel, the elder of James McIntyre's two younger sisters.

"Hi, Rachel," I said, forcing a slight smile. "Is your brother around?"

In spite of being a child of ten, and as such, somewhat smaller than myself, Rachel still managed to look down at me somehow, through those gold-rimmed spectacles of hers. "Hello, Lucy. I think so, but I'm not sure if I'm supposed to let you-"

"Rachel, who is it, dear? If it's the Jehovah's Witnesses again, can you please inform them that your father is a vicar for the Methodist Church, and that we are simply *not* interested?"

"Mum, it's Lucy - the one James used to go out with!" I loved the way she explained that, as if her mother might not know which *particular* Lucy she referred to otherwise - and she was clearly enjoying the "used to go out with" aspect. Rachel McIntyre was very much her mother's daughter.

Elizabeth McIntyre, for her part, was there so fast, and pushing her, slightly bemused, daughter unceremoniously out of the way. "I shall deal with this, Rachel. Go upstairs, and play with your sister."

"Shall I find out if James wants to-?"

"Rachel, go and play with Tina. I shall deal with the situation," reiterated the tall woman, with short, grey hair, her tone of voice authoritative.

"Mrs. McIntyre," I said, once Rachel had disappeared, "please can I speak to James? I've tried phoning several times, and he's apparently never at home. Rachel offered to ask him if he wanted to see me. He *is* here, isn't he?"

"Yes, he is. He's in his room, listening to whatever racket your generation listen to, on that personal stereo of his."

I actually smiled, visualising James lying on his bed, listening to his Walkman. I wondered what tape he was listening to - which particular track. "That's great. So, can I see him, please?"

"I don't think that's a good idea, do you? The fact is, James doesn't want to see you. He has a new girlfriend now. You must surely have heard. Lovely young woman. He met her at work."

I couldn't believe what I was hearing. "Are you actually telling me you *approve* of your eighteen-year-old son going out with a twenty-seven-year-old?"

"I wasn't sure when I first heard, but Erica is such an intelligent, well-mannered girl." She didn't say "unlike you", but she may as well have done.

"Can you just tell him I'm here, and let him make up his own mind?"

"My son has already made up his mind, Lucy. He doesn't want to see you any more. I would appreciate it if you didn't come here again - and in particular, would request that you don't approach via the back garden. I keep telling Stanley we must do something about that gate. Even the Jehovah's Witnesses, Mormons, and double-glazing salesmen, seem under the impression, that it's acceptable to enter our back garden, and hammer on the living room door."

I was officially in the same category as Jehovah's Witnesses, Mormons, and double-glazing salesmen. Marvellous. And I had no idea whether James had really indicated that he didn't want to see me. His mother had certainly never liked me, and was fully capable of lying, in order to prevent me from coming into contact with her precious son.

But maybe that wasn't it at all. Maybe he *didn't* want to see me. I had no way of knowing, and there wasn't, in any case, much I could do about it right then, so I muttered the nearest I could manage to a pleasantry, and turned away, before Elizabeth McIntyre could notice how close I was to tears. Not that it would bother *her*.

Did she really hate me that much? So much so, that she preferred to see James with someone like Erica Lee? And how the hell had Erica managed to get on Elizabeth's good side?

My head was spinning, and having momentarily considered heading straight for either Matt's or Charlotte's, I found myself wandering down the alleyway, and past the block of garages, belonging to residents of both Newton Lane and Greenfield Road.

So, there I was, back at my old school, of all places, sneaking through a gap in the wire mesh fence - an increasingly difficult feat, given that I'd put on more weight than I liked to think about, since leaving the dump. And of course, when I'd actually been at school, the gate to our playing field would have been open, so clambering through broken fences hadn't been an essential part of the process, for the most part - apart from after school, and at weekends.

Considering that no one was supposed to be there, it was fairly busy. A couple, in their mid-thirties, were walking a Yorkshire terrier. A gang of kids, possibly pupils from the school, were hanging around, smoking, and drinking cans of Stella and Strongbow. And a few other people were wandering around. It was probably more popular, as a venue, than some of the actual parks. There's something about a place being out of bounds, which makes it a more attractive prospect, somehow.

I ended up sitting on a bench, where I remembered sitting with James and Charlotte, and various other friends. It was covered in graffiti, even more so than it had been in our day.

Sweet that "Zoe loves Marvin" so much. Only hope things work out better for her than they have for me, and that she doesn't end up being dumped for some twenty-seven-year-old, and then have to endure Marvin's mother telling her how much better off her son is with said twenty-seven-year-old.

We all start off innocent, don't we? She'll learn, this Zoe, whoever she is.

It was weird, being in this place, as the sky became dark. Kind of cold too, so I only actually remained there for a few minutes - just long enough to get myself together, and stop shaking, following my encounter with Elizabeth McIntyre.

I then headed for my brother's. Well, that *had* been where I'd claimed to be going, right? I hadn't really thought up an excuse for my visit, but whatever. I'd think of something.

The McIntyres' gate had been freshly painted, but this one wasn't, and it sounded as if it could do with some oil as well. The garden path was littered with kids' bikes, a toy car, and a Space Hopper. Elizabeth would certainly have made Rachel and Tina put their bikes, and other clutter, neatly away in the shed, after use. I made it across the obstacle course in safety, and was about to knock on the door. But it was already ajar.

I would have gone straight in, except that I heard voices - raised voices. Matt and Clare, having another of their blazing rows.

"I'm sick of hearing your crap!" screamed Clare.

I'd never liked Clare. But she and my brother *did* have three beautiful daughters, with Baby Four on the way.

And since Matthew adored both Clare and the kids, there wasn't much I could say on the subject. I wished them well, of course.

"I don't care what you say, Clare - because I can't let this go. You know that, don't you?" My heart froze. Not my brother.

It was Steven Parker - Clare Smith's so-called "ex". I would know that irritating, nasal tone anywhere. I'd occasionally suspected that there might still be something between him and Clare, but had told myself my theories were ridiculous.

Until now.

Part of me wanted to run away, and not to hear another word. But I knew I had to stay. I had to know what they were arguing about.

Chapter Three

By nine, the party was in full swing, and most of the guests had arrived. We'd used a compilation tape of Sarah's "absolute favourites", since Matt usually sorted out the *DJ side*, and my eldest brother still hadn't turned up. Approximately every third song was by Spandau Ballet - but, knowing Sarah, that showed considerable restraint. Still, the atmosphere was okay, and most people seemed to be having fun. I wasn't sure whether Danny and Hannah would make their announcement in a moment, or wait for Matt to arrive.

It was then that I saw him - some guy I didn't recognise. Strange, as I'd thought I knew pretty much all of Danny's friends.

He was emerging from the kitchen, cracking open a can of Special Brew. I was in a lousy mood as it was, and already somewhat drunk. Well, why the hell not? I took a defiant swig of Stella Artois. If I had to be at this party at all, having just broken up with the love of my life, why shouldn't I get well and truly rat-arsed? How else was I supposed to endure the evening?

As for what I'd overheard at Matthew's place - that information had been deposited in the *really can't deal with this* box in my mind, and I simply wasn't allowing myself to dwell upon, or consider, any aspect of the situation. I needed to get through this party, and then I would decide what to do.

"Hey, cheer up, love. It may never happen." Evidently, he was drunk, too. Well, pretty obvious really, since he was on the Special Brew.

I thought of James. "Maybe that's the problem. Ever thought of that?"

"What do you mean?" Thinking was possibly not his speciality.

"Never mind. Who the hell *are* you, anyway?"

"Who are *you*?"

Bloody cheek. "I'm Danny's sister, if you must know. This is my mum's house, and I live here. I think maybe that gives me a right to be here, and to ask who you are."

"Oh, that's right. You must be Lucy, the crazy redhead with a foul temper. Now, let me guess. That's Sarah, the pretty one with the long, black hair." He nodded in my younger sister's direction.

Sarah was giggling about something, nothing, and everything, with best friends Fiona and Tracy. I was glad my sister was wearing jeans, as per usual - given that neither of her friends were wearing much of anything. Fiona, a tall, slim black girl, kept tugging at her red, Lycra miniskirt, looking painfully self-conscious. Tracy, short and plump, with shoulder-length, blonde hair, looked a little more comfortable in her own, somewhat revealing, black dress - but perhaps slightly *less uncomfortable*, would have been more accurate.

"And that one," continued Special Brew Guy, "who's dancing with a different guy every time I look: Catherine, presumably? The peroxide blonde, who likes to-"

"Okay, thank you - you've said quite enough. I don't care who you are, or why you're here. You're leaving. Blame it on my red hair and 'foul temper', if it makes you happy, but just bugger off. You're drunk, and you're not welcome in this house."

"You're not exactly sober yourself."

"That's my business. This is my home, and I'm kicking you out. I'll do it physically, if I have to. Don't underestimate me."

He had dark hair and blue eyes, and I supposed women might fancy him in general, although he wasn't exactly my type.

Well, I didn't really have a "type", apart from James. I'd never been seriously interested in anyone else.

Screw James bloody McIntyre. I wasn't going to think any more about him.

"What's going on here, Lucy?" asked Danny.

Birthday Boy looked good, in a pale blue shirt, and a pair of black Levis, although my brother had somewhat overdone the gel, in his dark brown, wavy hair. Anyone would think he'd gone into competition with Catherine, whose hair generally had the texture of cardboard, due to her excessive use of *extra hold* hairsprays.

"Hi, Danny. Can you help me to chuck out this weirdo? He thinks he can just walk in off the street and gatecrash your party, and he wouldn't even tell me his name."

Danny raised his eyebrows. "His name is Kev Tanner. He's Mark's cousin - you know, Mark Jordan, from work? He's around here somewhere, with Donna. Kev came with them." Danny and Mark both worked as mechanics at Harper's Garage, just outside the town centre.

"Right - well, at least you have some idea who he actually *is*, but I'm still not happy about the way he talked to me, in my own home. And he wouldn't give his name. Cousin of some guy you work with - that doesn't seem like much of a connection to me, but I guess it *is* your party. So, final decision - are we going to throw him out or not? He seems pissed to me, but it's up to you."

Danny chuckled. "Of course he's pissed. Kev's always pissed. But really, I don't think there would be many people left, if I kicked out everyone who's had a few too many tonight - and I don't like to think of you walking the streets, sister dear." He turned to Kev. "Sorry about this, mate. I did warn you about my sisters, and this is our Lucy in action."

Okay - so that was Kev Tanner's source, was it? Had my brother really told this drunken idiot that I had a "foul temper"? Thanks a lot, Danny - love you too, and all that. It might be true, but, hey - I did have good points too, right?

"Whatever." I was past caring. "I need some fresh air. I'm stepping outside for a bit." I was already heading back through the kitchen, pushing past a group of Matt's workmates, which served to remind me that I hadn't actually seen my eldest brother that night, as yet.

Which, in turn, reminded me of what had happened, only a couple of hours earlier. But I shoved the thought abruptly aside. Some things I didn't *want* to be reminded of.

"Aren't you going to need a coat or something?" Kev called after me.

In truth, it was obvious I needed a coat, and it hadn't really occurred to me, but it made me feel stupid to admit this fact, and I didn't want to start taking advice from the likes of Kev Tanner. "I'll be fine," I assured him, even though my cream silk blouse was paper-thin, and I would be frozen.

I stomped through the kitchen, and opened the door, which was seldom locked, apart from when no one was at home. I slammed the door with a vengeance, and sat down on the concrete step, at the side of the house. In spite of the temperature outside, the fresh air did calm me down somewhat. It was a relief to get away from all those people, for a couple of minutes - the whole *world closing in* feeling that often came over me in crowded rooms. Some nights, even my second home, the Red Lion, could feel overwhelming, for that reason.

I was almost ready to go back inside, when the door opened, and there was Kev Tanner.

"You stalking me or something?"

He smiled. Surprisingly, I didn't find it annoying when he smiled. It wasn't a smug grin, as I would have expected.

Either I was starting to like this guy after all, or I'd had way too much to drink.

Well, I'd definitely had too much to drink, of course. But still, I *did* like him.

What the hell was wrong with me? And anyway, it wasn't as if I could ever really like a guy again - not in *that* way - not after James.

"Do you smoke?" he asked.

I hesitated. I'd been trying to give up but, as he held out a packet of Marlboros, I knew I was going to have to give up some other time. I simply wasn't strong enough right then, not with all the crap going on in my life.

"And have my jacket, okay? Anyone can see you're freezing." He was already removing his brown leather jacket.

"Thanks." I managed a faint smile.

"So, you've broken up with your boyfriend?"

"Is there anything Danny *hasn't* told you? Yes, James McIntyre - and, as you probably also know, he's been seeing Erica Lee."

"Really? I actually didn't know that. Lovely girl, of course - but I always thought..."

"Me, too. Bi, apparently."

"I never realised that. Might have chatted her up myself, if I had - attractive woman."

"If you like that sort of thing - which my boyfriend clearly did. I therefore no longer have a boyfriend, and I'd rather not talk about it, to be honest. Not my favourite topic of conversation."

"Okay, no worries."

Neither of us spoke at all, for what felt like ages, but was probably more like thirty seconds. The silence felt kind of okay, though. The night air made it feel fine somehow.

"So, how about you?" I glanced at his left hand, which I'd noticed when he'd handed me the cigarette. "You're married?"

"I should take off that bloody ring, before I try to chat up girls."

"What's her name?"

"Deborah."

"Any kids?"

"Two. Gemma's eight, and Toby's six. And I'd 'rather not talk about it', either. It's all pretty boring, anyway."

"I don't think I'd find it boring," I said, "but fair enough. I get that you don't want to go into it. I can understand that."

He studied me for a moment. "How old are you, Lucy?"

"Seventeen."

"That *is* young."

"How old are you, then?"

"I'm thirty-one."

For some reason, I wanted to know how old Deborah was - but I knew I couldn't ask, especially now that the subject of Kev's wife and kids was officially closed.

I took a swig of Stella, draining the remainder. Stubbed out my cigarette. "I need another drink," I said. "Let's go back inside."

"Okay, but at least let me finish my fag first."

"I'll meet you in there." Trying to keep my tone casual, which wasn't working.

Kev used the hand that wasn't holding his cigarette - the one with the ring on - to pull me back down. He kissed me, and I let him, and soon, I was kissing him back harder.

Until the kitchen door opened, and there was Danny.

The world seemed to freeze, for one surreal moment.

Then, my brother said: "Matt and Clare have arrived, Lucy. Me and Hannah are going to make our announcement. Come through and listen - if you're not too busy."

And I didn't miss the look he gave Kev.

"Maybe I should be getting back." Kev's tone was indifferent, without a trace of remorse or fear.

"Don't do that, Kev. It's early. Let's grab some more drinks, like we said, and then we can listen to Danny and Hannah's announcement. It'll be fun." I heard my own words, but wasn't sure where they were coming from. Precisely how drunk *was* I, anyway?

Of course, Matt and Clare had brought the three girls. Typical. Surely they could have got her sister to babysit?

Bonita and Jess raced up to me, screaming my name, and demanding hugs. Jade wasn't interested, because Jade Ryman was a stroppy kid, who apparently didn't like anyone, and definitely did *not* appreciate hugs.

Bonnie was five at the time, and looked the most like their mother, with that curly, dark brown hair, and hazel eyes. The twins, aged four, although identical, with their fine, golden-blonde hair, and blue eyes, were easy to tell apart, as Jade's hair was shorter than Jessica's, and she was invariably the one who would be throwing a tantrum, bullying her twin, or answering her parents, or elder sister, back.

In a way, I was glad to be able to concentrate on the girls. It made it easier not to meet Clare's eye, as we all stood around, waiting for Danny and Hannah's "surprise" announcement.

"You Lucy's new boyfriend, then?" Jade demanded of Kev, making me realise that maybe it wasn't such a good thing, after all.

"Jade, be quiet," Matt told her. "Sorry, mate. You know what kids are like. How's it going? Deborah here tonight?" My eldest brother, although strikingly similar in appearance to Danny, was stockier in build, with lighter hair.

I could literally feel Clare smirking, even though I didn't look at her once.

I moved away, letting my brother talk to Kev, and joined my best friend, Charlotte Lyndhurst. We'd barely talked all night. I'd noticed her chatting to various people, including my cousin, Tara, but at the moment, she seemed to be on her own.

"I can't stand that woman," she said, tugging at her chestnut curls. I knew Charlotte referred to Clare.

"Not my favourite person either, right now," I remarked. "Sorry I didn't catch up with you before."

"That's okay. You looked busy." She nodded in Kev's direction. "Wouldn't have thought Kev Tanner was your type, Luce."

"You *know* him?"

"Vaguely. As much as I ever want to. He even tried it on with my mum, at one point - not that she was having any of it. I do understand though, given the situation with you and James. It's hard not to look for comfort sometimes."

I hugged her. "I love you, Charlotte."

She hugged me back. "You know I love you, too - but exactly *how* much have you had to drink tonight?"

"Who's counting, right? Not enough, if you ask me."

Once Danny and Hannah had finally got their announcement over and done with, Charlotte turned to me: "By the way, I didn't know Sarah drank."

My heart almost stopped. I couldn't believe how casual my friend's tone was. And seriously, I wasn't sure how much more crap I could actually deal with, in one lousy evening.

"Sarah? Holy shit, Charlie - she doesn't. Are you saying she's been *drinking*? She's fourteen bloody years old! Where *is* she?" I spun around, frantic and out of control.

Charlotte placed a hand on my shoulder. "Luce, calm down. We'll find her, okay? I knew you wouldn't be happy but, honestly, I don't think she's had more than a couple of cans. She did seem to be knocking them back a bit though, so I *was* concerned."

All in all, this party had turned into the biggest nightmare ever. Someone wake me up, right?

Chapter Four

It was precisely one week since Danny's twenty-first, and I had just endured the most stressful afternoon of all-time at my place of work - the Arthur Hart Partnership, an architects' office in town. I hated office work. It was either stressful or boring, or a kind of weird, simultaneous combination of both. Still, whatever, right? I had to do something for a living, and had yet to come up with any better ideas.

Having finally convinced my workmates, Amy and Ruth, that I really wasn't up for a drink after work, I was currently standing in a ridiculously long bus queue. Down side: Chances of a seat, non-existent. Plus side: At least my bus was obviously due. I turned up the volume on my Walkman, and lost myself, as much as I could, in Iron Maiden.

And still, my mind returned inevitably to James McIntyre. What the hell was wrong with me? Why couldn't I forget about him?

Well, one more attempt. Tonight. That was what I'd promised myself. I would try, once more, to talk to him. And if it didn't happen - that would be the end for me. I couldn't torture myself any more.

He might not even be at home, of course. He might be with her. With Erica.

Yeah, well - that would say it all then, wouldn't it? It would be my sign to give up, once and for all, and I would. I really would. If it meant living the rest of my life with a broken heart, then so be it. I'd reached the point at which I would rather accept total defeat, than continue clinging to the final threads of, basically futile, hope.

***

I rang the bell. Front door this time, as per Elizabeth McIntyre's request. A repeat performance, in many respects, in that Rachel answered again.

This time, she was clear as to her instructions, however. She did not remove the chain. "I'm sorry, Lucy. Mum said I was not to let you in." I detected a glimmer of a self-satisfied smile, although her voice was entirely emotionless and monotone.

I could feel the desire to fight draining from my body. I'd had a hard day, as it was. Didn't need to put myself through this.

It was as I was turning to leave, that I realised James had appeared, right behind his sister. "It's okay, Rach," he said. "Lucy doesn't need to come in. I'm going out."

The next thing I knew, he was taking the chain off, and opening the door. He grabbed his jacket. "We'll go for a walk, Luce. Is that all right?"

I nodded. I couldn't think of anything to say. Was it "all right"? Understatement.

Wow, he looked amazing - sexier than ever. I remembered so well, the moment, when I'd gazed into those large, almond eyes, and known that what I felt was way more than the friendship we'd shared since our infant days. I'd been eleven, at the time, and James, twelve. We'd been working together on an issue of the school magazine.

The feelings hadn't gone away, that was for sure. They'd intensified, over the years - at least for me. I couldn't believe how flustered this guy could still make me.

"But what do I tell Mum? She'll be back in a minute," said Rachel.

I could think of a few things, but was so delighted by my unexpected victory, that I couldn't feel uncharitable, even towards Eliza McIntyre.

James wanted to see me, after all. He had all along. It really had been his vindictive cow of a mother, preventing him. That woman was so controlling.

But what did any of it matter? He loved me. I knew it. He always had. We were destined to be together. Whatever might have happened between James and that Erica - I didn't even care any more, because I would forgive him. I wanted to be with the only guy I had ever, or would ever, love. What could *be* more simple?

"Let's go to *The Field*," suggested James - meaning, of course, our old school field, where I'd been the previous week, on my own.

I remembered our first kiss. That had been there, too. So many memories - a kaleidoscope of vibrant summer days. I tried to catch his eye, and read his expression, but James seemed different. Was distant: I could feel that, and it scared me. He had to love me, though. He couldn't simply have stopped, not after so long. We'd grown up together. I couldn't let him go: not now, not ever.

We reached our destination, and headed straight for *our bench*, as I'd known we would. The world around us seemed surreal. Every sound, colour, and aroma was amplified, and yet far away. I felt as if I was in what should have been a fairy tale, but already sensed that we weren't heading for a fairy tale ending. I sat down first, and James didn't sit as close to me as I'd hoped, so I moved closer anyway, but didn't touch him, even though I wanted to. I knew I had to hold back.

I noticed the couple with the Yorkshire Terrier, the same couple who'd been there last week.

I read the same graffiti. Zoe and Marvin, Marvin and Zoe. I wondered who they were. Would they end up together? Married with six kids?

Or had they broken up already?

What did it matter?

Was it even Zoe who had written the graffiti? Maybe she didn't even like this Marvin. Maybe one of her friends had just written it for a laugh. Or perhaps she *did* like him, but he'd never looked twice at her.

"So, how have you been, Luce?"

"Okay," I said, even though I'd never been less "okay" in my life. "And you?"

"Fine, thanks. Looks like I'll be getting promotion at work soon, which isn't bad going. I thought it would take years, to be honest."

"Congratulations. I knew it wouldn't take you years. You were always going to be successful." It was true. James was just one of those people. He achieved his goals in life, but without walking all over others to get there - something I'd always loved about him. One of the many things.

"There have been other changes in my life, too. I imagine you've heard."

I felt slightly sick. Forced myself to hold his gaze. "You mean Erica?" I had to stay in control here, and try not to react emotionally. "I *did* hear, but I wasn't sure what to make of it."

"She was temping, in our Accounts department. That's how we met. I'm actually surprised we didn't meet sooner, given that she lives around the corner from my mum and dad's."

Yeah, same house she'd lived in with my cousin. But I resisted the urge to mention that.

"We've been dating for nearly three months," he continued. "I should have told you before, but I wasn't sure if it was serious."

"And *is* it?" Fiddling with a gold chain I often wore. A seventeenth birthday present from Mum. James had bought me one, very similar, for my sixteenth, but it must have snapped, whilst I was wearing it. I'd felt for it, and it hadn't been there any more.

"I think so, yes."

"But she's so *old*," I blurted out, in spite of myself. "You can't have a relationship with someone who's practically thirty."

"Twenty-seven, not 'practically thirty.'"

"Get real. Twenty-seven is near enough thirty, James. I don't understand what the two of you could possibly have in common."

"Well, I wasn't going to mention this, but you must admit, you're being hypocritical here. How old is Kev Tanner? A few years older than Erica, I believe?"

"What the hell has Kev Tanner got to do with it? I'm not seeing Kev."

"Maybe not, but you were getting pretty intimate with him at your brother's party, by all accounts."

"So you're jealous? Is that it?" Hope fluttered, like a persistent moth, clattering around in a lampshade.

"No, Lucy, I'm not - because our relationship is over, and I'm with Erica now."

"Why go on about it, then?"

"I wasn't. I was simply pointing out that you're attracted to older men, and my being attracted to older women is no different."

"But what about us? Surely it meant *something*?"

"It was a childhood romance. It was fun, but nothing like what I have with Erica. When you find that sort of relationship yourself, you'll understand - trust me."

"Don't fucking patronise me, James McIntyre. Just *don't*, okay? And, as for trusting you - that was clearly my mistake all along." *Please stay angry. That way, you might manage not to break down.*

"I never meant to hurt you, Lucy. I *am* sorry." He sounded sincere, and I knew, in my heart, that James hadn't hurt me on purpose, but that didn't make it any easier. Nothing did, or could.

"But I love you." My voice was seriously cracking now. Not crying had been too much to ask, of course. "I've always loved you. Maybe I didn't say it before, but you must have known that. I thought you loved me, too."

He could have hugged me or something, surely? Even just as a friend? Was that too much to ask?

"I'm sorry," he repeated, inadequately. "I ought to be getting back. Will you be okay, if I leave you now?"

"You already are, aren't you?"

"No, I mean-"

"I know what you mean. You want to go home, now you've finished dumping me for some thirty-year-old, who doesn't even know if she fancies blokes or women."

His expression hardened. "I would prefer it if you wouldn't make personal comments about my girlfriend, and I don't know what you think you're achieving, when you twist the facts like that. Have some self-respect. It can't possibly make you feel better, when you come out with that sort of rubbish." His voice was like steam-ironed cardboard. At that moment, he reminded me of his mother and Rachel, and part of me almost hated him. Almost.

"I'm sorry, James. It's just that...you know..." I was crying harder by this point, and couldn't find words for what I needed to express, let alone get them out. "We *are* still friends, aren't we?"

He looked awkward. "Do you think we *can* be?"

"Yes. Yes, of course." How could he even ask?

He shook his head. "I think a clean break would be healthier, Lucy."

"What are you saying? I don't understand."

But I did. I realised precisely what he was saying. It was over, completely over - the relationship, friendship, all of it. There was nothing left. James didn't want me in his life any more. As simple as that.

So I watched him walk away, and I didn't beg. Bloody "self-respect", right? Didn't have much of that left, but I had to hold on to the remaining fragments of my pride. I knew that. I'd been comprehensively dumped, and doubted I would ever be the same again. Something had died inside of me.

Chapter Five

"You don't have to go out, on my account," I assured Charlotte's mother.

"I know that, love," said Valerie Lyndhurst. "I just get the impression the two of you need to talk. And I've been promising my sister I'd visit."

Val looked a lot like her daughter, with that curly, chestnut hair, and the hazel eyes. They'd always seemed more like sisters, in many ways - partly because there was only fourteen years between them.

"I've always envied you for having such a cool mum," I told Charlotte, once Valerie had left, and the two of us were sitting in the kitchen, drinking coffee, and scoffing way more chocolate biscuits than either of us could get away with.

"I know," said Charlotte. Morning sunlight filtered through the window, behind my friend's head, illuminating the blonde highlights in her hair. "I understand in a way, but you don't know how lucky you are. I'd give anything to have brothers and sisters."

"I can't imagine being an only child," I admitted. "There are pros and cons, of course." I smiled, faintly. "You can have our Cath, if you like."

Charlotte reached across the table, and took my hand. "It's fine, you know. You don't have to pretend you're okay."

"I'm not really pretending, Charlotte. It's just - well, there's so much going on in my head right now. I don't know where to start."

"It doesn't matter really, as long as you start somewhere. We've got all day. That's what Sundays were invented for. Well, either that, or to hang out at church, but neither of us are into that shit."

"None of our lot ever were, apart from Sarah. Well, at one time, that is. I don't think she's attended a service for a while." I reached for a Bourbon. "Why are we talking about church, anyway?"

Charlotte shrugged. "Killing time, until you tell me what's on your mind. I'm guessing at least part of it, is connected to James."

"Have you spoken to him?" I took a sip of my coffee, noticing the skimmed milk I'd come to associate with coffee at the Lyndhursts'.

"In passing, a few times. He *does* live next door. He hasn't really given much away, though."

"Well, basically, he dumped me - doesn't want anything more to do with me, not even as friends."

"That's a bit OTT, isn't it?" She hesitated. "*Unless...Lucy, I have to ask this.*"

"What?"

"Did you cheat on him?"

"No - the other way around. You must have heard about James and that Erica."

"Yes, I know, and we'll get to that - but I mean, *before* James and Erica. That guy, Kev Tanner..."

"That wasn't before James and Erica. I'd never met him, until he showed up at Danny's party."

"That answers that one, then - in which case, I really can't understand where James is coming from. About Kev Tanner, by the way - I'd steer well clear, if I were you. He's bad news."

"Charlotte, what *is* this? Me and Kev - that was a one-off drunken incident. My whole world is falling apart here. What does it matter about some guy I snogged at a party, after my boyfriend had already dumped me for a lesbian?"

There was a new expression in Charlotte's eyes that confused me, even more so than her going on about Kev Tanner. A definite reaction to what I'd just said.

"What's wrong now?" I asked, when it became apparent that my friend wasn't about to fill the silence.

"It doesn't matter," she replied, although clearly, it did - but it was equally obvious that I wasn't going to get any more out of her, for the moment.

"Well, anyway, there's no need to worry about me and Kev. He's not my type, and he's way too old for me."

Charlotte nodded. "You don't need a guy like that in your life."

"No, of course not," I agreed. "I've been worried about Sarah, too. She's never touched a drop of alcohol before, and she went crazy at that party, for some reason. I've spoken to Fiona and Tracy about it. They said it was like she totally flipped. Apparently, Tracy did have a couple of cans herself, and persuaded Sarah to have one, but my sister didn't want to stop at one."

"Well, we're all a bit like that at times, aren't we? And if Sarah hasn't had any experience with drink, I guess it went to her head. I honestly wouldn't worry about it. I bet she woke up with one hell of a hangover the next day, and she probably won't want to go through that again in a hurry. You know the drill."

I wasn't so sure, but had the feeling, as I sometimes had in the past, that Charlotte would never get it, when it came to my wanting to keep Sarah safe. I probably *was* overprotective, because she was my kid sister, and who *wouldn't* be protective of a younger sister, right?

But I honestly felt that, in Sarah's case, she *needed* protecting. She was so innocent - so very fragile. It scared me, to think of her having to face so many of the things that Catherine and I had taken in our stride, because she wasn't like either of us. Sarah was a good girl, but it was possible to be too good for this world, and sometimes, I wondered how she would survive what life could potentially have to chuck at her.

If only I could keep her safe, then everything would be all right. But, at that party, I'd taken my eyes off her for too long - and I could never let that happen again.

"I guess you're right," I said, because it was easier.

Charlotte knew I was totally ignoring what she'd said on the subject. I'd mentioned it, knowing what she would say, and knowing equally well, that I wouldn't take any notice whatsoever of my friend's opinion.

"Anything else? I mean, before we return to the subject of James and Erica. There *is* more to discuss there, but I think we need to leave that until last."

There was more about James and Erica? Shit. How much more could there *be*? And did Charlotte seriously expect to divulge that much, and then change the subject?

"There *is* something else, not connected to James and Erica," I said. "I was actually planning to save *that* until last. It's huge."

"Tell me now."

"It's about Matthew." I waited for her reaction, and pretty much expected my friend to agree with my initial judgement, that this item should be left until the end.

She blushed, as I'd known she would. "Go on."

"I overheard a conversation between Clare and that Steven Parker. He was over their place, the night of the party. They don't know I heard anything, and I haven't said a word to anyone." I drank some more coffee, appreciating the caffeine. "The baby Clare's expecting is Steven's, not Matt's, and there's a good chance Bonita is, too. I don't think Clare knows, one way or the other, with Bonnie."

"Are you sure? You're basing this on some overheard conversation. You need to be careful here."

"Oh, I'm sure. You know as well as I do what Clare's capable of - and, believe me, what I heard was in no way vague. They spelt the details out clearly enough."

"How about the twins?"

"They weren't mentioned. Presumably, they *are* my brother's, but when you're dealing with the likes of Clare Smith, it's anyone's guess. I always knew she couldn't be trusted."

"Me, too." Charlotte's eyes filled with tears. "How could she do this to Matt? He's the sweetest guy in the world." She hesitated. "But, honestly - you wouldn't *tell* him, would you?"

"You think I shouldn't?"

She held my gaze. "It would break his heart."

"I know that, but surely he has a right to know?"

"Some right. It would destroy him, Lucy."

"You want me to lie to my own brother?"

"It's not lying. Clare's told the lie already."

"It's a lie by omission. I can't believe you want me to cover for her. You hate her as much as I do."

"More, if anything. But I love Matt more than I hate Clare, and anyway, you *do* agree with me. That's why you haven't told him already."

I couldn't answer that. My friend was right.

"Lucy, listen - about James and Erica. There *is* more to say on that too, but I think we're going to need something stronger than coffee."

***

For want of anything else alcoholic, Charlotte and I were sharing a bottle of red wine, which my friend had informed me was "some cheap shit". In fairness, that aspect didn't make a significant difference, from my own point of view, since I never did know one wine from another. Hey, if it contained alcohol, and you could therefore get drunk on the stuff, that was fine by me. We'd moved from the kitchen to the lounge, so that we could sit in the "comfy seats".

"I won't lie to you, Lucy. James is my friend, but I think he's handled this badly. He should have had the guts to end your relationship sooner, and I still don't think he's been entirely honest about how serious things have become between him and Erica. It's wrong that he's treated you like this, after you guys dated for so long."

"I don't think I can hurt much more than I've been hurting already. You reach that point, in the end. Are you saying they might be moving in together or something?"

"I think he's already spending more than half of his time at Erica's place, so yes, I suppose it's only a matter of time. Also, she's wearing a ring, which looks suspiciously like an engagement ring to me."

"She *isn't* - you know?"

"If she is, it must be early stages, so she probably isn't keen for people to know yet - but to be honest, I *did* hear, from a reliable source, that Erica's pregnant. I'm sorry, Luce. I know it's not fair to dump it on you like this, but what else can I do? It's not as if you're not going to find out, sooner or later."

I couldn't speak. Could barely even breathe, let alone form coherent words and sentences. I polished off my wine, and Charlotte took the glass from my shaking hand, and refilled it.

I needed a cigarette too, but remembered that Charlotte's mother, in common with my own, wasn't keen on smoking in the house.

"Let's go outside, for a moment. I expect you could do with a ciggie," said Charlotte, reading my mind.

In truth, it wasn't particularly difficult to read. I was predictable enough, after all. Boring, really. I was boring, had to be. That was why James didn't fancy me any more. Why he preferred Erica to me.

I nodded. I went out to the hallway, where my denim jacket was hanging, and grabbed the packet of Marlboros from my pocket, along with my lighter, grateful for the fact that it was a new packet. This was no time to be running out of fags, that was for sure. I followed Charlotte through the lounge, to the patio doors that opened on to the small, untidy back garden.

Charlotte didn't smoke herself, but was content to stand around, while I got my fix.

"You know," I said, at length, "I do wonder how Tara feels about this. After all, she was living with Erica, not so long ago."

"Tara's okay about it."

"How do you know?" Then I remembered: "You were talking to her at the party, weren't you? Did she say something?"

"That's the other thing I need to tell you. Tara's fine about James and Erica. She's with someone else herself."

"Really? I had no idea. Proves how much our family talk, I suppose - my own cousin, and I don't even-"

"She's with me."

"Don't wind me up. I'm not in the mood. Are you seriously trying to tell me you're in a lesbian relationship with my cousin?"

Charlotte looked me in the eye. "Yes, that's what I'm saying. You don't disapprove, do you?"

"Of course not, but I'm having trouble getting my head around it. I mean, you're not gay. You can't be, because I know you're in love..." *Shit, don't say it, Lucy.* We'd never mentioned this specifically before.

"Of course I've got feelings for Matt," said Charlotte. "It's always been unrequited, though. He doesn't see me as anything more than his kid sister's best friend, and once Clare came on the scene, that was pretty much that, in any case. He doesn't notice me, or any other woman."

"But you fancy Matt, and you therefore fancy guys. Surely you're not saying you're bisexual, as well? I've heard this 'bisexual' thing too much for my liking lately, and I'm not buying it."

"It's real, Lucy. So many people out there are bi - including me, and yes, including Erica."

I finished my cigarette in silence. Then I told her: "I love you, Charlotte. We'll always be friends. But I need some time, to get my head around everything."

"I understand." She placed a hand on my arm. "I'll show you out, but call me later, and we'll talk some more. I know it's a lot to take in."

"Sure," I almost whispered.

I felt slightly unsteady. Wondered how strong that wine had been, or whether it was the shock - probably a combination of the two.

I walked rapidly, as if desperate to reach my destination, even though, in reality, I had no idea where I was walking *to*.

Chapter Six

It being Sunday, every shop in the local precinct was closed, and the, normally hectic, place was deserted. The only sign of life was a group of, somewhat obese, pigeons, devouring the remains of someone's takeaway.

Cigarette butts littered the ground, surrounding the bench on which I sat, and I might almost have felt guilty for my own contribution. Except that I was past caring.

Charlotte and Tara. James and Erica. Erica's pregnancy. The engagement. Matt and Clare, the kids - and Steven Parker. It was all spinning around in my mind, on an endless loop and, the more I thought about it, and tried to make sense of it, the more bizarre and totally senseless it all seemed. I didn't understand anything or anyone any more. Why couldn't we all just go back to being kids? Life had been simpler then. I hadn't needed to smoke nearly as much either, although admittedly, the habit had been there, to some extent, since I was twelve.

"Lucy?"

I nearly jumped out of my skin. "Holy shit, don't *do* that. I..."

"Don't suppose you've got one of those going spare?" asked Kev - meaning the fags, of course.

Kev Tanner. Where the hell had he sprung from?

"I guess so," I replied, somewhat reluctantly handing him one. I didn't particularly want to leave myself short, and the rate at which I was smoking them was crazy - but I probably needed to slow down anyway, and he had pretty much caught me off guard. That, in itself, was becoming something of a tradition. "You shouldn't creep up on people like that, you know."

"I didn't. You were totally zoned out - in a world of your own. Hardly my fault."

"What are you doing here, anyway? It's Sunday," I said. "All the shops are closed."

"I noticed. And the answer is, same as you, I guess."

"Which *is*?"

He shrugged. "Sitting around and smoking, in a shopping centre, where all the shops are shut anyway, because it's Sunday."

"I don't know if it's you, me, or both of us, but I think this conversation must be one of the most pointless I've had in a long time, although a recent one with my ex would probably be in contention for *that* title."

"The ex who's with Erica Lee now." It was a statement, not a question.

"Do you think she's *that* pretty?" I blurted out.

"Well, she's not bad," he replied, his tone upgrading the term "not bad" to more like "stunning".

"Prettier than me?"

"You expect me to *answer* that?"

"Forget it. You already have."

"I haven't," he said. "And, no - not prettier than you. Not even close. Forget about her, yeah? And her stupid boyfriend. He sounds like an arse."

I laughed.

And then we kissed for the second time, and forgetting about James and Erica started to seem like a fairly achievable task.

Chapter Seven

It kept coming back to me in flashes: especially, for some reason, the moment when Kev Tanner had unhooked my bra. His touch had been neither gentle nor rough. It had been firm. I'd liked that - wanted it. Wanted him.

I could still smell the blend of hash, tobacco, Doner Kebab remains, and dirty laundry. The Tanners apparently rented two rooms in that house. Effectively, that one was Kev's. Deborah lived in the other, with Gemma and Toby. Bathroom and kitchen facilities were communal - shared with the other residents. How a family lived like that was beyond me. How old had Kev said the children were again - eight and six, right?

It made no sense, and yet, he made me feel alive, in ways I never had before. I couldn't wait until tomorrow night. I was finally going to meet up with him again. We'd arranged it yesterday lunch-time, after meeting, by chance, in town.

"You okay, Luce?" said Sarah. "You were miles away. I asked if you wanted another cup of tea."

"I told you, Sarah. It's a bloke - got to be," said Catherine. "Honestly, there's nothing but crap on TV tonight. I should've gone out, but I'm broke, as per usual. Plus, Tom's working late again. He's so boring."

"Next candidate?" I suggested. "And don't assume we're all on the same level as you, Catherine Ryman." I knew I was being a hypocrite, even as I heard the words leave my own mouth.

I'd had sex with someone else's husband. What right did I have to judge anyone?

It wasn't as if I remotely regretted it, either. I couldn't wait to get my hands on him again.

At that moment, the key turned in the front door. I glanced at my watch, frowning slightly. Mum was back early from her sister's. It was almost as if that woman didn't trust her own daughters - for *some reason*, right?

However, when the lounge door swung open, it wasn't Mum who walked in, but Danny. He'd come straight from work, by the looks of him. I hoped, for his own sake, that he wasn't planning to make physical contact with Mum's somewhat expensive - as we were being constantly reminded - olive-green, velvet three-piece suite.

"Some point in you moving out, if you ask me," observed Catherine. "You must have been back ten times since-"

"Nice to see you all, too. Lucy, can we talk?"

"Sure. What about?"

He grabbed my arm. "Upstairs, okay? This won't take long."

"Secrets, Sarah," said Catherine. "We know when we're not wanted, don't we? Bet this is, in some way, connected to whatever guy Lucy-"

"Catherine, shut the fuck up, okay? This has got nothing to do with you." He was dragging me now.

"Danny, you've lost it," I told him, "and take your hands off me. I don't mind talking about whatever's bugging you, but I don't appreciate being dragged around. I'll come with you of my own accord, but *no one* forces me to do *anything*. Have you got that?"

My brother relaxed his grip upon my arm. "Fine, whatever." No apology, though.

I turned to Catherine. "And Danny was right about one thing. This is none of your business, so keep your opinions to yourself, sister dear."

I caught a glimpse of Sarah, out of the corner of my eye, as I followed Danny out of the room. She looked scared, and I could tell she was about to cry.

"Now look what you've both done," said Catherine. "Feel better, now you've reduced our little sister to tears?"

But there wasn't anything I could do for Sarah, so I just had to trust that Catherine would comfort her. Danny meant business. I knew this side of him too well. He didn't lose his temper every five minutes, like Matt, Cath - and, okay, myself. But when Danny got mad, he really didn't *do* half measures.

***

My brother slammed the bedroom door behind us. "I'll come straight to the point, Lucy. You were seen with that piece of scum, Tanner."

"Had your spies checking up on me, have you? So I was seen with Kev Tanner - big deal."

Behind Danny's head, Spandau Ballet looked on. It felt as if they were listening in, although why they would want to was anyone's guess.

"Don't try to tell me there's nothing going on. You were all over each other, from what I heard."

Danny had to mean yesterday, of course. I wondered who'd spotted me. But, whatever. That was this bloody town for you.

"I didn't say there was 'nothing going on'. It's actually none of your bloody business what is or isn't going on between me and Kev. Where do you get off, treating me like a naughty school kid? You're only a few years older than I am - remember? You act like you're my dad, instead of my brother."

"So you don't deny you're seeing him?"

"I don't deny anything. I don't have to. What part of 'none of your business' don't you understand?"

"You're my little sister. That makes it my business - and you *are* still under eighteen."

"The age of consent is sixteen, I think you'll find. I'm old enough to work full-time. That makes me an adult, as far as I'm concerned."

"I'm not debating this with you. Do you have any idea what you're getting into? Apart from the minor detail of being married with two kids, the guy is also a drunk, a junkie, and a pusher, not to mention a complete fucking psycho. Come a long way since dating the vicar's son, haven't we?"

"Leave James out of this," I said. "And, if Kev's so bad, why invite him to your party? It was you who insisted on letting him stay. Kind of hypocritical, don't you think?"

"Well, you certainly changed your tune pretty fast, once he turned on the charm. I thought you had more sense, to be honest."

"I like him."

"You'll just have to learn to unlike him then, won't you? You're not seeing him any more."

"You can't tell me what to do."

"I swear, Luce - me and Matt are going to fucking kill the bastard, if he lays his filthy hands on you again."

"Then don't expect me to visit you in jail. I'm going out with Kev, and I couldn't give a shit what you or Matt, or anyone else, has to say. It's my life, and I'll do what I bloody well want. Don't let me hold you up any longer, bruv. You did say this wouldn't take long, and I'm sure Hannah's missing you."

Chapter Eight

We'd reached the latter half of October already, and I found myself wandering around town, looking at the various Halloween window displays, ranging from tacky to somewhat impressive. The past few weeks were a hazy blur.

It was Saturday afternoon. Following a "quick drink", in a hotel bar in town, with Amy and Ruth, I was almost as pissed as I was pissed off - having been treated to Ruth's "views" on my relationship with Kev.

Everyone seemed to be having a go: from Mum - that morning; to my brothers; to some stupid girl from work, whose opinion I could tell myself didn't matter. Still, it was one more person, turning on me, and I could have done without it. Who were they to judge me, anyway? Like they were all so bloody perfect, right?

Tears stung my eyes, which I hastily wiped away. I wasn't going to cry, not over comments made by someone as insignificant as Ruth Mason.

Pumpkins. Witches. Skeletons. The images danced in front of my eyes, even as I turned away from those shops, and headed for an off-licence, where I purchased some cans of Tennent's Super, on impulse. I hadn't used to like the mega strong lagers. Was losing my grip.

***

I clambered through a gap in the wooden fence panels, as per our usual routine. An easy enough feat in jeans and trainers. Not ideal in a skirt and high heels, as I'd discovered, the previous week. Fortunately, this was very much a jeans and trainers day. Just as well. Performing this task whilst drunk was a sufficient challenge, without the added difficulties presented by inappropriate attire.

Of course, as it turned out, the back door was not ajar. Kev usually left it open for me, when I came by prior arrangement, on the specified day, at the time of appointment. I didn't know for sure that he would even be there. And I didn't know that Deborah and the kids *wouldn't*.

My heart was thudding, and sweat dripped steadily down my back. I'd actually done it: shown up unexpectedly, at a random time on a random day - the one thing Kev had warned me never to do. The logical part of my brain was still there, in the background, begging me to see sense and leave, before the situation escalated. But I was too pissed to give a damn what that part of my brain had to say, on the subject.

I peered through the glass pane in the back door. Couldn't see anyone. I strained to hear voices, but again - could distinguish nothing. Maybe no one was at home but, since people, for the most part, lived upstairs here, it was difficult to tell.

I hammered on the door a couple of times, before giving up, and going around to the front, where I rang the doorbell. No answer. I repeated the action a few times. Still nothing.

At that moment, I looked up, and spotted Kev, checking who was there from the window. I stood, waiting for him to come down, and answer the door to me. Waited some more. Rang the bell again. And again. And finally, I stood there, my finger glued to the bell. The part of my brain that controlled my behaviour, ensuring that it was in any way rational, had clearly taken a vacation.

After a good five minutes with no response, I sat down on the doorstep, and reached into my carrier bag. Took out one of my cans, and cracked it open. If Kev was going to make me wait, might as well make the process a little more bearable, right?

I could sit there all bloody night, if I had to. Kev Tanner was sure as hell not going to ignore me.

When the door finally opened, and Kev appeared, I actually jumped. Got to my feet quickly, however - and he dragged me inside, and shoved me into the kitchen. Half of my Tennent's Super got spilt in the process, and I placed the remainder on the kitchen table. Left shoulder and both arms burning, from the force he'd used.

"What the hell are you doing?" he demanded. His eyes, in that moment, were cold and hard - his voice barely raised, but full of what felt almost like hatred.

"I'm sorry," I practically whispered, my voice beginning to crack.

"Don't fucking cry. I don't need that, on top of everything else."

I nodded, willing the tears not to come, although a couple streamed silently down my cheeks.

Kev's face relaxed, and his eyes returned to normal, and I half thought I'd imagined how angry he'd been, only a moment earlier.

He hugged me. "It's not that I'm not pleased to see you, Luce. You know that, don't you? But you can't ever do this to me again. Deborah will be back in about an hour, with the kids."

"I won't do it again," I heard myself saying. "I won't, I promise. I just miss you so much."

"I miss you, too." And we kissed, and suddenly, all seemed fine with the world.

I was barely coming up for air, when I heard voices, and the spell was broken. Everything became crazy again, as Kev launched directly into panic mode.

Deborah and the kids. They were early.

He shoved me into the downstairs loo, and slammed the door. Opened it momentarily, and shoved my open lager can into one of my hands, and the carrier bag, full of additional cans, into the other.

"Lock the door," he instructed, his voice low but firm.

And off he went, to greet his wife and kids.

"We can't stop," said a female voice, its owner apparently approaching. "The kids both went at my parents', but I neglected to go myself, and now I'm bursting. Plus, Gemma forgot her leotard, which wasn't too helpful. Go and fetch it now, Gem. I'll just...Kev, let go of me! What the hell are you doing?"

"You can't use *that* loo."

"Why not?"

"Why would you want to? It's disgusting." A statement which I wouldn't have refuted, observing, as I was, for want of anything else to do, the mold on the walls.

"So, what's new? Kev, what are you actually *on* today? I'm bursting here."

"Go upstairs, woman. Just bloody well do it, okay?"

"Fine. We'll talk about what your problem is, when I'm not moments away from peeing myself."

Just when it seemed as though that little drama was resolved, however - Deborah, or the voice I understood to be her, returned. "Farooq's in there, having a bath. Kev, I'm serious. I don't even care what you've got stashed in there. I just need the toilet, before I literally wet myself."

"Just hold on, okay? I'll sort it." I could hear Kev, charging up the stairs. "Right, you Paki bastard - out, now!"

I took a large swig of lager. I'd never known Kev to be blatantly racist before. Could taste the bile in the back of my throat.

"I be have the bath!" Farooq was yelling too, by this point. "You can wait few minutes - no? Or she can be use other toilet?"

"Like hell! My missus needs a piss, in her own home, in her own country! I'll give you ten seconds to dry off and come out, or I'll kick the fucking door down!"

"Okay, calm down, man! I come out! I not like that you be the racist!"

"I not like that you be a Paki bastard, but do you hear me complaining? One - two..."

Kev had reached seven, by the time that, apparently, Farooq emerged, and Deborah was able to use the upstairs toilet.

It all went quiet for a while, until I heard Deborah asking Gemma whether she had her leotard ready.

"Yes, Mum," said the girl. "Can we go now? I'm going to be late for my class."

"Yes, we're leaving right now," her mother assured her. "Whatever you've got in the downstairs loo, Kev Tanner - and I really *don't* want to know - make sure it's gone by the time we get back. Come on, you two - and Toby, what did I tell you about picking your nose? I gave you a tissue, so use that, please."

The front door slammed, and they were gone.

"You can come out now," said Kev. "Say anything, Farooq, and you're a dead man."

"I not be care you have woman in there," said Farooq, who was still in his dressing gown, his thick, curly hair wet. He looked about nineteen.

"I'm Lucy," I said. "Lucy Ryman."

Farooq nodded, in my direction. Then, he looked at me a little closer. "I maybe meet your sister? She has same eyes, and she is Ryman."

He knew Catherine? Well, why not? Catherine certainly knew plenty of guys, in this town. "I *do* have a sister, Catherine, who's probably about your age."

Farooq shook his head. "I do not know Catherine. I meet maybe another sister, or a cousin, called Sarah. I think I meet her at pub?"

"I do have a sister called Sarah," I told him. "That's my younger sister. She does go to the Red Lion with us, so I suppose it's possible you met her there."

"I do not think was Red Lion. I not be go there. Maybe was King's Head?"

"I doubt it. She's fourteen years old, and not exactly the type to be hanging around at the King's Head." I'd had enough of this conversation already. What *was* this guy's agenda?

"Okay, I guess I make mistake," said Farooq, with a shrug. "I dress now, and then I be go out. See you later, Kev."

"Whatever," muttered Kev.

I was heading for the door, but Kev grabbed my arm. "You don't have to go yet, Luce. Deborah won't be back for an hour or so. I've had all the crap from that now, so you might as well stay."

"Let go of me, Kev Tanner. I'm out of here. You have some nerve, if you seriously think I want to stay, after everything that's just happened."

Kev released me, without further protest, and I left via the front door, which Deborah had slammed, roughly five minutes earlier.

Chapter Nine

For once, I'd been seriously tempted to give Friday night at the Lion a miss. Had Charlotte not been so insistent, I almost certainly wouldn't have bothered.

"My round, Luce," my friend announced. "Your usual?"

I nodded - my "usual" being a pint of Stella. The whole thing was predictable and, for the first time ever, seemed boring, and completely pointless. But what the hell, right? Easier to go through the motions sometimes. Go with the flow. Let life happen around you.

Charlotte finally returned from the bar, a good twenty minutes later, and placed our drinks on the table. Holy shit, weekend nights out were so overrated. "Look, there's Danny and Hannah." She indicated a table in the corner, by the fruit machines, where my brother and his fiancee were sitting. "Do you want to join them?"

"What do *you* think, Charlotte? You know I haven't spoken to either of my brothers in over a week."

"Then, maybe it's time to."

"Yeah, or maybe not. This was a bad idea. I did warn you I wasn't in the mood."

"Well, you can't shut yourself away forever."

"Sounds okay to me."

"It's not 'okay', and I won't let you do it. It's not good for you to sit at home, and wallow in self-pity."

"Whatever you say. Let's drink up, and then we can move on."

"Where to?"

I rolled my eyes. "The Red Lion isn't the only pub in the world, you know. The Royal Oak, maybe - or The Horse - I don't know, anywhere."

Charlotte held my gaze. "I'll make a deal with you, okay? A quick drink and then, if you still feel like it, we'll move on: to the Royal Oak, The Horse, or wherever you happen to fancy. But *first*...."

"Yeah, fine, whatever. Anything for a quiet life." That said, we took our drinks, and made our way through the crowded bar, towards Danny and Hannah's table.

***

Approximately ten minutes of small talk ensued, principally between Charlotte and Hannah, who had nothing much in common, and had never hit it off.

Until finally, Danny turned to me: "So, how've you been, Luce?"

"Not great, but that's how it goes. And you needn't worry about Kev Tanner, by the way. I think it's safe to say, that's over."

"I can't say I'm sorry to hear that." My brother looked almost as tired as I felt.

"I wouldn't expect you to, Danny. What would be the point in lying?" I was playing with a beer mat, wondering whether to give in and have a fag. Since I hadn't been planning to stay at the Lion for long, I'd been hoping to hold out, but to do so was becoming increasingly difficult.

"I *am* sorry I lost it the other day, though. I don't know what got into me."

"Fine. Apology accepted." I managed a faint smile. I wasn't *that* mad at Danny. Never could be. I thought the world of both of my brothers.

"You should come over to our place some time, Lucy - and you too, Charlotte," he said.

"Yes, you must," Hannah agreed, actually sounding almost enthusiastic.

I put down the beer mat, and reached into my bag for those cigarettes. I had to rummage, in order to find my lighter, and by the time I'd located said item, Matthew and Clare had arrived, and were approaching our table.

Bloody marvellous. That was all I needed.

"I finally persuaded Clare to let her sister look after the kids," announced Matthew.

"Good job," said Danny. "You have to take a break sometimes, Clare. What can I get you both? Usual, Matt?"

Translation: pint of Heineken. Matt nodded. "Cheers, bruv. And Clare's still on the orange juice."

"Lucky me." Clare was in one of her strops, and I had a feeling, from the outset, that her bad mood and my own were going to make for a lethal combination.

Why hadn't I trusted my instincts, and stayed at home? I tried to catch Charlotte's eye, to indicate that I hoped to leave shortly, but she was talking to Hannah again. Holy shit, surely those two weren't actually getting on, after all? Well, whatever. All I knew was, I had to get out of that place, before I exploded.

"Don't be like that, babe," said Matt. "It's only for a couple more months, and you know the kids are worth every moment."

"Yeah, especially when you're not the one who actually has to give up drinking, or go through the agony of childbirth. It's all very well for men to come out with crap like that. You haven't got a bloody clue."

"I'll get the drinks in, then," said Danny.

"We'll come with you," offered Hannah, clearly meaning both herself and Charlotte.

Ever get the impression you're being deserted?

To my credit, I did try - I really did. But it only ever took that girl a matter of minutes. "So Lucy, is it true, what I heard about you and Kev Tanner? You *do* surprise me. I thought you'd be moping around over James for *at least* five minutes."

"Clare, I told you not to mention that," warned Matthew.

"No, Matt," I said. "If Clare has something to say, she should say it. She just might need to be careful, because I could say a few things about her, too."

Bloody hell, shut up, Lucy. Don't go there. She's winding you up, okay?

"Of course, I could understand if it was Catherine," she persisted, undeterred. "I mean, not being funny, but hardly *discerning*, is she?"

I was livid. "Hardly discerning" - and Clare *was*, right? The fucking bitch.

At the end of the day, Cath was single, with no kids, as yet. She might be a slag, but so what? That was nothing, compared to what Clare was doing to our Matt.

"I need some air," I announced, and practically ran out of that pub.

The relief of being hit by the cold night air made me realise how true that statement had been. At least outdoors, I could breathe. It had been so hot in the Lion, which was becoming increasingly packed, as the evening progressed.

More people were arriving, all the time. I tried to keep my gaze fixed upon the row of shops on the other side of the road, all of which had long since closed for the day, of course: the post office; one of the many estate agents', which seemed to be so abundant of late; and our local branch of Nationwide, where people would form ridiculously long queues each Saturday morning, due to the fact that the branch closed at midday, on the one day when most of us could actually get there.

"You okay?" I turned to face Danny.

"I'm fine," I assured him.

"You sure, Luce? I know Clare can be a bit much at times, but you shouldn't let her get to you. You don't normally, or not to that extent."

"Yeah, well - maybe I'm feeling fragile right now."

He lightly touched my shoulder. "I know."

I was about to tell Danny to give me a couple more minutes - that, after that, I would go back inside.

At which point, Matt emerged - and my eldest brother clearly had no intention of being as easygoing as Danny had been.

"Matt, Lucy's a bit upset," said Danny. "Maybe you should-"

"*She's* upset? That's a good one, bruv."

"Leave this, Danny," I said. "I'll talk to Matt. You go back inside, okay? We won't be long."

Danny looked dubious. "You're sure?"

"Yeah, I'm sure."

He shrugged, and headed back towards the public bar entrance, but not without giving Matt a look, that spoke volumes.

"All right, out with it - are you going to tell me what Clare's supposed to have done? You were trying to pick a fight with her, from the moment we arrived."

"Yeah, like she didn't say anything at all to provoke me."

"Cut the crap, Lucy. I've known you all your life. You meant something specific when you said that you could say 'things about her too', and you can either tell me what the fuck you meant, or go back in there and apologise - or preferably, both."

"If I tell you, the second stage might not seem so necessary. Which will it be, Matthew - the truth, or making the peace, and shutting up about the whole bloody thing?"

This was happening too fast, and I knew it. I was losing control of the situation. How could I even consider telling Matt? Hadn't Charlotte and I talked about this?

Agreed what the right course of action - or inaction - was.

It would destroy him, Lucy.

Matthew looked me in the eye. I caught a glimpse of his torment, in that instant. He knew there was something huge - but surely he could have no idea *how* huge?

"The baby isn't yours," I said. "Bonita might not be, either. Clare's been going with that Steven Parker."

The world seemed to freeze momentarily, until Matthew visibly reacted.

"How did you find out?" His words came out mechanically.

"I was at the house. I heard them talking, Clare and Steven."

"When?"

"The night of Danny's party."

"That was over a month ago."

I forced myself to meet his eye. "I know, and I'm sorry. I didn't know whether to tell you, but Charlotte and I both thought..." I let my voice trail off, knowing I shouldn't have mentioned having talked this over with my friend, without saying a word to Matthew himself.

But he didn't seem angry about any of that, as I might have expected.

"What are you going to do?" I asked.

"Nothing," he said. "There's nothing to be done about it."

"Are you leaving Clare - or do you need time to think it over or something?"

"No, I'm not going anywhere."

"I don't understand."

"You think I should leave her, right?"

"I don't know, but - how can you just accept it?"

He didn't reply. Looked straight past me.

"Matt? I said-"

"I heard you. I was thinking, okay?" He paused. "I don't really accept it, but there's nothing I can do about it, and I love Clare and the kids. Anyway, I already suspected."

"You suspected? What, that the baby isn't yours? And possibly Bonita, too? That Clare has been going between you and Steve, the whole time?"

Matt nodded. "I suspected all of that. Now you've confirmed it. I don't know how much it helps me to know for sure, but I guess, at the end of the day, it makes no odds."

"Are you going to insist that she ends things with Steven?"

"Not even that. If she has any conscience, and if she wants to, she'll stop of her own accord." There were tears in his eyes - the first real sign of emotion. "Who have you mentioned this to, Lucy? Have you told Danny? Our sisters, or Mum?"

I shook my head. "Only Charlotte."

"Thanks. I'd appreciate it if you could keep it that way."

"Okay," I almost whispered.

"Shall we go back in, then?"

I nodded, but then impulsively, I hugged him. "I love you, Matt."

He didn't say anything, but he hugged me back, and I knew that all I could do was to be there for him, if and when everything ended up falling apart.

Chapter Ten

It was one of those clock-watching Monday afternoons at work.

"Even the switchboard's dead," announced Ruth. "Only two calls since I got back from lunch."

"I'm not complaining," said Amy. "Makes my life easier. I fancy filing my nails, but kind of a cliche, isn't it? Still, got to do it some time, I suppose." That said, she fished her nail file out of her handbag, and started work.

"I hate how it's all or nothing around here," I remarked. "I'm glad it's more often hectic, though. At least then, I don't have time to think about how I could be in a million other places, instead of stuck here, wasting my time."

"Such as the pub, Luce?" suggested Amy.

"Well, I guess that would be *one* option. It would certainly be better than being here, doing sod all."

"But, when you think about it - wouldn't you be paying some pub good money, for the privilege of sitting around, doing nothing?" said Ruth. "Here, we're actually getting paid to sit on our arses all afternoon, doing absolutely nothing. It's not so bad, when you look at it that way."

"If there was anything around here that I could get even remotely pissed on, I might be inclined to agree with you, Ruth," I told her. "As it is, I'll take an afternoon in my local, any day."

"Life isn't all about 'getting pissed', you know," said Amy.

"It *isn't*?" said Ruth, in mock horror, and we all laughed as if it was the funniest thing anyone had said, in the history of time. Boredom has that effect on people.

At which point, the switchboard lit up, and Amy put down her nail file, and answered.

Ruth and I were still laughing, but we stopped abruptly, catching Amy's expression.

PAULA PUDDEPHATT

"Yes, yes - she's here. Lucy, it's your brother, Danny."

"Dan - hi. Is everything okay?"

"Not really, Luce. It's Clare. She had a fall, and had to go into hospital. She's okay, but the baby..." His voice trailed off, as it started to crack.

The baby didn't make it.

Steven's baby, of course - but what did any of that matter? Matt had loved that unborn child as his own.

"I'll ask if I can leave work early."

"You don't need to do that. You're finishing in an hour or so anyway, aren't you?"

"Yeah, I am - but I'll see if I can get off a bit earlier. We're not exactly rushed off our feet."

I wanted to be there for Matthew.

Roughly ten minutes later, having negotiated with one of the partners, I left the Arthur Hart Partnership offices. Took the escalator to the ground floor, out of habit. Most people used the lift, but Amy and I often walked together, and she was terrified of lifts, due to her claustrophobia. At that moment, I could imagine how that must feel: the walls of the lift seeming to close in, and pure panic, at the thought that the door might never open. Having held up my hand, by way of acknowledgement, to Miranda, who worked on Summit House's main reception desk, I headed for the exit, and pushed through the revolving doors, into the street.

Where I immediately saw him. Kev Tanner. Shit, that was all I needed. He was sitting on a wall, directly opposite to the building, drinking. And had spotted me, of course.

I wondered whether he'd been sitting there on purpose, waiting for me to emerge, but it didn't seem likely, given that he couldn't have predicted my early departure. Had I been working until five-thirty or later, as per usual, he would have had a pretty long wait.

I tried walking straight past him, but could hear him calling my name.

Someone nudged me. Some girl, who worked in another office within Summit House. "I think your boyfriend's calling you," she told me.

"He's not my boyfriend." My tone was abrasive.

She looked taken aback.

"Sorry - and thanks. It's complicated - you know?"

The girl I had only ever seen around, looked understandably bemused, but forced an awkward smile, before going on her way.

I gave in, and talked to Kev.

By the time he'd walked with me to the bus stop - not my usual one, but the Number Seven, to take me directly to the hospital - well, we hadn't said much, but had arranged to meet on Wednesday night. And I couldn't pretend not to know what the outcome would be.

It didn't seem to matter how useless Kev was, or how consistently appalling his treatment and attitude might be. I gave in every bloody time, because I wanted to. In the same way as Matt wanted to stay with Clare, in spite of everything.

Chapter Eleven

"Can you help me to lift this one?" asked Charlotte, indicating a large box, next to her bed, in the chaos that was her soon-to-be-former bedroom.

Charlotte had lived in this house since the age of four: herself and her mum, and their various pet cats, hamsters, and gerbils.

"Sure." I wasn't, after all, here to reminisce.

I was here to provide practical support to my friend, during her moving process.

The process of moving in with my cousin, Tara - now that Tara's ex-girlfriend had gone off with my ex-boyfriend. What could you *do*, though? Life went on.

I started to lift the thing, but had to effectively drop it. "What the hell have you *got* in here, Charlie?"

"Books mainly," replied Charlotte. "Some records and tapes. Do you think we should leave that one for James?"

"James?"

She nodded. "He said he'd pop over, at some point - see if I needed any help. It probably won't be until tomorrow."

"If you mentioned that I was likely to be here *today*, it definitely won't be until tomorrow." I knew I sounded jaded and cynical. Well, I *felt* jaded and cynical. "And no, we *don't* need to leave anything for James. Just give me a moment to catch my breath, okay? We're perfectly capable of moving a few boxes, without having to depend upon some guy. Whatever happened to Women's Lib, anyway?"

***

We were in the kitchen, drinking coffee and recovering, having moved all that we sensibly could, and a good deal more.

"My back's killing me," I said.

"Mine too. I guess we should have left some of it for James, after all."

"Whatever. He was never that great anyway, when it came to lugging stuff. But hey, he *is* a guy, and we're supposed to depend upon them for bloody everything, right?" I took a much-needed sip of coffee. "Except that you actually don't. Maybe you have the right idea."

"Being a lesbian isn't a lifestyle choice."

"It is to a point, if you're supposed to be bi."

"Maybe - guess it depends how you look at it. Anyway, Luce - how are you?" She took my hand. "And your brother and Clare?"

"I'm okay, and I guess Matt and Clare are pretty much carrying on," I said. "Not much choice really, when you've got three young kids to think of."

"No, I know. They must be devastated, though."

"Yeah."

"Do you think it makes it more complicated for Matt - since he knows the baby wasn't...?"

"I don't think that part makes any difference. I told you how he reacted when I told him, Charlotte. He half knew already - and about the possibility of Bonita being Steve's, too. He didn't consider leaving Clare, at any point."

"And you don't think that could ever change?"

"It seems unlikely, if he's still with her, after all she's done."

"Well, you know your brother best. Personally, I'd say it depends whether she gets rid of Steven. He should clear off and let them get on with it, but if he doesn't, and Clare keeps on messing around - I can't see Matt putting up with it indefinitely. She should appreciate what she has in him, I know that much."

"Yeah, she should." Charlotte was preaching to the converted on that one, and we both knew it.

"It's a pity you didn't make it to Donna's party. It was crazy, but a lot of fun." She referred to Donna Mann, Mark Jordan's other half.

"Whatever. It's not really my scene." I'd been hoping for a change of subject, but could think of more interesting subjects than Donna and Mark.

"Kev was there, at one point. I probably shouldn't say this, but he was flirting with Cath."

"Yeah, well - what do you expect? She flirts with every guy she meets. He flirts with at least every other woman. I couldn't give a damn."

"*Sounds* like it."

"Sarah didn't go, did she? I'm more worried about her. Catherine and Kev can both take care of themselves."

"Not that I know of." Charlotte looked perplexed. "Sarah wouldn't go to something like that, would she? I can't see your mum allowing it. And I wouldn't have thought it was her 'thing', in any case."

I frowned. "It isn't Sarah's 'thing', but lately - I don't know, not entirely sure what's going on with that girl."

"Growing up, I suppose. She *is* fourteen."

"Yeah, I guess so. Hopefully, it's just a phase."

"How about you and Kev? Is it on again?"

"Yeah, it seems so. No matter how many times I tell myself I can't possibly get back with him, it doesn't work. As soon as he's actually there, and talking me around - I can't turn him away, Charlie. I'm crazy about him. As in, literally can't stop thinking about him."

"And you think you're in love, of course - which is debatable, if you ask me. It sounds more like infatuation."

I rolled my eyes. "It's *Sarah* who's fourteen, not me."

Charlotte didn't get the chance to respond because, at that moment, her mother came through, accompanied by James and Erica, who had apparently just arrived.

Bloody great.

Well, Charlotte and I would just have to chat some other time, because I sure as hell couldn't deal with this, on top of everything else.

My heart didn't seem to have registered that I was over James McIntyre. The moment I saw him again - it was all still there, those bloody feelings. On my side, at least.

How could it be, when I was totally messed up over Kev Tanner now?

"Lucy - hi. Good to see you." He looked about as comfortable as he had the day he'd dumped me, and avoided direct eye contact.

"Hello, Lucy," said Erica, sounding neither friendly nor unfriendly: totally neutral, and unaffected.

I silently cursed my messed up hair, and the fact that my clothes were soaked with sweat, following my recent exertions. I couldn't have been more of a contrast with the beautiful, elegant woman my ex had dumped me for, with her glowing complexion, flawless make-up, and not a curly, auburn hair out of place.

"Hi," I said. "Yeah, good to see you both, too. I must be getting off, though. I'll catch up with you soon, Charlotte."

"Don't leave on our account," said James. "We were only dropping by briefly - while we were passing, you know. We can't stay."

And, that said, he and Erica couldn't get out of there fast enough.

At which point, Charlotte's mother, whose departure I hadn't even noticed, returned. "Lucy, love - I've got your brother, Danny, on the phone. He says it's urgent - that he tried Matt's number, but got no reply."

I followed Valerie into the living room, where she handed me the receiver. "Danny?" My heart was thudding. It seemed to be one thing after another.

"Luce, it's Sarah. She's in A. and E. Catherine will come and pick you up, in the next few minutes. She'll explain what's happened. I'm going to keep ringing around - try to get in contact with Matt or Clare."

"But, Danny - what the...?" He hung up on me.

I stood there, holding the phone, like an idiot, until Charlotte and her mother came through.

"What's wrong?" asked Charlotte.

"I don't know. All he'd say was that Sarah's in A. and E." As I replaced the receiver, I realised my hand was shaking.

Chapter Twelve

Matthew was pacing, whilst the rest of us - Danny, Hannah, Catherine, and myself - sat around in Hannah's mum's, somewhat cluttered, living room, with its awful combination of mulberry walls, lime-green three-piece suite, and fuchsia curtains. Cynthia Jackson was at work, so we had come here to talk.

"I don't give a shit what any of you say. Our little sister was raped and dumped - left for fucking dead. She shouldn't even have been served in that pub, and the police are doing sod all. I think it's time we sorted this ourselves."

It was two days since Sarah's attack, and she was at home, and recovering well from her physical injuries - but not coping nearly as well, from a psychological point of view.

Danny got to his feet, and went over to our eldest brother. He placed a hand on Matt's shoulder. "I'm not disagreeing with you, bruv. We can't just walk into the King's Head, and start smashing the place up, and knocking every other person's lights out - that's all I'm saying. What we need is answers, and we have to stay calm."

"Fuck calm. Sarah's fourteen years old. The landlord of that place dies for this, in my book - along with the pervert who did this to our sister, and anyone else who was in on it."

"Is this about Sarah at all, or your male egos?" suggested Catherine.

"Cath's right," said Hannah. "This doesn't help Sarah - doesn't help any of us. There's no need for any of you to be going down that pub, making things worse. The police are dealing with it."

"Like hell," said Matthew.

"I agree with Matt there," admitted Danny. "The police have done nothing, apart from half accusing Sarah of bringing it on herself, by being drunk, and practically bragging about some mutual, backscratching arrangement they've got with the King's Head dealers."

"Exactly," said Matt. "I can't just sit around here any longer, drinking tea and doing nothing. I'm going down there."

"I'm coming with you," said Danny.

"You're not, Danny. I'm asking you not to." Hannah stood, and moved towards her fiance, but he and Matt were already walking away.

"I'm coming too," I announced, getting to my feet.

"Don't be stupid, Luce," said Danny.

"Don't you call me stupid. If I am, you are. She's my sister too, and I'm bloody well coming, whether you like it or not."

Matthew and Danny exchanged glances. Both knew me well enough to realise I meant business. I really hoped neither of them could see how much I was shaking, as I could feel them relenting, and I wanted the three of us to be out of there, before either of my brothers had the chance to reconsider.

Matthew nodded. "Okay, Lucy."

"Have you both gone completely crazy? You're taking Lucy?" Hannah was becoming hysterical.

"Yeah, Lucy's coming." Danny's tone was decisive: The thing was settled. He gave Catherine a look that she understood: Her job was to take care of Hannah. It was down to the two of them now, to wait for news of Sarah, via Mum or Clare.

***

It was hard not to love the fact that the music blaring from the jukebox in that little pub, created vibrations that could be felt in the street outside. Within, it was a different zone, and the heavy metal and rock they played there, was definitely my kind of music. Posters, mainly featuring heavy metal bands and related imagery, covered much of the wall space, and a decent percentage of the ceiling, too.

The place was basically a dive though, and every other person, at least, had clearly been stoned, whenever I'd ventured inside.

That afternoon, the pub was by no means busy, especially given that it was Saturday, but it was well known that the regulars didn't necessarily hang out in the bar itself. Although less so at this time of year, they would tend to congregate outside, on the car park wall - there being no garden, as such - drinking and getting high.

A pale, thin, somewhat sick-looking woman stood behind the bar. She wore a black Lycra dress, which left almost nothing to the imagination.

Matt came straight to the point: "Where's the fucking landlord?"

The barmaid shrugged. "He's around, I guess. Who's asking?" Her expression was vacant, tone of voice vague and distant.

A bald man, aged about fifty, appeared in the bar, right behind her. "It's okay, Sasha. I'll handle this."

She nodded, and trudged off to serve a customer, who had started to bang his pint glass on the bar.

The landlord, as I guessed him to be, turned to Danny, ignoring both Matt and myself: "Long time, no see, Dan. Saw your ex in here, a couple of weeks ago. Stunning as ever, but who *is* that weirdo she's hanging around with?"

"I wouldn't know, Rex," said Danny. "I haven't seen or spoken to Mel since we split. I'm marrying my fiancee, Hannah, next year."

"Cut the crap," suggested Matthew. "I gather you guys know each other, but *whatever*. We didn't come here to discuss my brother's love life. Sarah Ryman - that's our little sister. Our *fourteen-year-old* sister, I might add. Name ring a bell? We want to know why she was served in here on Thursday afternoon, and which bastard raped her."

I placed a hand on Matt's shoulder. He couldn't lose it. We needed answers, not simply a brawl.

Rex indicated that we were to follow him, and took my brothers and myself upstairs. Behind the scenes, the King's Head was no less of a dive than the bar.

Rex showed us into the living room, where all was dusty and dirty, chaotic and disordered. The three-piece suite was obviously supposed to be cream, but the thing was filthy. However, that was the least of our worries right then, so we sat down, regardless.

"The girl you're talking about: tall, slim; long, dark hair, and pretty?" said the landlord.

"Yeah," I answered. "That sounds like Sarah. Go on."

My brothers were livid, that this guy had referred to our sister as "pretty". I'd watched them both visibly react, when he'd said that. But Sarah so obviously *was*, that to me, it was naturally part of the physical description that anyone *would* use.

"Came in on her own," said Rex, "but ended up chatting to the Bryant girl."

"Kirsty Bryant?" Danny sounded alarmed.

"Who's that?" I asked. "She's not connected with *the* Bryants?"

"Younger sister," confirmed Danny. "She's in Sarah's year at school, so they would know each other. They aren't exactly friends, though."

Rex shrugged. "Wouldn't know. She's *your* sister, mate. They were definitely getting on okay that afternoon."

"Who served them, anyway? They're clearly both kids," I pointed out.

"I would contest 'clearly', particularly in the Bryant girl's case," observed Rex, in the process of lighting a fag. He considered for a moment. "It might have been Sasha. Probably Roxy, too. Hard to pin it down. We get a lot of customers."

"You don't look rushed off your feet right now," I noted.

"Like hell they are. It's crap to claim this place would be so busy, you couldn't possibly figure out who served a couple of school kids, on a Thursday afternoon. Anyone can see it's dead in here." Matt was close to flipping.

"Rex," I said, "was she with Kirsty the whole time? Did they leave together? This is important."

Again, Rex shrugged. "I think a whole group of them were sitting together, at one point. A couple of the Bryant lads were there, and one or two others. I went through this with the cops, you know."

"Yeah, well - we thought maybe you would remember something you didn't mention to them." This from Danny. It was then that I noticed the expression in his eyes, but I couldn't quite define it.

Then, I remembered, and a chill ran through my whole body. That hard, cold stare: It was the old Danny. Before he'd settled down, and even started to get old and boring, and do things like getting engaged to Hannah Jackson. It was the Danny who would have known scum like Rex, to begin with.

And I'd been worried about Matthew losing it, because he was the one with the temper, in general. But now, that was the least of our problems, because if *Danny* lost it - he would *really* lose it. Matt knew as well, and the shock of realising that his younger brother was on the verge of going completely nuts, somehow took the edge off his own fury.

And in the crazy moment, that happened almost too fast for any of us to realise what had transpired or how, it was Matt who managed to grab the knife from our brother's grasp, before Danny himself, or all three of us, ended up on a murder charge.

"You have completely lost the fucking plot, Danny Ryman," said Matt, as he dragged his younger brother away.

The landlord was in a heap on the floor, and shaking. If Rex knew anything at all about what Danny was capable of - and it seemed probable he did - he knew he could have been a dead man.

Just when I thought I couldn't take any more, I saw him: heading towards the pub, with three other men. They'd come from the direction of the car park, of course: two of the six Bryant brothers, an Asian guy, whom I recognised to be Farooq, Kev's housemate - and Kev Tanner himself.

I looked my boyfriend straight in the eye, and he held my gaze. I knew, in that moment, that he'd nothing to do with what had happened to Sarah, but I wasn't so sure about his so-called "mates". Those Bryants were nutters. I couldn't believe Kev would deal with the likes of them.

Then again, I *could*. Business was business, for Kev, after all - and the Bryants were major dealers, in this town. As was Kev himself. I'd known the score, from the start.

But, whatever happened, I couldn't and wouldn't, let my brothers hurt him, so I concentrated on assisting Matt, with leading a, now shaking, Danny, away.

I felt momentarily dizzy, as I left that pub, with my two brothers - Matthew driving this time, even though we'd come in Danny's car.

Shit, Kev hung around with some dodgy types. I knew that, but hadn't twigged before, that he had connections with the King's Head lot. I wasn't sure how many more "surprises" I could deal with, but it seemed as if they just kept coming.

Chapter Thirteen

The following weeks passed in a blur. On Sarah's own insistence, our brothers and I "dropped it". As in, stopped trying to find out what had gone down, and who had been responsible for her attack.

As far as I knew, both Matthew and Danny had stuck to that, although with those two, you could never entirely be sure.

She told the police the same - that she couldn't deal with any more of their interrogations, and wouldn't give evidence.

Sarah claimed she "wanted to forget about it all", although she didn't appear to be doing that.

And events reached a point of crisis, when my fourteen-year-old sister was discovered to be pregnant.

Mum, with almost clinical efficiency, arranged for her to have an abortion, and Sarah didn't say much, but went through with the operation.

After the termination, Sarah withdrew. For a week, she stayed in our room, mostly lying in bed, and staring at the ceiling.

Mum was advised to send her back to school, and my sister complied, without protest. She started to eat properly again, and to sleep at night, and get up and dressed every day. She was functioning.

Functioning, but nothing else. She was going through the motions, and none of us could reach her any more.

And then, she changed again, when she started to hang around with Kirsty Bryant.

"Forget about Sarah, just for a moment," said Kev. We were sitting on his bed, but had yet to rip each other's clothes off, for once. "There's nothing you can do."

I looked at him for a moment. "Do *you* have brothers and sisters, Kev?"

He shrugged, avoiding my eyes. He didn't like me mentioning his family background. In truth, there wasn't much he *did* like me mentioning.

"You're an only child?" I pressed.

"No, I'm not. I've got a bitch of a sister, who would interfere in my life, given half a chance. I'm not into all this family shit like you are, Lucy. You know that, and you should learn to respect it." He was lighting another joint. That was his answer to everything - that and drink.

I took a swig of my own Tennent's Super. Well, I could relate to the latter, admittedly. I shouldn't be drinking the mega strong stuff, on a regular basis, but that was what Kev tended to have in his fridge.

Still, I'd got him to admit he had a sister. That was progress, considering the amount Kev had divulged about his family background, since we'd met. I knew he didn't get on with his parents, and evidently, he didn't have much time for the sister, either.

"Will you *ever* let me in?"

He didn't reply. He reached under my blouse, and was trying to unhook my bra. I wanted him so badly it hurt, but his lack of response to my question stung, and I froze. "Don't," I told him. "I don't want it."

"You do. You know you do," he said, but removed his hand, anyway.

"Why won't you talk to me? I hardly know a thing about you."

"I'm not in the mood for this."

"You never *are*. I thought you liked me." I wished I didn't sound so much like a whiny seventeen-year-old. I'd only ever tried to be real with Kev, and yet, my words always sounded stupid and immature, when I said them out loud.

Of course, Sarah felt Mum had bullied her into the abortion, and I couldn't deny that there was some truth in this, but then again, I could also see Mum's point of view. She had to do what she thought was best, in the interest of her own child, after all. I mean, how could Sarah have coped with a baby, at her age? It would have messed up her whole life, right? And the child of a rapist, at that. Every time she looked into her son or daughter's eyes, she would have seen her attacker, staring back at her - or, at least, that *could* have happened.

We would never know now. That kid would have been my nephew or niece.

I couldn't help remembering that Valerie Lyndhurst had had Charlotte at fourteen.

And Sarah wasn't coping now, that was for sure.

Kev had been no help. He never was. I didn't know why I couldn't forget about him, but somehow, I never could.

Still, that particular evening, I'd had enough. "I'll catch you some other time," I told him, as I stood and headed for the door.

"Fine, whatever."

I slammed the door of his room - followed by the front door, on my way out. Some bloody boyfriend - but I'd given up deluding myself that I simply wouldn't bother with Kev any more. It had never worked so far. Somehow, he always found a way to make me come back for more.

***

When I arrived home, I found Matt there, flicking through channels on the telly.

"Hi, Matt. I didn't know you were coming over."

"Yeah, well - couldn't stand it at my place any longer. I had to get out, before Clare and the kids drove me up the wall."

"No one else around?"

"No. Mum was going out, as I arrived, and haven't seen anyone else. I guess Catherine and Sarah are out partying, since it *is* Friday night." He hesitated, actually lifting his fingers from the remote control for a moment, and turned to face me. "It doesn't seem right to think of our Sarah 'partying', does it? She's growing up too fast for my liking."

"She isn't 'growing up', Matt - more like losing the plot, if you ask me."

Matt nodded. "I know what you mean," he said, starting to play with the remote again. "So, how about you? Not seeing your psycho boyfriend tonight?"

"Just been there. I guess I'd had enough, too," I admitted.

"You're breaking up with him - again?"

"Don't sound so hopeful, because, no. We're still seeing each other. Sometimes I need my own space, that's all. Why don't you turn the telly off, if there's nothing you want to watch?"

"I like changing channels."

"It's bloody annoying. Kev does that for hours."

Matt slammed down the remote. "Don't compare me to that piece of shit, Luce."

"All I said was...Oh, never mind. How's work going?"

"Same old shit, I suppose. It pays the bills."

At that moment, the doorbell rang.

I opened the door to a tall, thin woman with pale skin, and fine, blonde hair. "Lucy Ryman?"

"Yes. I'm sorry, do I know...?" I didn't finish my sentence. There was no need. I felt momentarily light-headed. I knew instinctively who she was.

"No, you don't know me, Lucy - but I believe you know my husband. I'm Deborah Tanner."

"You'd better come in," I said.

"Thanks."

I led her through to the living room. "Hello, Matt," she said, on seeing my brother. They knew each other? He'd never mentioned that.

Come to think of it, though - I did vaguely remember Matt talking to Kev at Danny's party. Hadn't he asked after Deborah? I hadn't thought much about it, but he must know them both.

"Hi, Deborah," he said, standing up. "It's okay, don't mind me - I was about to head home."

"You don't have to go, on my account," said Deborah. "I'm sure me and Lucy can go in the kitchen or something."

I ought to have been concerned about being invited into the kitchen by my boyfriend's wife. Like, was she planning to grab a knife or something? Yet, somehow, I sensed I had nothing to worry about, in that way.

Matt touched Deborah's arm lightly, as he passed her, and the compassion in his eyes, as he looked into hers, almost made me cry. After everything Matt had been through in his own relationship, I supposed it was natural he would feel for Deborah. "I honestly wouldn't have stayed much longer anyway, Deb. Clare will go crazy, if I'm not back soon. I'm surprised she hasn't been on the phone already, chasing me up."

Chapter Fourteen

"So, you know Matthew?"

Deborah took a sip of her tea. "Yes, I've known Matt for years - and your other brother, Danny. Both nice guys."

"Kev's cousin, Mark, works with Danny, right?"

"Oh, yes - that's right. Mark Jordan's bad news, of course - and I've always felt sorry for his girlfriend, Donna. She was such a pretty girl - still is really, but completely messed up on the drink and drugs." I realised why her voice sounded familiar. I'd heard it before, when I'd been the hidden item in their downstairs loo.

"I don't really know her that well, but I know what you mean. Look, Deborah - you didn't come here to talk about my brothers, or Mark Jordan and Donna Mann."

"No."

"You have two kids, you and Kev?"

"Gemma and Toby, yes - but I'm sure Kev's told you about them already." As she flicked a stray hair from her face, I noticed her gold wedding band: the only item of jewellery Deborah was wearing. "He adores Gemma, worships her, more than he ever did me, or ever will you. He's the reason that girl is so spoilt, and a nightmare to deal with. Totally ignores his little boy, most of the time. I don't know what to say to Toby, when he asks if Daddy favours Gemma. I lie of course, but there isn't much point. How old are you, Lucy?"

"Seventeen," I replied.

"I thought so. You're even younger than the last one."

"The last one? There have been others?"

"A few, yes." I somehow knew she wasn't telling me this in a bitchy way.

"I didn't expect to like you." As soon as the words were out, I wanted to snatch them back. "I'm sorry. That sounded bad."

Deborah smiled - faintly, but it was definitely a smile, genuine and unforced. "It didn't sound bad, and I like you too, Lucy. I didn't really expect to, either."

"How old are *you*, if you don't mind me asking?"

"Twenty-nine. And it's okay, if you thought I looked older. People generally do. Life hasn't been easy, especially these past few years. I guess it's taken its toll."

"You look fine."

"I look awful. Lucy, you have to realise what you're getting into with Kev. I'm not here to threaten you, or tell you to stay away from my husband. He's going to have affairs. I don't like it, but I'm used to it. But when I heard he was involved with you, and that you were Matt and Danny's sister, and not much more than a kid..." Her voice trailed off. There was so much sadness in her grey eyes. "I've got to be heading off soon. I need to pick Gemma and Toby up, from my parents' place. Just take care, okay?" She was getting to her feet.

"Yes - yes, you too, Deborah," I said, as I showed my visitor out.

Like, seriously - how weird had *that* been?

And Deborah Tanner was lovely.

Chapter Fifteen

"Sarah, listen - I'm worried about you," I said.

My sister and I were in the Red Lion, where the Christmas decorations were in full force, reminding us that we had somehow reached December already. I didn't know where the time went. Apparently, it got worse, the older you got - according to Mum, at least. The artificial Christmas tree was huge, and decorated with silver tinsel, and gold and silver baubles.

"Don't be. I can take care of myself."

"But you *aren't*, are you?"

"I don't really know what your problem is. I only want to have some fun. After all the shit I've been through lately, surely I'm entitled to that?"

"You don't seem to go around with Fiona and Tracy much now. I thought they were your best friends."

Sarah rolled her eyes. "So I've made new friends. Fiona and Tracy are okay, but they never want to *do* anything."

"You mean, they don't want to go out getting drunk every night, like you and Kirsty have been, for the past fortnight?"

"You're exaggerating. We go out and have a laugh. Mum reckoned I had my whole life ahead of me, and I was so young, and all that crap. That was how she justified bullying me into an abortion I didn't really want. And I hate myself for giving in to her, even more than I hate her for making me feel I didn't have a choice. So, don't tell me I don't have a right to live for the moment, and be young, and go to nightclubs, or anything else I feel like doing. What else *is* there? Studying for exams and playing my stupid cello, because that stuff keeps Mum happy? No way, Lucy - not any more."

"Sarah..."

But, of course, Danny, Hannah, and Matthew all arrived, and my moment with Sarah was lost - not that I'd been getting far, anyway.

Sarah barely said, "Hi," to the three of them, before announcing: "I'm off now - said I'd meet Kirsty at the Royal Oak."

I grabbed her arm. "Why the Royal Oak? Can't you meet her here?"

"Kirsty doesn't like the Lion - says it's boring here, and I'm inclined to agree with her."

"The Royal Oak isn't exactly that exciting. It's dead in there, half the time."

"No, it's not great, but anything's better than this place, and it's not as if we'll stay in there long. It's boring, just to sit in one pub, all night. That's what old people do."

"Kirsty's words again?"

"Not particularly. We both think the same way, that's all. Kirsty gets me, which is more than most people seem to, right now."

Danny turned to me, once Sarah had left. "What was *that* all about? I take it you asked about her new boyfriend?"

"You're optimistic, Dan. I didn't get that far."

"It's that Farooq, who hangs around with *your* boyfriend," said Matt.

"We don't *know* that," said Hannah.

"Yeah, well - let's hope, for his sake, it isn't true," Matt observed. "He'd better like fucking hospital food, if it is."

I remembered that afternoon at the house, when I'd first met Farooq - the day Kev had "hidden" me in the downstairs loo. Hadn't he said something then about knowing Sarah? I'd dismissed it, at the time. Now, I was beginning to wonder.

Chapter Sixteen

"But why here, Sarah? I don't understand." In truth, it was unusual for Sarah not to be hanging around with Kirsty and her crowd, of late - and the case progressed from unusual to suspicious, given that she and my brothers had insisted on meeting at The Horse.

"Lucy, please stop asking questions. All I know is, Matt and Danny said we should meet them here, because it's quieter, and we would be able to talk. You know what it's like at the Lion, people coming up to us all the time."

"Yeah, well - that's because it's our local, and it's where our friends and family go. Are you sure you're okay? I'm worried now."

"Yes, I'm okay, or as okay as I'll ever be. It's not about me."

"So, who *is* it about - Catherine, by any chance?"

"You *know*?"

"No. You just told me. So it *is*. I did wonder, since she's the only one not coming. A sibling meeting with one sibling missing, and I know she isn't really working late. It was obvious Danny made that up on the spot. He's such a crap liar."

"Oh, look - there they are," said Sarah, and I noticed Matt and Danny, approaching - conveniently saving Sarah from having to respond.

Once the four of us had our various drinks, and the pleasantries were out of the way, I came straight out with it, in typical Lucy style: "So, come on, then - what's this all about? Whose fiance has Cath been screwing this time? Not pregnant, is she?"

It was instant, the change of expression on each of my sibling's faces. "She *is*, isn't she?"

"Yes, she is," said Matthew.

"Well, that didn't take much guessing, did it? Honestly, I thought she'd have had the sense to take precautions. It's not as if she's exactly naive, is it? So, go on, then - whose is it? I take it she does *know* whose it is."

"She knows," said Danny.

"Shit, he isn't married, is he?"

"Yes, he is," replied Danny. "To Deborah Tanner."

My heart was hammering. This wasn't real - wasn't happening. "You're saying it's Kev's? No way, Danny. She's winding you up. I bet she's got off with Rupert again. I told Amy she couldn't trust that bastard."

"No, Lucy - it's Kev's," Matt insisted.

"But when would they...?" Then I remembered what Charlotte had said about Donna's party, and I felt slightly sick.

I'd barely even *cared*, when Charlotte had mentioned Kev flirting with my sister, at some party. It had seemed so insignificant.

But it hadn't been, had it? And they'd done more than dancing and flirting.

"Donna's party," said Danny, confirming my fears.

I had to get away. "I need time out," I said, before racing off to the ladies'.

***

"Luce, are you in there? Are you okay?"

I was grateful to Sarah for having left it a good ten minutes, before following me. I used the last of the bog roll in that cubicle to wipe my nose, and took a deep breath, before emerging.

I saw my reflection in the mirror by the basins, and it wasn't pretty: eyes red raw, mascara all over my face, hair in a total mess. I would have to make at least some sort of effort to freshen up, before I could go back out there. Reached into my bag, and located my hairbrush and make-up bag.

"I know what you could so easily say, Sarah - what Matthew and Danny will both say," I admitted, as I got to work on my hair.

"I'm being a hypocrite, by getting upset, when Kev isn't even mine to begin with. It's Deborah who ought to be upset, not me. He's *her* husband, after all. I bet they said all of that, didn't they? When they were building up to this little meeting."

Sarah didn't hesitate for long, but it was enough. "No one thinks you're a hypocrite, Lucy. But I suppose they *did* say some of that, yes. They were going through all the implications, trying to make sense of the situation."

"There *is* no sense. It's a bloody mess. How could she do this to me, Sarah? Surely there are enough guys out there she could have got off with? She doesn't really like him, does she?"

"No, I don't think so. I think they were both just drunk. It didn't mean anything to either of them."

"But it means something now - at least if she has the baby." I immediately realised what I'd said. "Sarah, I'm sorry."

"It's okay. You can't spend the rest of your life not mentioning abortions, in case I go off the deep end. But, in answer to your question, I don't think Cath views that as an option."

I didn't say anything. Finished brushing my hair, and started to apply my make-up.

Sarah remained with me, not speaking, until I was done - at which point she asked: "Shall we go back in now?"

I nodded. "Yeah, okay - got to face it some time, right?"

Sarah ruffled my hair, and I didn't mind, even though I'd just brushed it, and she'd messed it up, all over again.

We returned to the bar, only to find that our brothers had been joined by Amy Clark, from work, and her fiance, Rupert Oakwell.

Rupert - another of Catherine's many conquests. This was too much. I could feel the tears welling up again.

I gave Sarah a look, that clearly indicated my desire to escape, and the sooner, the better, but it was too late, because Amy had seen us already, and was calling out and waving. Wearing a dusky pink, silk dress, my friend looked even more glamorous than usual, and radiant, as she clung to Rupert's shirt sleeve.

For his part, Rupert looked handsome, impeccably turned out, and bloody uncomfortable, as if he wished he could be almost anywhere else.

I felt a moment's renewed hope, at the prospect of my earlier theory being perhaps somewhat more likely than my siblings had credited. Perhaps Catherine didn't even know whom the father was, which, in harsh reality, had to be another possibility.

It was when Amy attempted to hug me that I broke. I pulled away from her, and ran out of that pub, tears streaming down my face.

Yeah, well - that was *it*. As I stood there, in the car park, not caring about the wind and rain, or how cold it was out there, I felt a sense of clarity, along with the rage and sadness.

I was through with both of them: Kev Tanner and, even more so, my sister. His betrayal - well, it was crap, made me sick to the stomach, but what did I honestly expect?

But my fucking sister. No way - you didn't do that shit to your own. And it brought back memories of past betrayals. So many - ones I had systematically shoved aside, because - well, because Catherine *was* my sister.

Or used to be. I was done with that now.

"You screwed it up, Catherine," I said, aloud, tasting the rain water, along with my own tears. "I'll never forgive you this time."

Then I realised that Sarah was standing there, watching me. "Let's get you home, Luce," she said, taking one of my freezing hands in her own.

Chapter Seventeen

The following evening, I was in Sarah's and my bedroom, with both of my sisters.

Catherine and I had been screaming at each other non-stop, for at least twenty minutes.

Sarah had come in about ten minutes ago, and was desperately trying, and failing, to act as referee. "Will you two both just calm down?"

"Stay out of this, Sarah," said Catherine. "I thought you said you were meeting Kirsty?"

"I'm not going. I'm hardly in the mood. I wanted to call her, before she left, but Mum's still on the phone. No idea who she's been speaking to, but she's been on there for half an hour. She goes mad if I'm on the phone for more than ten minutes."

"Oh, I can tell you the answer to that one," I said. I realised how sore my throat was, after all the yelling and crying.

"Yeah, like - it's her who pays the bill, not us," said Cath. "It's still hypocritical, though."

"I didn't mean that part - and, for your information, I'm not so sure it *is* Mum who pays the phone bill, or most of the other bills around here. She works part-time, stacking shelves. Dad pays for almost everything. And *that*, by the way, is who Mum's talking to."

Sarah's face became instantly pale. Judging by visible reactions alone, I would have guessed *she* was the one in trouble. "Dad? Are you sure?"

"Yeah, pretty much. I listened in for as long as I could stand. She was telling him about Catherine."

"You don't think he'll kick me out? He can't do that, can he?" asked Catherine.

"He owns the house," I replied, "so yes, he can."

In walked Mum, right on cue. "Your dad's coming over," she announced. "He wants to talk to the three of you."

"Count me out," said Sarah. "I'm meeting Kirsty."

"I thought you said-" I began.

"I changed my mind. Going out suddenly seems like a good idea, after all."

"I'd prefer it if you stayed," said Mum, "and it might be better if you changed into something a little less revealing."

Mum did have a point. Sarah's miniskirts were shorter than Catherine's, these days. Dad would hit the roof, if he saw his "angel" dressed like that.

"Forget it," said Sarah, pushing past our mother.

Cath was following her towards the door, but Mum grabbed her eldest daughter. "No way. *You* are going nowhere, young lady."

"Let go of me, Mum - and you can relax, okay? I'm only going to my room. I might as well get a head start on packing." Her voice was cracking, and Catherine hardly ever cried.

The front door slammed, and Sarah was gone. Mum could have prevented her, of course - but hadn't made more than a tokenistic effort to do so. I was grateful to her for that. I didn't know exactly what had gone on between Dad and Sarah, in recent weeks, but she'd been the only one of us who had ever meant much to him. And my younger sister had worshipped our dad - but then, something had changed, which Sarah hadn't talked about, not even to me.

I didn't have long to dwell on any of that, though. It couldn't have been more than two minutes after Sarah's departure, when the doorbell rang.

Chapter Eighteen

Nearly two weeks later...

Sarah held on to the side of the bath, and vomited into that. Her puke seemed to mock Mum's OCD tendencies, reflected in the otherwise gleaming and immaculate white bath. My sister had got some sick in her beautiful long hair. I looked away. Didn't want to feel sick myself, and I was starting to.

And there I had been, expecting a relaxing afternoon, having actually got off work early. All of that had gone out of the window, the moment I'd got home, and found my sister, in her current state.

Then I saw them, and for a moment, the whole world seemed to freeze, and I froze along with it. Stared, transfixed, at the empty Paracetamol packets, scattered around the side of the bath.

I reached out and grabbed one. "Have you taken *all* of these, Sarah?"

She threw up again.

"Sarah, this is important. Tell me what you've done. Have you taken an overdose?"

"Yeah," she managed, half gasping, half sobbing, and then she gagged, but wasn't sick that time.

She was wearing her navy and grey school uniform, but whether or not Sarah had actually attended, was anyone's guess.

"Where's Mum?"

"Town." Mum had mentioned that she might meet up with her friends, Freda and Beatrice, for coffee and a catch up.

"I'll see if I can get hold of Matt or Danny," I said, grateful for the chance to get away, albeit briefly.

My hand was shaking, as I reached the landing. Snatched the phone, and dialled Matt and Clare's number. I almost forgot the final two digits, in my confusion.

No reply. I started to panic, as I hung up. Tried Danny and Hannah's number instead. That was just ringing, too. Shit, what now?

I was about to hang up, when I heard Hannah's voice. "Hello?"

"Hannah, it's Lucy. Is Danny there?"

"No, he's not home from work yet. I've literally just walked through the door myself."

"Can you tell him to come over, the moment he gets in? Sarah's sick."

"Yes, of course. What's wrong with-?"

"Please, just give Danny the message, Hannah. I need to keep trying to get hold of one of my brothers."

Unless I could contact someone within the next few minutes, who could drive and had access to a vehicle, I'd have no option but to call an ambulance, to take my sister to A. and E.

I tried the garage where Danny worked, and was informed that he'd left, so I hoped he would be home any minute, and receiving my message.

I even rang the Inland Revenue, where Cath worked, but was predictably given the runaround, by the usual incompetent staff, who played their routine trick of: "I'll just put you through to someone who can help you." My call was sent to at least three random extensions, by which time I was ready to scream, and I slammed down the phone.

I wasn't even sure whether Cath was still going into work, but had a feeling she would be. Danny had told me she was staying, on a short-term basis, with a local friend, but I hadn't exactly pushed for more details. It was hard to believe that it was under a fortnight, since Dad's visit. It all felt so distant, at that moment - almost inconsequential.

I was considering whom to call next, and was on the verge of ringing 999, when I heard someone unlocking the front door.

I practically threw myself down the stairs, and met my brother in the hallway.

"Danny - I've been calling Hannah, and your work."

"Well, obviously I wasn't *at* home or work. I was on my way here. I *will* need to give Hannah a ring, to let her...Lucy, what *is* it? What's happened?"

"It's Sarah. We need to get her to A. and E. She's OD'd on Paracetamol."

Chapter Nineteen

"I'm going to see if I can get hold of any of the family," said Danny. "The nearest payphones are at the front of the building, near reception."

I nodded. "Have you got enough change?"

"Yeah, I should have, thanks. You all right to stay here with Sarah?"

"Of course, Dan - no worries. I'm just glad that nurse finally brought her a commode, or potty, or whatever you'd term the thing. How can they leave a young girl like that, screaming and crying her heart out, thinking she's about to pee herself?"

Danny shook his head. "Search me, sis. I don't think they give a fuck about patient dignity, but that's how it is, I guess. They're overworked and understaffed, but aren't we all?"

"Exactly. Oh, and Danny - I think she was serious about Mum, when she said she didn't want to see her. Things aren't right between them, and I don't think it would be a good idea for her to show up."

"I'll keep it in mind. Try to get Matthew or Catherine over here, at some point, but I'll encourage Mum to stay away, if I can. Might not be easy, though."

I returned, once again, to our sister, who was calm right now, but clearly still feeling the discomfort and pain in her body. She'd been sick multiple times, and looked pale and exhausted.

They kept asking her the same questions, the doctors and nurses - making her answer, repeatedly: what time she'd started taking the pills, how many she'd taken, and why she'd done it.

Sarah was in no way vague about the question of motivation, however confused she might be on some of the other points: "I wanted to die. I killed my baby, and I wanted to die, too."

How could it have come to this? How had we let our little sister get to this point? I needed to know she would be okay. She couldn't die. We all loved her so much. Surely she realised that?

A nurse approached, and addressed myself, rather than my sister. "We're transferring Sarah to a ward in the old building," she informed me. "Will you be wanting to stay with her?"

"Yes, of course - but our brother has just popped out, to phone some family members. Can we hold on until...?" But I didn't finish my sentence. Danny was back. "They're moving her," I told him.

"Is your mother coming?" asked the nurse.

"No," said Danny. "Our eldest brother and my fiancee are both on their way, though."

Sarah started to cry again. "I don't want Mum here."

"Sarah, she isn't coming," Danny assured her. "That's what I just said."

***

This second ward, although noisy and hectic, was somewhat less so than A. and E. There was a Christmas tree, by the nurses' reception area, with a fairy on top, and a single piece of sad-looking, silver tinsel, thinning like the hair of an elderly relative. It looked like something rescued from the bottom of a family's Christmas dec box - and, knowing the NHS, it quite possibly *was*.

The rest of that weekend became a blur of images and events, in my mind. The medics tried to pump Sarah's stomach, but it freaked her out, and they apparently couldn't do it. Then, they gave her some sort of antidote, and she had to stay attached to this machine, at all times. Once she became physically capable of doing so, my sister was allowed to go to the toilet by herself, rather than using a commode, as long as she remained attached to the machine - which could be wheeled around - via various tubes.

We took it in turns to stay with her - Danny, Hannah, Matt, Clare, and myself. Catherine visited once, briefly - and our brothers arranged this in such a way that she and I wouldn't bump into each other, for which I was grateful.

And Mum did come a couple of times, in the end. The hospital staff were pushing for it, with Sarah being underage, and Mum herself became, understandably, insistent. Sarah hardly said a word to her, but at least there wasn't a scene - only that awful sense of hostility in the air.

***

On Monday morning, I phoned the Arthur Hart Partnership, and spoke to Amy, since none of the partners were available, at the time. I told her I was staying with Sarah - as opposed to asking. The way I saw it, the worst they could do was sack me. Both of my brothers and Hannah had to go into work, and Clare had the kids. I wasn't prepared to leave Sarah on her own.

"I hope Sarah will be okay, and do give her my love, of course," said Amy. I could sense an unspoken "but..." to her statement.

"Thanks, Amy," I said. "There's a good chance I'll be in tomorrow, but I can't say for sure."

"I understand, Lucy. I hope the partners will too, but I'm only in a position to pass on your message. Could your mum not stay with Sarah?"

"No, that's not appropriate. It *does* need to be me. I'll be in touch again, when I can."

"Okay. You take care, Luce."

***

"I don't even feel sick any more," Sarah told me, as we sat together, over twenty-four hours after my phone call to Amy. The Arthur Hart

Partnership, along with most aspects of my normal existence, felt distant - memories from another lifetime.

"That's good," I said, but I knew where this was going.

"Why aren't they letting me go? I thought I was going to be discharged, once they took me off the machine."

I reached out and took her hand. "They need to do some more tests first. It won't be too much longer, sis."

As if in direct response to this conversation, a nurse approach Sarah's bed - a tall woman, of about thirty-five, with fine, mousy hair. "How are you feeling, Sarah?" she asked.

"I'm okay. When can I go home?"

"I can't say precisely, dear. We *will* need to do some tests, just to check you haven't damaged your internal organs. What I'm about to do now is, test your heart, to make sure everything's functioning okay."

"My *heart?*"

"It's routine, love - an ECG. We need to establish whether the tablets you took have done any permanent damage, in which case we *will* have to provide further treatment."

Sarah burst into tears. "But I'm only fourteen." I would never forget how vulnerable she looked, in that moment.

The tests confirmed that, thankfully, Sarah was fine - but they still weren't letting her go, and she was starting to go up the wall.

"Even if Mum has to come and collect me, I don't care. I just want to go home, Lucy," she told me. There was desperation in her eyes.

I hugged her. It was the best I could do. "Hang on in there - please. You'll be home soon enough." Tears slid down my cheeks. It was the first time I'd cried, since this whole nightmare had commenced. "Sarah, I'm so glad you didn't die."

"I think I am, too," she said. "I do love you, Luce. I'm so sorry."

"I love you too, and you haven't done anything to be sorry *for*. If anything...I don't know, but I guess I feel like there must have been something we - or I..."

"There was nothing you could have done, nothing that would have changed my mind. And you possibly saved my life, you and Danny, by getting me here when you did."

"You really wanted to die, didn't you?"

"Yeah, I did."

"Because of the baby." It was a statement, not a question.

"It feels like nothing will ever be okay again."

"It will, Sarah. You have to believe me, and keep fighting. Promise me you'll never do anything like this again?"

"I promise." I could feel that she meant it, and I was so grateful for that.

***

Mum did come that evening, along with Matthew, Danny, and Hannah. Sarah was being assessed by a psychiatrist - the final obstacle, which my sister would need to face, before she could be discharged. The rest of us were sitting on plastic seats, in a waiting room, around the corner from the office in which the interview was taking place.

"I don't understand why it took them so long to get this doctor to see her," said Mum, who was pacing again.

"It *is* the NHS, Mum," said Danny. "Why don't you sit down? You're making all of us jumpy."

"I can't. I wish I had one of my pills." Reference, the Valium, which Mum had been routinely popping for years. The doctors had become increasingly reluctant to prescribe her the drug, of late. Frankly, I could see their point.

That said, I was no better. I was shaking, and wasn't sure how much longer I could go without a fag - that, or a drink, or preferably both.

Hannah glanced at her watch. "They've been nearly an hour. I hope there won't be a problem."

"Of course there isn't a problem," I said. "Why would there be? They just have to ask a ton of questions, and fill in the paperwork. They always drag these things out."

"I'm sure you're right," said Hannah, but of course, I knew full well that the purpose of this assessment was for the psychiatrist to decide whether Sarah would be *allowed* to come home. There was a chance that she'd be admitted to a kids' psych ward - if they felt she was "a danger to herself".

After a further ten minutes, Sarah emerged. "I can go home," she told us. "I've got to see my GP, to discuss antidepressants, and see the shrink again, for an outpatient appointment, in February." She didn't sound as relieved as I would have expected, considering how much she'd been going on about wanting to leave the place, but at least she was coming home. That was all that mattered, as we could work on the rest.

***

That night, in our room, Sarah said to me: "It's interesting, that the shrink asked me whether I was going to take another OD - like, if I was going to, I would hardly be likely to tell him, would I? And, when I said I wasn't, he automatically believed me."

"Sarah, I thought we talked about this. You promised me you'd never..."

"I know. I'm not saying I'm still suicidal. I'm just saying, it does make you think, that's all."

I couldn't shake the feeling of uneasiness, that something still wasn't right with Sarah. "Try not to overthink it," I said. "You need to move on - try to put this behind you."

"Yeah, I guess so."

"Things have been crap lately - and I mean, for me, too. But we *will* get through this. It's almost Christmas. We'll make it the best one ever, okay? And 1984 is going to be so much better."

"George Orwell didn't think so."

"Yeah, well - what did he know? The way I look at it - things have pretty much reached rock bottom, so it's got to get better."

"I hope you're right, Luce."

I hoped so, too. I couldn't take much more.

Meanwhile, I was ready for an early night. Amy had somehow persuaded Arthur Hart, the senior partner himself, to let me keep my job, and I would have to make sure I wasn't late, for my first day back.

Chapter Twenty

It was March 1984, and I was in the Red Lion with Charlotte and Tara, trying to convince them that I really didn't want a party, for my birthday, the following month.

"You have to do *something*, Lucy," Charlotte insisted. "It *is* your eighteenth."

"It will be yours in June. We'll have a double celebration then."

"No way. You don't get out of it that easily. We've got to have a party."

"I'm inclined to agree with Charlotte," said Tara, preventing her glasses from sliding down her nose with one hand, whilst adjusting a hair grip, in her short, blonde hair, with the other. "I didn't do much for my eighteenth, but I've always kind of regretted it. That's why I had such a huge party for my twenty-first, I guess."

"I remember," my friend remarked.

"You surprise me, Charlie. I barely remember a thing about Tara's twenty-first. We were all totally rat-arsed that night."

"Oh, I know," said Tara. "It was a right laugh though, wasn't it?"

"I can't really say, can I? Since I don't actually remember. I think I've just about recovered from the hangover, over two years later."

"We should have it at our flat, if you don't fancy a club. That would be cool. Invite absolutely tons of people."

"No, Tara - thank you, but no. I do appreciate the offer, but I'd rather just have a quiet drink here, with family and a few close friends."

"Lucy, are you turning eighteen or eighty?" said Charlotte.

"I don't care if I'm being boring, Charlotte. I don't want a lot of fuss. You can invite a few extra people here, and call it a 'party' if you want to, but nothing more. And please don't arrange any 'surprises'. I mean it when I tell you I don't want some big deal eighteenth birthday party, so just don't push it, okay? It's my round. Same again, for both of you?"

That said, I went to the bar - and saw Kev Tanner, for the first time since our break-up. Holy shit, why had I actually come here tonight, anyway?

"Hi, Lucy. Fancy meeting you in here."

"Well, it *is* my local. What are you doing here, anyway?" I could feel the sweat on the palm of my hand, soaking the note I had ready to pay for the drinks.

Shit, keep it together, Lucy. Could you make it slightly more obvious that you still fancy the crap out of him?

"Same as you, I guess. About to order a drink, since it's a pub."

"So, enjoy your drink, then."

"Don't be like that. I came to find you, obviously."

"You're wasting your time. I told you before, Kev. It's over, and I don't want to talk to you."

"I've broken up with Deborah. I thought that might interest you, but I guess not. I'll go," he said, already turning away.

"No - wait." I grabbed his arm, touching his leather jacket. My head was spinning. Only Kev Tanner could come out with something like that, and then walk away again. "It was a shock to see you, that's all - and I *am* here with Charlotte and Tara tonight. It wouldn't do any harm to talk, though."

Kev shrugged. "I'll give you a call some time. Maybe you can fit me into your schedule - when you're not too busy with Charlotte and Tara, of course." And then he left, and that was that.

"What did Tanner want?" asked Tara, when I returned with our drinks, a few minutes later. "I hope you told him to fuck off, in no uncertain terms. It's the only language arseholes like that understand."

"Tara, leave it," said Charlotte.

"It's okay, Charlotte. If Tara wants to say something, she's free to do so. But I don't actually need advice on how to handle my ex-boyfriends. It's bad enough that I get this crap from Matt and Danny." I downed my pint in three. Never could manage it in one, as I'd seen Kev do. Got to my feet. "I've had enough for one night. Speak to you both later."

Chapter Twenty-One

The Red Lion was packed. I don't think I'd ever seen it so busy. And the noise, and the heat, and the screaming insanity of it all, made me want to turn and run away, there and then.

"Holy shit, Charlie - you've invited half the world." But, of course, she didn't hear me, over that bloody racket.

Everyone was there: from Amy and Ruth, to barely remembered cousins and second cousins, some of whom I knew for a fact, no longer lived in the UK. This was crazy, out of control, and everything I really hadn't wanted.

No choice, but to smile my way through the ordeal, and endure the incessant screeches of: "Happy birthday, Lucy!"

I wondered when it had happened - that Charlotte and I had grown apart, to the extent that she no longer understood me. I didn't honestly know if I'd always hated crowds as much as I did, right then. Probably not. It had built up somehow, over the past year or so.

What I *did* know was that, at one time, my best friend would have twigged that my reluctance about a big party was serious - not some sort of attention-seeking ploy, to encourage her, in conspiracy with Tara, to create the most mega eighteenth birthday party, in the history of time.

I forced myself to breathe naturally, fighting back the tears that were threatening, and only hoped that getting drunk would help. There wasn't much else I could think of to do, at that moment.

***

I was finally starting to feel somewhat relaxed, when Fiona and Tracy approached me. The alcohol definitely *had* taken the edge off, and I was chatting and giggling with Amy and Ruth. I might have known that couldn't last.

"If you're looking for Sarah, I think she left with that Kirsty and her cronies," I told them.

"Yes, we know," said Tracy. "That's why we wanted to talk to *you*. About Sarah. Can we go outside or something? It's too noisy to talk in here."

"Yes - yes, I suppose so, Tracy." I looked at my workmates. "Back in a minute, guys." And I followed Sarah's friends, out to the car park.

"We're just really worried about Sarah, especially after - you know, everything she's been through," said Fiona.

"She's always hanging around with Kirsty Bryant, that weirdo Farooq, and their crowd," added Tracy. "She acts like she doesn't want to know me and Fiona any more."

"She blanks me half the time lately, but I still don't want to give up on her - not after we've been friends for so long."

"Since primary school. She's changed, though - really changed. Sometimes it's hard not to leave her to it."

The way these kids were looking at me, it was as if they seriously expected me to wave a magic wand, and make everything better. They didn't seem to take into account that I was only a few years older than they were.

"I really appreciate that you've both stood by Sarah, and I hope you won't stop," I said. "She needs genuine friends now, more than ever. I can't disagree with you about anything you're saying, but what are you asking me to do?"

"You're Sarah's sister," said Tracy. "She listens to you. Can't you talk to her? Me and Fi aren't getting anywhere, Lucy. She's heading for a disaster, if she carries on the way she has been. She's always getting drunk, and I don't think she's taking drugs, but it's only a matter of time, with that lot she's been hanging around with."

"Believe me, Tracy - I've tried to talk to Sarah, and at one time, I would have agreed with you that she does listen to me. If not me, she might at least listen to one of our brothers, or Mum. But now -

I just don't know if she does. That doesn't mean I won't try, though. Of course I will. Please, don't give up on her. She's so lucky to have friends like you two."

"We're lucky to have her, too," said Fiona. "We just want the old Sarah back - the Sarah we knew."

I didn't say anything. I didn't think that was realistic at all. Sarah had been through too much, and I doubted if she would ever be the same again. I could only hope, with all my heart, that she would come through this somehow. There was still a spark that hadn't died, and I would catch it sometimes, but as for "the Sarah we knew" - no, she wouldn't be back. Sarah's childhood, her innocence, were gone. Her illusions had been shattered, and in a way, my own illusions had died, the moment that that happened.

Still, Fiona and Tracy both looked so young - *were* so young - and their hearts were good. Their innocence remained very much intact. So I simply nodded, holding back the tears. I needed to get away, before I broke down entirely, so I made my excuses.

In a toilet cubicle in the Red Lion, I cried, steadily and silently. This was my eighteenth birthday party. *Happy birthday, Lucy.*

When I finally emerged, feeling comparatively calm, and as ready as I would ever be to face all those people again, I spotted Kev Tanner's face, swimming towards me, through the sea of faces, and I knew what I was going to do.

I grabbed his arm, before he could even speak, loving that familiar sensation of touching his brown leather jacket. Once I'd dragged him out into the car park, and snogged him, in full view of anyone who cared to watch, I announced: "I've had enough of this. Let's go down the Royal Oak. It's quieter there."

Kev grinned. "You're abandoning your own party?"

I nodded, and we walked off together, in the direction of the other pub. Charlotte would be mad at me, of course - but she would get over it. Anyway, I was mad at her too, for doing this to me, in the first place, so that made us even, as far as I was concerned.

Chapter Twenty-Two

"Are you going to help me lift this cupboard, Danny?"

I had to focus on the practicalities. Every glance at Sarah's cello case, or the Spandau-covered walls, made it that much harder. Still, everyone leaves home eventually, and I wanted to be with Kev.

"You're taking that? I thought it was Sarah's."

"No, it was both of ours, really. It had some of her things in, but mostly mine. Now, are you going to help me, or do I have to lift the thing on my own? I lugged enough crap for you and Hannah."

"Of course I'll help you," said Danny. "I'm just surprised you need to take so much stuff. Surely Kev has cupboards there already? Deborah can't have taken all of it to her parents', can she?"

"She did take a few bits, but they didn't really have that much furniture, to start with. I honestly don't know how they managed, with two kids and almost no storage. I'm having one of the bookshelves too, but I think we'd be better off taking that to pieces, and putting it back together when we get there."

"I don't suppose Kev had much need for bookshelves."

"That proves what you know. He does have a bookshelf. It's just jam-packed already. He reads a lot as it happens, or maybe not so much so lately, but he *has* read widely. He writes poetry, too."

"Yeah? Drug-induced creativity?"

"Danny, just help me with the bloody cupboard, okay?"

That said, my brother and I both focused on the task in hand, and managed to get the cupboard, followed by various other items, out into the street. There, we were assisted by Danny's mate, Ivor, into whose van we loaded the items in question.

"You know, I'm not exactly a fan of Kev Tanner," said Danny, when we were finally done, and about to set off on the journey to my new home. "Matt feels the same. Still, I hope it works out for you, Luce."

"Thanks. I hope it works out for you and Hannah too, and I'm not her number one fan, since we're being so honest here."

"Yeah, well - you don't have to be her 'number one fan', but Hannah's not a drug dealer."

I practically laughed at the image of Hannah, dealing drugs down the King's Head, even though it wasn't really funny at all, and my brother did have a point.

"And, Lucy - I know you won't like me saying this, but if you're ever in danger..." He lightly touched my arm, whilst looking me in the eye.

"I'll be fine," I said. "Don't worry."

***

That night, Kev made love to me, and I knew no one else needed to understand, because there was another side to him. There was to everyone. And I was in love with Kev Tanner, and was going to be with him, no matter what anyone said.

Kev kissed my forehead, as I lay there, in his arms. "Your family don't exactly approve."

"That's their problem. I'm over eighteen now. I make my own decisions."

"And this is really what you want?"

"You know it is."

Then, he looked me in the eye: "I love you, Luce." He'd never said the words before, not even once, and I knew, in that moment, that he meant it.

"I love you, too," I said, brushing away a couple of tears.

"You can't leave me now. You know that, don't you?"

"I only just got here. Why would I be leaving?"

There was something in his eyes that actually almost scared me, even though I'd never been happier. "I mean it, Luce. You can't leave me, not ever. I need you."

"I'm not going anywhere," I assured him, and we kissed again, and then he just held me really tight, and he was crying.

And I wasn't scared by it any more. Instead, felt overwhelmed by love - and protective of this man, who had finally let down his guard, and given me a glimpse of his vulnerable side.

***

I woke up in Kev's arms, and he kissed me briefly. Then, extricated himself, and got out of bed. He was starting to dress already.

"Kev, can't we just stay in bed? It's Saturday. I don't have to go to work. I thought...you know..." Trying to conceal my disappointment, and keep my tone neutral.

"Stay in bed as long as you need to, babe. There's no hurry, if you need a lie in."

"That's not what I meant. You know it isn't."

He came over and kissed the top of my head. "I'd stay if I could, but I do need to go out. You know how it is."

"Business?"

"Yeah. I'll only be a couple of hours, tops."

"I guess I'll see you later, then." Not much else I *could* say.

Chapter Twenty-Three

"I feel bloody stupid, dressed like this."

"Kev, please stop sulking. You look fine." I took a moment to apply crimson lipstick, instead of my usual lip gloss, still not certain the resulting look was *me*. "Toby's being more mature about this than you are, and he's seven."

"I'm more surprised Gemma's apparently loving it. She hates your family."

"She likes party dresses more than she hates my family. I guess that's a compliment, of kinds. Your suit looks fine, you know, apart from the trousers. The leg length isn't right, but I've still got time to take them up. It would look so much better."

"Stop fussing, Luce. You can't go sewing up a pair of trousers that don't even belong to me. I borrowed this suit off Mark, remember?"

"I'm sure he wouldn't mind. I could always-"

"Leave it, okay? The trousers stay as they are. Anyone who doesn't like it can fuck off, as far as I'm concerned."

"Yeah, well - you might want to tone down your language a bit, when we get there. Both of my nans and my aunt, Sylvia, will be there."

"I'll be on my best behaviour, babe."

"I'm serious."

"Did I say I wasn't?"

"Oh, and call my mum Helen, instead of Mrs. Ryman."

"We've been through this before. She *told* me to call her Mrs. Ryman."

"That was when you first met her. I've spoken to her about it since. Hannah and Clare both call her by her first name. You're as much family as either of them."

"Not for much longer. Hannah's marrying Danny this afternoon, remember?"

"Yeah, well - if that's the criteria, then how about Clare? She's not married to Matt."

"They've got three kids."

"There's a few things I could say about that, but I don't want to put myself in a bad mood today. Weddings are supposed to be happy events, believe it or not."

"It's the bit after the 'happy event' that people don't consider. If they thought about that, no one would bother."

I didn't say anything. Kev was so cynical about marriage. Did he honestly expect me to have no feelings of my own, on the subject? But it was a door he had not only shut, but double-locked, in his mind. Two kids were also "more than enough", apparently. Well, I wasn't in a tearing hurry for either marriage or kids, but I wasn't quite ready to write them off.

"Is your sister coming?" he asked.

"I would hope so. I'm sure even Sarah can tear herself away from Farooq and Kirsty, for long enough to attend her own brother's wedding."

"I wasn't talking about *Sarah*."

"Catherine wouldn't *dare*. I'd bloody kill her."

"She might. It's *her* brother's wedding, too. I could do without the hassle."

"She isn't coming, so there won't *be* any hassle. I'm going to see if the kids are ready. We need to be leaving fairly soon."

***

As it turned out, the wedding and reception went fine - well, apart from Matt and Clare's girls playing up throughout, which had been more or less expected. And some sort of incident - at the reception, at Mum's - involving Jade and Gemma.

Still, I actually really enjoyed the day, on the whole. Some of those moments are the ones I will always look back on. It was that feeling of security, of being a couple - Kev and me.

It was a sunny July day, a family wedding, and there were moments when we just looked at each other and smiled, and I was so proud, to be there with the man I loved.

Kev was bloody uncomfortable, for the most part, of course - and yet, there were times when I felt him relax, however briefly, and really be present.

It was everything I could have dreamt of. Everything. It was real, and I knew, even then, that it couldn't last. But at least I had something to hold on to. Remember.

And now, after all that has happened, I still think about that day. After all, we need to remember the good times, don't we? No matter how things may have ended. Nothing can destroy our memories, or extract them from our hearts and minds.

Chapter Twenty-Four

"It's only a couple of hours, Luce. I've got to meet Jake down the pub."

Kev and I had been living together for approaching five months, and the honeymoon period, such as it had ever been, was over.

"Jake Bryant? Kev, you know I can't stand that piece of shit. What do you have to meet *him* for?"

"Business, babe. You know how it is. I don't particularly like the guy either, but needs must."

"Right - well, good to know where your loyalties lie, anyway."

"I can't avoid the entire Bryant family, just because you have an issue with the kid sister. Be reasonable."

"Whatever," I said, taking my frustration out on the stain I'd been trying to remove from the basin. "I'm wasting my breath anyway, but can't you take the kids with you? Well, obviously not to the King's Head, but can't you drop them off at Deborah's parents' or something?"

"This is my access time. Deborah's probably made her own plans. Anyway, I don't want to give them back. This is my time with them, not hers. It's my right, to see my own kids. And leave that bloody sink alone. The stain's been there for years, and it's never bothered me half as much as your obsession with getting rid of it."

I slammed down the cloth I'd been using. "Stay here with them, then. You won't see them if you bugger off at barely noon, and stagger back in the small hours."

I noticed that, this time, he didn't even bother to deny that this was how long he would be away, or that he would be "staggering back". "I don't know what your problem is," he said. "They haven't been bad."

"*Toby's* no problem, of course."

"I don't like what you're implying."

"I'm not 'implying' anything. I'm telling you straight out that your daughter's a nightmare. Sure, she's been on her best behaviour, but I could see that look in her eyes. The second you walk out of that door, she'll be making my life hell."

"Keep your voice down. They'll hear you."

"I don't care. Gemma knows exactly what she's doing. She's a nasty piece of work."

"She's nine years old."

"She's not right in the head."

"That's a joke, when you consider your nieces, especially that Jade."

"That's for Matthew and Clare to worry about, even if it *is* true. Anyway, I'm not making you babysit Jade, am I?"

"Lucy, I'm going out, and that's all there is to it. They're your bloody step-kids. It won't hurt you to look after them for a couple of hours.

"They are *not* my step-kids. We're not married. You're not even technically divorced yet, so don't try that one on me. Gemma and Toby are your responsibility."

"Fine. Chuck them out in the street, then. I'm not arguing with you any more. I'm late enough, as it is."

"You can't just..."

"Screw you, Lucy. I'll do what I fucking well want. You got that?" Kev grabbed my arm, and looked directly at me. There was something in those eyes that terrified me into sudden silence - a tangible threat of violence in the air, that I'd experienced a couple of times lately.

I felt myself slipping away. Gone - the stubborn, defiant girl, who didn't take shit from anyone. She was replaced by the wreck I became, whenever Kev managed to make me feel this way - as if I was nothing. Less than nothing. Filthy, worthless.

***

"Dad slept with your sister, too - that's what I heard. She got pregnant, and had a baby boy. That's our half-brother, technically - mine and Toby's." Gemma looked up at me, with those huge blue eyes, as she spoke, all the while playing around with that crimson hair band, that she so often wore in her curly, blonde hair.

"Haven't you got any homework to do?"

"Done it. It's all pretty easy. I'm not thick, like your niece, Jade. They couldn't get her into nursery, or even playgroup, and she's going to be in remedial group, once she goes up to the juniors at St. Andrew's."

"Something else you 'heard', Gemma?"

"Yes, as it goes. My best friend, Lila - she knows everything."

"Everything? As much as that? I *am* impressed."

I began to seriously wonder how Deborah coped with this kid. Gemma's attitude stank.

Yeah, well - if Kev thought he was going to pull a trick like this on me again, he could forget it. I might be getting sick of Gemma, but lately, I was growing equally sick of her dad.

She had to have got it from *somewhere*, right?

I smiled reassuringly in Toby's direction - poor lad, cowering in the corner, as per usual. He must have been the butt of Kev's cruel jokes, yelling, threats, and probably at least some degree of actual violence, throughout his childhood, thus far. It couldn't not have had some effect.

What I'd seen of Kev's interactions with his son and daughter were, of course, the tip of the iceberg. But I'd seen more than enough for me - much more than I cared to witness, or could ever justify.

Chapter Twenty-Five

"What's wrong with you?"

"Nothing," I replied, but the fact that I'd pulled away from my boyfriend, and practically leapt out of bed, clearly contradicted my statement. I was in the process of looking for something to wear, which task was proving to be less straightforward than one might imagine. "Kev, why do we have to live like this?"

"Like what?"

I picked up a pile of dirty laundry, discarded on the floor. "We don't even have a laundry basket."

"So buy one, if you're that bothered."

"I wanted to do a wash earlier, but Farooq put on a load, practically the instant the couple across the corridor took theirs out."

"So now you want your own personal washing machine, as well as a fucking laundry basket? Anything else, Your Royal Highness?" Kev was lighting up. I hated that he had to smoke in bed. Apart from anything else, it was bloody dangerous. "You know, Deb mostly used to hand wash, and she had two kids, as well. I don't see what you're moaning about."

"Don't you want anything from life, apart from surviving day after day, and making dodgy deals, with your so-called 'mates' down the King's Head?" I searched his expression for something - anything, other than indifference and apathy. "Wouldn't you rather have our own place, than live in a shithole like this?"

"Right - you mean, a nice, four bedroom detached house, in the pretty part of town, like you lived in with Mummy?"

"I'm not talking about a four bedroom house, but surely we could afford our own flat or something? I hate living like this."

At that moment, the doorbell rang.

"Leave it," said Kev.

I was going to at first, but whomever it was started to hammer on the door. It seemed stupid to ignore it, and end up with a brick through the window.

"You don't even know who it is. It might be for someone else." I was getting sick of ignoring the front door or phone, every time I was instructed to do so.

Kev grabbed me. "I *said* to leave it. I don't give a fuck who it is, and as for the other residents, no one's home anyway, and I'm not the fucking butler, for that lot."

"No one's asking you to be. *I'll* get the door."

"I'll check who it is first, okay?" Kev went over to the window. "There you go, Luce - just some whore. I told you it wasn't worth the bother."

I looked for myself. "Kev, it's Donna, your cousin's girlfriend."

"As I said - some whore."

Donna had reached the stage of crying and shouting obscenities. She was here because she needed a fix. We both knew that.

"I'm going to let her in," I told him.

"Whatever. I'm sick of arguing the toss with you, but she's wasting my time, and her own."

I went down and opened the door to Donna. Her long, white-blonde hair was dishevelled, and there was a wild, crazy form of desperation in her grey eyes. Her jeans and T-shirt looked as if she'd been wearing them, day and night, for at least a week, which was entirely possible.

When I'd first met Donna, she'd been stunning, and as vain and fashion-conscious as our Cath. A few years down the line with Mark Jordan - and, let's just say, the way of life was taking its toll. At twenty-five, Donna Mann could have passed for forty.

"I need to see Kev," she said, barging past me.

I followed her upstairs. She hammered at the door of Kev's and my room, which he'd locked behind me. I reached into my pocket, for my own key, and opened up.

"Donna, what a pleasant surprise. What can I do for you?" I didn't see why Kev had to be sarcastic, and wind the girl up even more. She was clearly at rock bottom, as it was, and he was either going to supply her or not.

"I'm going to the loo," I said - because I genuinely needed a comfort break, and it also served as an excuse for me to leave them to it, for a few minutes. Kev didn't like me hanging around, when he was "talking business", and I wasn't too keen on hearing about it, anyway.

By the time I was washing my hands, Kev had reduced his cousin's girlfriend to a sobbing, screaming wreck. I dried my hands, as well as I could, using the threadbare, beige hand towel, unlocked the bathroom door, and headed back to our room.

"I'll do anything. You know I will. I'll give you a blow job, like last time." I was standing outside the door, key in hand, when Donna came out with that - and I unlocked the door, and stood there, looking my boyfriend in the eye.

Of course, he turned on Donna. "You fucking whore. Like I'd touch you with a barge poll. Get out!"

"No! You've *got* to help me. Please, Kev - I'm begging you."

"Fuck off."

"All I need is-"

He grabbed her. "To fuck off, Donna. All you need is to fuck off, and leave me and my girlfriend alone. But, before you leave, you can tell Lucy you were lying. I've never touched you in my life. Just because you and Mark carry on like that, doesn't mean we're all into prostitution and casual sex."

"Let go of her, Kev," I told him. "She doesn't have to tell me anything, or cover for you."

"There's nothing to fucking cover for. I've not touched her."

"Fine, whatever you say - but we can discuss that later. I want you to let go of Donna."

The row continued for several minutes, with Kev still refusing to release Donna. She struggled to free herself but, as a fragile woman, who probably weighed under six stone nowadays, she didn't stand a chance. My desperate attempts to help, in this respect, were equally futile. Kev was way too strong for either of us, or even both of us, put together.

The three of us ended up outside the room - and when it happened, it happened so fast. And yet, for a moment, everything seemed to switch into slow motion in my mind, as I watched Donna falling. Kev had chucked her down those stairs, almost casually, as if she were some inanimate object, of no value whatsoever.

I pushed past him. Raced downstairs, risking an injury myself. Donna was lying at the foot of the stairs.

There was one terrifying moment, when I wasn't sure. She wasn't moving, and there was blood. She'd cut her face. Then, Donna did move, and she was crying again. She was alive.

I knelt beside her, where she had fallen. "Are you okay? Should I call an ambulance?"

"You fucking dare," said Kev, who had followed me downstairs. Then, he actually kicked Donna's injured body.

"You bastard. You could have killed her. You really don't give a shit, do you?"

"No, I don't. She's a slag. Just chuck her out with the other rubbish, although I don't expect the bin man would touch anything as soiled as *that*. I'm off out. I'm supposed to be meeting Jake and Farooq down the pub, and I'm running late, thanks to all this bullshit and drama."

"Have you got *no* compassion?"

Kev's reply was in the form of the look he gave me, before continuing to walk towards the front door, which he slammed behind him.

I turned my attention to Donna, who was at least sitting up now. "Do you need an ambulance, Donna?"

She got to her feet. It had obviously taken every ounce of her limited strength to do so, however, and the girl was clearly in agony. "No - thanks, but no. I'll be okay."

Donna left, and it wasn't until she had been gone for about five minutes that it really hit me, and I finally broke down.

I called Charlotte in tears, and told her exactly what had gone down.

"You've got to leave him, Luce. You must be able to see that."

"It's not that simple, is it?"

"Yes, it is. If you showed up here, or at your mum's, or one of your brother's - you know none of us would turn you away, don't you?"

"It won't come to that, Charlotte - but yeah, I know - and thank you. I do need to see you, though. We've been like strangers lately."

"Well, I keep saying you should come over. We're going to Tara's mum's tomorrow, but Sunday afternoon would be good for me. That said, if the case becomes urgent - well, I gave you a key, so come any time."

"I'll be okay," I said, and realised my words were identical to Donna's. And she hadn't exactly been "okay", either. "Oh, and Sunday sounds good. Thanks, Charlotte."

Chapter Twenty-Six

"Tara was saying earlier - we've hardly seen you since the wedding," said Charlotte.

The flat was decorated very much in Charlotte's style, with plenty of pale grey and pink. It was certainly less cluttered than it would have been, had my cousin lived there alone.

"Yeah, it does feel that way. Where *is* Tara, anyway?"

"Had to pop out to the shops - shouldn't be long. She probably realised we'd want to catch up though, so she might take a detour."

I nodded. "I still can't get used to - to things as they are. Are you happy?"

"Yes, very much so. It would be easier if everyone was happy *for* us, but you can't have everything in life, and the people who matter most are supportive. Mum's been amazing, of course."

There was a brief silence, during which I focused on stroking the two cats - Ada, Tara's ageing tabby, and their more recent arrival, a black-and-white rescue cat, Matilda - who were competing for my attention.

"It went well, didn't it - the wedding, I mean?" said Charlotte.

"Oh yes, I think it was always going to. Danny and Hannah are so bloody perfect together. Makes me sick, but I'm pleased for them too, of course."

"I half wondered if Catherine would show up, to be honest."

"I'm glad she didn't."

"Yes, I suppose you're right. It wasn't the time or place."

"If I ever see Catherine Ryman again, it will be too soon." I reached for my tea, and took a couple of sips.

"How's Sarah?" asked Charlotte.

"Drunk, mostly. Hanging around with Kirsty Bryant and her lot - hardly talks to Fiona or Tracy any more. She's seeing that Farooq - the one who lives at the house."

The house. The phrase echoed in my mind. For some reason, I still didn't call it *home*. It was always "the house". That was how Kev referred to it, too. It didn't feel much like a home, even though we both lived there.

Lived - or maybe *existed* would have been more appropriate.

"Have you seen Primrose? She's the sweetest thing ever - could really see James in her eyes, although she looks a lot like both of her parents, I thought."

"Saw her briefly, yes. I can't say I noticed her eyes, but she's beautiful, of course. All babies are."

"Sorry, Luce. I guess it must still feel a little strange for you. I just assumed - well, because you're with Kev now and everything..."

"I'm fine about the baby, Charlotte. Why wouldn't I be? I'm with Kev now, as you said. Why should I care about James and Erica, and their damn baby, anyway? I couldn't care less, if you must know." Holy crap, I was shaking.

Charlotte came over, and sat next to me on the sofa. She hugged me, and I stopped fighting the tears. My friend stroked my hair, tenderly.

I hadn't felt close to her for so long. There had been a feeling of distance and disconnection between us, but in that moment, Charlotte and I honestly felt like best friends again.

"I don't know how I feel about James and Erica," I said. "I guess I *am* jealous in a way, but I don't want him back. It isn't that. I mean, if everything was going well with Kev..."

"Which it isn't?"

"No. I mean, it was good at first, or at least, I told myself it was. I guess it was never great, but that's life, right? No relationship is perfect."

"Of course not. Some are considerably further from that ideal than others, though."

"You're telling me. It's awful, Charlotte," I admitted. "Kev's getting out of control, with the drink. And drugs. He's using more hard drugs now. It was mainly hash before, but now - it's heroin mostly, some cocaine, and pretty much anything else he can get his hands on." I hadn't intended to blurt out any of that, but then again, I either talked to my friend or I didn't, right?

"Well, you knew he was into drugs."

"Yeah, and I lived with it, but it wasn't this bad before. Is it hypocritical, that I'm willing to overlook him getting customers hooked on that crap, as long as he doesn't get too messed up on the stuff himself?"

"It *is* hypocritical, but it's also understandable, and it's not up to me to judge, is it? The thing is, me and Tara - we've smoked a bit of hash, and been around people who were into hard drugs. And, let's face it, Luce - we all like a drink or ten sometimes. But, seriously, Kev Tanner - he's out of our league."

"He's out of his own league."

"Well, you know what I think. I mean, that thing you described, with Donna - how can you keep on living with the guy, after something like that?"

"Two reasons, I guess. I love him, and I'm also terrified. He said once that, if I ever left him, he'd kill me first, and then himself."

"Threats and emotional blackmail? Lucy, that's completely out of order. Surely you can see that? And how the hell can you love someone who treats you like that - who, in your own words, 'terrifies' you?"

"I didn't say I liked everything about Kev - but there's another side to him, and I do still love him. I think about walking out sometimes, but I don't think I could, not really."

Tara came in, at that point, and Charlotte and I left it there, with the heavy topics of conversation. It was good to have said some of that, even though it changed nothing, in practical terms.

And it also helped just to be around Charlotte and Tara, and have their company, for a change. Even a temporary escape from my situation was something, and made a huge difference.

Chapter Twenty-Seven

It was June 1985, and I'd been living with Kev for just over a year. I had a feeling the situation couldn't go on for much longer, but also knew I must focus upon the matter in hand.

Because, if I was close to breaking point - Sarah was even closer.

I was on the verge of giving up, when the front door finally opened. "Mrs. Bryant?"

"Yes." The woman, with shoulder-length, grey hair, might have been in her fifties - maybe not even that old - but she had a look about her that was old before her time. She was pale, and excruciatingly thin. Emerald eyes, full of fear, stared at me, from the skull that was her face.

"I'm Lucy Ryman," I explained. "Sarah Ryman's sister."

She looked blank for a moment. Then, seemed to make the connection. "Oh, Sarah - Kirsty's friend. Her *sister*, you say?" She still appeared somewhat confused, but then, Kirsty's mother wouldn't exactly have been expecting me to drop by.

"Yes, that's right. Can I come in, please? I wanted to talk to you."

"Of course, dear," she said, leading me through a cluttered entrance hall, and into the living room.

The place was, at first glance, much as one might have expected. A mess, basically. Yet, somehow - not quite as I had imagined. It was certainly untidy, but didn't stink of drink and drugs, as per the King's Head.

Was I prejudiced to have expected Kirsty's family home to be exactly like the King's Head pub?

"I'm sorry it's such a mess," she said, as if reading my mind. "My eldest son and his girlfriend brought their three over first thing, and I was clearing up after their visit, when my daughter-in-law showed up, with her newborn, and...I'm sorry, dear. You don't want to hear this boring family stuff."

I smiled, in spite of myself. "It's okay," I said, "and I know a bit about large families myself. I'm the second youngest of five, and my eldest brother has three kids. My sister-in-law, Hannah, is expecting her first."

"Oh yes, I remember now. Sarah mentioned being the youngest, and having several brothers and sisters."

Mrs. Bryant moved a pile of Lego from a faded green armchair, so that I could sit down. She reached for one of the many photographs that were lined up, in cheap-looking frames, on the mantlepiece, along with a few, mainly brass, ornaments, most of which were dusty.

The photo frame she handed me was covered in dust, too. I instinctively brushed it off, as I took it from her.

"These are my seven kids. I'm hoping to persuade them to pose for another, this time with the grandkids. Eleven, and one great grandson."

I looked at six men, ages ranging from early twenties to about thirty, and Kirsty. All of Kirsty's brothers were tall and thin, with wavy, ginger hair. Two, including one I guessed to be the eldest, wore glasses. Kirsty, with her peroxide blonde hair, clearly sporting dark roots, stood out a mile, being the only girl, and obviously the youngest, and not having the characteristic red hair. I recognised two of the brothers as Jake and John, who frequented the King's Head.

"Would you like a cup of tea or coffee?" asked Mrs. Bryant.

I considered for a moment, aware that I was becoming a little too comfortable here. Wasn't I supposed to be addressing the issue of Kirsty Bryant being a bad influence on Sarah? The fact that I actually *liked* the mother wasn't helping me to stick to the point.

"Coffee, please - white, one sugar," I heard myself saying, almost against my own will.

When she handed me the mug, I noticed her hand shaking. In fact, she was shaking in general. She could have a drink problem, but somehow, I didn't think so. Even though it wouldn't have been too far-fetched, considering the reputation of the Bryant family, as a whole. My guess was that she suffered from anxiety, in common with my own mother.

Having raised six Bryant lads and daughter Kirsty, it was easy to imagine that day to day stress levels would be significant.

It was doubtful, when I left three hours later, whether I had achieved much towards my original goal: persuading Mrs. Bryant to actively do something about controlling her teenage daughter's behaviour. Still, I had more of an insight into Kirsty's background, and had even encountered two of her older brothers, at one point - one of whom, Jake, I already knew.

I was considering all of this, as I walked home, several coffees, and a few slices of fruit cake, later. Home, as in Mum's, since I couldn't immediately face returning to *the house*.

And that was when I spotted James and Erica, with their little girl, Primrose, and instinctively dived into a random alleyway. My heart was pounding, and for one awful moment, I believed I was actually going to throw up.

But the wave of nausea passed, as swiftly as it had arrived, and I was sure they hadn't seen me.

James wanted to be friends again. That was what Charlotte had told me, several times. I didn't know how I felt about that any more. I'd never wanted to stop. I wouldn't have, either - could even have accepted about his relationship with Erica.

It was the way he'd gone about it - and *now* he wanted to be friends? Good for him. I had no idea whether I wanted that or not.

My mind was processing everything. He'd looked well - and Erica, stunning, wearing a floral dress, with blonde highlights in her auburn hair, and a glowing complexion.

As for Primrose - she was undeniably cute. And yet, it hurt so much to look at her, even for an instant: the final knife twist, in a sense. James and Erica had their perfect little girl, the one James and I should have...

Don't go there, Lucy. Just don't, okay?

Anyway, I was with Kev now. It might not be going great, but that was reality - adult life and all that. Behind the scenes, no relationship was perfect. No, not even James and Erica's - even if it *did* do a damn good impression.

I brushed away a couple of tears, as I emerged from the alleyway, and continued heading in the direction of my family home.

And I still hadn't solved my original problem, either. I still had no idea what to do about the fact that Sarah, at sixteen, was going off the rails, under the influence of Kirsty Bryant and Co.

***

It was Sarah who answered the door. My sister had short, blonde hair now, and wore a ton of make-up. Was looking more like Kirsty Bryant, by the day.

But that was the least of my problems, right then. Something had happened. Sarah's purple mascara was smudged, and her eyes were so red, that they were approaching burgundy. "Luce, we've been trying to get hold of you."

From the direction of the lounge, I heard other members of my family, crying. Someone had died.

"Is it Nan?"

"No, not Nan," said Sarah.

I knew then that it had to be Mum's elder sister, Sylvia, who'd had a heart attack, in recent years. I tried to recall my aunt's age - fifty-five, perhaps? Not old - I was certain of that much. And they had been close. Mum must be heartbroken.

"Lucy, it's Bonita."

I stared at her, not understanding. "What *about* Bonita? What's going on here? I thought someone had *died*."

"*Bonita's* dead. Let's go upstairs, okay? I need to tell you what's happened."

Chapter Twenty-Eight

I had barely entered our old bedroom, since moving out. The walls looked bare without the Spandau Ballet posters. They were painted a different colour, too: peach, instead of the usual pink.

I sat next to Sarah, on her bed. At least I recognised her bedspread - and that was still pink. "How did...?"

"Clare was taking the girls to her sister's. From what I can make out, Jade was playing up, bullying Jess, and Bonita was trying to keep the peace - all the usual stuff, you know. Of course, I wasn't there, and Clare's hardly said a word, so most of what we *do* know has come from Julie Rollins and her mum."

I nodded.

"Clare was stressed out," continued Sarah, "the way she gets sometimes, but worse than average, I guess. She was having a bad day. She just kept yelling at the kids. Then, Jade pulled Jessica's hair really hard, and Jess was screaming her head off, and Clare was trying to deal with them both. They were waiting to cross the road, at the time - Carrington Avenue, so not far from Edwina's house. Bonita saw Julie, with her mum, across the road. She said: 'Mum, that's Julie from school,' but Clare was too busy dealing with the twins, so Bonnie raced out into the road by herself. Clare tried to grab her, but too late. She was hit by a lorry. Died instantly." Tears were streaming down Sarah's face. "I can't believe it, Luce. She was seven."

I hugged my sister, with a sense that I was going through the motions. I could feel the tears sliding down my cheeks, taste them in my mouth, but I didn't feel as if they were really my own. It felt as if this was happening to another family, on a film or something, and I was watching, watching from a distant land, and feeling the emotions, but they weren't mine. None of this was happening. I could stop watching, at any point - could hit *Pause* or *Stop*, *Fast*

Forward or *Rewind*. Then it would all be over, and we could get back to normal, and stop pretending that this tragedy was real.

That Bonita, our Bonnie, had been knocked down by a lorry. That Bonita was dead.

***

There was a box of tissues on the dining table, of which Mum and Hannah had clearly been making good use. Danny was stroking his, heavily pregnant, wife's light brown hair, his own eyes red. Tears slid steadily down Edwina's fat cheeks, as she sat with her arm around her younger sister.

Clare, for her part, was not crying. Sat, almost expressionless, staring at the russet table cloth.

"Lucy," said Mum, "no one knew where you were, darling."

"Where's Matt?"

Sarah looked anguished. "He needs some space, Luce." However, she nodded in the direction of the kitchen, knowing I would go to our brother, anyway.

He was sitting at the table, drinking brandy straight from the bottle. I closed the door behind me.

"Matt," I said, "I'm so sorry." I tried to fight the tears, but failed.

My brother didn't respond at all. Didn't even look up at me - just sat there, ignoring me and drinking.

"You shouldn't be drinking that stuff," I told him, knowing that to do so was useless.

For a moment, which felt so much longer than it must actually have been, nothing happened - nothing at all. The silence continued.

Then, Matt looked at me for the first time since I'd arrived: "That Steven's coming over, you know. She called him right away - reckoned he had 'a right to know'. Like fucking hell. I told her: 'If you call him now, it's finished between us.' She told me it was finished already - so that's that. The relationship's over, and it's ironic, because for so long, it seemed like the worst thing that could ever happen - and now, it really has, and I don't even care."

I came closer to him, and put my arms around his shoulders, which were full of tension. "You and Clare are both in shock. Neither of you are thinking straight."

Matthew shook his head. "It's over," he said. "I'm tired of it all, and I can't live a lie any more."

"Where are the twins?"

"Edward and Vera's." Edward and Vera being Clare's parents.

Matthew was crying now, too. He finally let me hug him, collapsing like a dead weight into my arms. I just held on to him, still not really accepting that any of this was real.

He only pulled away when the doorbell rang. We were both waiting for Steven's voice, but it was Charlotte and Tara. I could hear them asking after me.

"You'd better go," said Matt. "I'll be okay."

I looked at him. Somehow, I doubted that. But I nodded anyway, sensing that he did need space. We would just have to make sure, as a family, that he wasn't given too much.

I hugged my cousin briefly, and my best friend a little longer. We were all crying. None of us could think of a thing to say to each other, and we somehow knew not to try.

"Mum sent her love," said Charlotte, eventually. "James, too. He wanted to come with me and Tara, when I told him - but he wasn't sure if that was appropriate, and I didn't know, either."

"It would be good to see him," I said. "He's always welcome. He should know that."

Charlotte nodded. "Thanks, Luce. I'll tell him you said that, and I'm sure he'll be in touch, as soon as he can." She paused. "I don't think he planned to bring Erica or Primrose, by the way. I can clarify, if you like."

"Either way, Charlotte - James is welcome. I don't have a problem with Erica, and certainly not with little Primrose." I was surprised at my own words, and more so to realise, as I spoke them, that they were the truth.

Life really could change in an instant, and I didn't even know who that girl was, who had ducked into an alleyway, to avoid seeing her ex-boyfriend with his wife and kid.

My mind was gradually making the connections, joining the dots. I thought about Tina, James's little sister, with her white-blonde curls, and vast collection of Sindy and Barbie dolls. She was the same age as Bonnie - had been three weeks old, when my niece was born. They were in the same class at school, and were friends, although not best friends. Tina's best friend was Julie Rollins - the girl who, along with her mother, had witnessed the accident.

I stayed at my family home that night.

Chapter Twenty-Nine

Less than a month after Bonita's death, Danny and Hannah's son, Joshua Daniel, was born. The emotions of the whole family were, needless to say, all over the place.

Matt and Clare remained together, but barely. Jade was getting into more fights than ever at school, whilst Jessica became increasingly withdrawn, spending most of her time alone, in a fantasy world of her own creation.

Sarah was still up and down, drinking way too much, and spending most of her time with either boyfriend Farooq, or Kirsty.

James and I were friends again, and I was even getting on okay with Erica, although part of me would always feel that she was too old for James, and just not right for him somehow. Maybe a tiny part of me would always be in love with him, and yet, our friendship felt like enough, and comfortable. I enjoyed being able to hang around with both James and Charlotte. And sometimes, Matt would join us - maybe for a quick drink at the Lion - which seemed to do him good.

As for Kev - what can I say? It wasn't working, and I knew what I had to do, but still, was too scared to do it.

Or *had* been, until now.

It felt surreal. There I was, in that too-familiar room, with Charlotte and James, stuffing my belongings into bags.

"A lot of this furniture is yours, isn't it?" said James.

"Yeah, but I'm letting it go. There's enough at my mum's, and I can always buy more."

"Lucy's right," said Charlotte. "We just need to get her out of here. It's not safe."

"Don't be dramatic, Charlotte. Kev's not that bad."

"Yeah? Then, why did we have to come here when he's out - and why are we rushing to get this done, before he comes back?"

I didn't reply. My friends and I continued to grab anything and everything, and were about to leave. Then, we heard the front door opening. It was probably Farooq. He often came in at around four in the afternoon, on Saturdays.

Except that it wasn't Farooq. The door of our room opened, and Kev was standing there.

"What the hell is going on, Lucy? What are those two doing here?"

I froze, exactly as I was, my hand on the zip of a bag, which I'd stuffed full of clothes, mostly T-shirts and underwear. Before I could do anything to stop him, Kev grabbed the bag, and emptied the contents on to the floor.

"Please, Kev - just let me go. You must know as well as I do, things haven't been working between us."

"You want to go - what, with these two? What *is* this, some sort of three-way relationship, with your lezzy girlfriend and McIntyre?"

He grabbed Charlotte and flung her across the room, as if she was nothing: exactly as he had with Donna. How could I have blocked that out - told myself that Kev wasn't really like that? He *was*.

I was checking that Charlotte was okay, when Kev got hold of the one he really wanted to hurt: James.

He'd been livid about our revived friendship, and never had trusted me, when I'd assured him repeatedly, that James was a friend, and nothing more.

Kev had him pinned against the wall.

"Let go of him, Kev. I'll never forgive you, if you hurt him."

Kev released James, but continued to glare at him. "Thought you were meant to be with Erica Lee, mate - converted her from being a lesbian with Lyndhurst's now-girlfriend, if we can keep up with your twisted relationships?"

"Erica McIntyre," said James, obviously struggling to keep his voice from shaking as much as his body - and yet, determined to defend the most important relationships in his life. "We're married, with a daughter, Primrose. Charlotte and I are Lucy's oldest friends, and she asked us to help her today. We were concerned for her welfare."

"I should fucking kill the pair of you, and if you don't get out of our home, I will. I'm not letting you drag Lucy into your kinky, three-in-a-bed thing - or however many in a bed it *is*, what with Erica, and Lucy's cousin, and whoever else is involved."

"They *will* leave, and I'm going with them," I said. "I'm not moving in with Charlotte and James, and we're not in some sort of 'three-in-a-bed' relationship. It's you who's 'twisted' and 'kinky', if you actually think that way. I'm going back to my mum's."

"Like hell." He totally lost it, at that point, and started knocking whole shelves of things down, and smashing things ups, and generally trashing what had been as close as we had had to a home together.

"You'd better go," I told James and Charlotte.

"Come with us," said James.

"We can't just leave you here, Luce," added Charlotte.

I shook my head. I'd been here before, with Kev going nuts like this, and knew I had to talk to him. I was still leaving, but I couldn't not talk to him first. It wouldn't work, not now. "I'll be fine."

"We can call the police, if you like," said James.

"No, James - please, don't do that. It will be okay. Me and Kev just need to talk. Thanks for your help, and I'll call you both later."

I'd been wrong, anyway - to try to leave without saying a word. Then again, I had been - *was* - terrified.

And yet, I could predict that the smashing up of everything in sight, could only last for so long - and I knew, in that moment, that Kev wouldn't hurt me. Not this time.

It was almost immediate, once the door slammed, and James and Charlotte were gone. Kev collapsed to the floor, and broke down entirely.

I knelt down beside him, stroking his hair, as if he were a newborn baby, and then I kissed the top of his head.

"Don't go, Luce." The anguish in his eyes, and seeing him cry, was a knife that twisted, deep inside of me, and it was all I could do not to start crying myself.

"I have to." Later, I would cry. I would probably cry right through the night. I couldn't see myself getting much, if any, sleep, after this.

"You don't. Things will be better, I promise."

"They won't. You know they won't."

"So, what about the kids? You're walking out on them, too?"

"We didn't have any," I said. "The kids are yours and Deborah's."

"Don't try to make out you don't care. I know you do. Even Gem's accepted you. I spoil Gem, and can't deal with Toby. Deb spoils Toby, and can't deal with Gemma. You're great with them both."

The lump in my throat was becoming dangerous. "I think the world of Gemma and Toby, but don't use your own kids to emotionally blackmail me. That's cheap."

And I left, grabbing one random bag, out of those packed by my friends and me.

Chapter Thirty

You know that feeling, when the logical part of your brain is telling you that you'll be fine without someone - that the person caused you nothing but heartache and drama, anyway - but somehow, your heart won't agree?

That was where I was at. I couldn't stop thinking about Kev, and breaking down.

Monday tomorrow. I hardly dared to consider how I'd get through the day - the *week* - at work. Every damn thing seemed to trigger some memory or other. One minute, I'd think of something that filled me with rage. The next, something that brought out the other side: tenderness, compassion, and love. There was no denying it. I *did* still love him. I always would.

I was hanging on by a thread, and even basic, day to day functioning felt almost impossible.

Still, life *did* go on. It had to. And we were all supposed to be meeting at Danny and Hannah's - sort of a first sibling get together since Josh was born - except minus Catherine, and apparently, minus Sarah, too.

"Hi, Lucy," said Danny, showing me through to the lounge, which was decorated with blue and white balloons. "No Kev?"

"He couldn't make it."

I could tell, from Danny's expression, that it was taking every ounce of his willpower to resist making a sarcastic comment. Hannah must have him under instructions not to. I'd asked Mum and Sarah not to mention that I'd moved back in with them. It was all too raw, and I wasn't ready for questions.

Besides, this was supposed to be about Josh.

And, in truth, even if I *had* still been with Kev, he wouldn't have come. He would have made up some lame excuse, and gone to meet his mates down the King's Head, as per usual.

But, as I said, Josh. It was about him, and that was who I wanted to focus on here: not myself - and not Kev Tanner.

Just when I was about to ask where Hannah and the guest of honour actually were, they appeared. I approached them, and impulsively reached out to touch my baby nephew, who immediately began to bawl.

"Thanks a lot, Lucy. It's only taken me three hours to get him to sleep," snapped Hannah. She handed the baby to Danny. "Your son - you sort him out, for once." That said, she stormed out of the room again, slamming the door behind her.

"I don't know what the hell is wrong with her," said Danny, a good five minutes later, having finally managed to soothe Josh, and even got the cutest smile ever out of the child.

"He *is* adorable, isn't he? He has your eyes. Can I hold him?"

Danny handed Josh to me. "You know how to support his head, don't you?"

I rolled my eyes. "I looked after all of Matt's girls. I should know how to hold a baby by now."

"I know, but Hannah said to make sure..." His voice trailed off. "Honestly, she's driving me around the bend. She used to be such a calm person." His voice was low, almost a whisper. I wasn't sure if that was more for Josh's benefit or his wife's, but I was guessing, the latter.

"And now she has a newborn baby, Dan. You're saying that's made even *Hannah* a little stressed?"

"'A little'? It's like being at Matt and Clare's. I mean, they've always been like that, haven't they - rowing constantly, and chucking objects around, and stuff like that?"

"For as long as I can remember," I admitted. "Then again, they do have small kids, too." *One less, of course - but that's another subject not to be dwelt upon. Focus on Josh, Lucy. Danny, Hannah, and their firstborn son.*

"Matt and Clare would be like that, with or without kids. I know plenty of people with kids who aren't completely crazy. Mum was never like that, for a start."

"She had her moments."

Danny didn't get the chance to respond, before Hannah was back. She marched over to me, and demanded that I give Josh to her.

"I might have known you couldn't be bothered to hold him, even for a few minutes, Danny Ryman."

"Hannah, it wasn't Danny. I asked if-"

"Stay out of this, Lucy," said Hannah, as she stormed out of the room once more, with Josh in her arms, who predictably started to cry again.

I placed a hand on Danny's arm. "She'll be okay. Talking of Matt and Clare, what time are they due?"

"Anyone's guess - but I spoke to Matt earlier, and he said they'd definitely be here. Sarah isn't coming, though."

"I know. She reckoned she was 'busy'. I think that translates as 'getting drunk with Kirsty Bryant' - and that's if we're lucky."

"*That's* lucky?"

"It is, when the alternative is that Farooq. Of course, our sister has never had 'exclusive rights'. Farooq's into 'open relationships'."

I'd seen it all, of course - having lived in the same house as Farooq. Sarah stayed over sometimes, but she definitely wasn't the only one.

"Yeah, well - don't encourage me to think too much about that piece of shit, or I'll go over there right now and punch his fucking lights out. I know Matt feels the same."

"He isn't worth doing time for, and you're a husband and father now."

"I know. That's seriously all that's stopping me, Luce." He hesitated. "I did ask Catherine, but she said she couldn't come, because you wouldn't like it."

"Really? Whatever gave her *that* idea?"

"You ought to get over it, you know. It isn't just about her and Kev, is it?"

Just as well that, at that moment, the intercom rang, and Danny was diverted by the need to let in Matt, Clare, and the twins. Hannah returned with the baby, and seemed comparatively calm, for the first time since my arrival.

Matt appeared stressed, as ever, and Clare looked pale and sick. She'd lost at least a stone in weight, since Bonita's death.

Jade whacked Jessica around the head, and Jess started screaming and pulling her sister's hair. In fact, I didn't know if it was good or bad that Jess was retaliating. That was out of character, and not good to see, but then again, she'd always let Jade get away with too much.

"Behave, the pair of you!" yelled their mother. "I'll be taking you both straight back home otherwise."

"Good," said Jade. "I never wanted to come, in the first place. I was gonna hang around with Carys and Becky. There's nothing to do here."

"Where's Sophie?" asked Jessica, referring to the ginger rescue cat Danny and Hannah had taken in, when they'd first lived together. Jess had always loved petting her.

I saw the interest in Jade's eyes too, and had to look away. Jade had enjoyed tormenting Sophie, every bit as much as Jess and Bonnie had loved stroking and playing with the animal.

"She's at my mum's, darling," explained Hannah. "She was showing signs of jealousy, when we first brought Josh home, and we couldn't risk having her here any more."

Jessica made her way over to Hannah, and her baby cousin, and started to take an interest in him instead, holding his little hands in her own. "He's so cute," she said, her eyes shining.

"He's ugly," said Jade. "I hate babies. I wish Sophie was here, so I could pull her tail."

Matt shot Clare a warning glance. He sometimes tried the *just ignore her* method, when Jade came out with things like that, whilst Clare tended to react to everything - increasingly so. It was obvious she viewed my brother's approach with contempt. Saw it as nothing more or less than letting Jade *get away with it.*

"No Kev, Luce?" asked Matt, turning to me.

Partly just something to say, of course, to move the subject away from Jade's comment. Still, I could have done without him starting too, having already had that exact question from Danny. "Couldn't make it," I replied.

Clare didn't say anything sarcastic. I almost wished she would, because I knew she had lost her *edge*, since Bonita's death, and even the absence of her sarcasm, in these moments, actually almost hurt. Served as yet another reminder that everything had changed. The family no longer functioned, even in its usual dysfunctional style.

"I saw James and Erica the other day," said Matt. "They'd been visiting Elizabeth and Stanley - caught them as they were leaving."

I smiled, politely. Of course, I was past the stage of being actively upset, every time I heard about James and Erica, and their kid. James and I were friends again, after all - and really, Erica wasn't so bad. Yet, the healing process wasn't linear, so it seemed. There were still moments when it was too much.

Matt, seeming not to notice my ambivalence, reached into the back pocket of his jeans, took out a photograph, and handed it to me. "He gave me this, but she's grown, even since this was taken." Primrose McIntyre wore a little cream dress, with bright yellow daisies on it. She was squinting at the camera, indicating a sunny day, and smiling like an angel.

I felt suddenly dizzy. It wasn't about Primrose, or her parents, any more. I knew that Clare had to have noticed, too. That dress, that bloody dress. It was like one of Bonnie's.

It happened so fast, after that. Clare ran out of the room, and Matthew looked at me, in confusion. He didn't even realise what he'd done. Men never *did* pay much attention to detail, with clothes and the like, but still, I couldn't believe he hadn't twigged. Danny and Hannah looked somewhat confused, too.

"The dress," I said. "Bonnie had one exactly like it."

"Shit," muttered Matt, as he raced after his girlfriend.

Jessica looked close to tears - Jade, halfway between bored and mildly amused. Josh didn't seem bothered either way, and had fallen asleep again, in his mother's arms.

Chapter Thirty-One

It was decided that Clare needed a complete break. After staying with her sister, Edwina, and family, for a few days, Matthew took her up to Durham, to her aunt's. He wouldn't comment on how long she was likely to be away. Matt himself, on Mum's insistence, and that of us all, returned to the family home, with the twins.

I watched as, yet again, my mother, who seemed to have aged at least ten years, in the past couple of months alone, attempted to deal with Jade.

"You *will* pick up that Lego, Jade. All of it. I'm not prepared to do it for you, and your dad will be too tired to deal with this, when he gets home, after a hard day's work."

"Make Mum come back and do it then. It's *her* job. She hasn't got anything better to do."

"Jade, we've been through this already. Just clear it up. You made the mess, and it's your responsibility to tidy up after yourself."

"There's fuck all you can do about it, if I don't. You're not my mum, and I don't even do what she says, let alone you."

She got a slap, at that point. "You are *not* to use language like that, Jade Ryman."

"I hate you! You can't fucking well hit me! I'll get the NSPCC on to you!"

I couldn't take any more. I'd moved back home expecting some degree of peace, away from Kev and the nutters he hung around with. But nowadays, my family home was no sanctuary.

I retreated to my room - technically Sarah's too, although she hadn't slept there at all for the past three weeks, and had only been back a couple of times.

I happened to glance over at Sarah's cello, in its case. I walked over to it, and touched the once-treasured item, brushing off a layer of dust.

I heard the front door open, and slam shut, and somehow guessed that it would be Sarah. It *was*, and she was, predictably, drunk.

I drowned out the noise of her argument with Mum, by putting on my Walkman, and turning up the volume as far as it would go. Some compilation I'd borrowed from Charlotte. I would still catch the occasional word from the row, and the silences between each track were agony.

The side ended, and I pressed *Fast Forward*. Why did they leave so much bloody silence at the end? There was room for another entire song on here.

I slammed the machine down on the writing desk, and went downstairs. I couldn't ignore this any more.

"I can't deal with this, Sarah - I really can't. I've got enough on my plate, with the twins. If you want to live with your so-called 'boyfriend', you know what to do: Move out. See how long you survive, out there in the real world."

"See, Nan? I could go to the NSPCC about this. Me and Jessica shouldn't have to live this way, being hit and living with drunks. It's against the fucking law. They'll have to take us into care, and put you all in prison for child abuse."

"If you like your chances, and you think you'll do better in care, you do that, Jade. I'm at my wit's end, dealing with your nonsense - I know that much. Sarah, where do you think *you're* going? I was talking to you."

"To my room, okay?"

"It's okay, Mum," I said. "I'll talk to her."

"Fine. I hope you have more luck than I have. It's time you went to your room too, Jade. Your sister has been in bed for hours."

I left Mum to argue the toss with my niece, and followed my sister upstairs.

Sarah lay on her bed, staring at the ceiling.

"You can't go on like this, you know," I told her.

She didn't respond. I was beginning to think that maybe Mum was right, and that I wouldn't have any more success than she had.

"I can't go and live with Farooq, Lucy," she said, finally. "We broke up."

"Sarah, look - I'm sorry. You're better off without that piece of shit. I know it doesn't feel that way right now, but-"

"Who says it doesn't? *He* didn't dump *me*, you know. I ended things. He treats me like crap, and I'm sick of it - sick of him and Kirsty, and all those people. I just couldn't handle the way Mum laid into me, the moment I walked through the door. Do you really think she'll kick me out?"

"No, of course not," I said. "I'll talk to her, okay? You need to get some sleep, Sarah. You can barely keep your eyes open, and you don't look as if you've slept in weeks."

I closed the door lightly behind me, feeling sure that Sarah would soon drift off.

As I stood on the landing, I heard something that was starting to worry me. Jessica was in what was currently her and Jade's bedroom - Cath's old room, and before that, Matt and Danny's. And my six-year-old niece was talking to herself again.

Well, as Matthew and Sarah had both said, when I'd mentioned it to them, this was hardly uncommon. It wasn't, sure, and I had certainly talked to myself at times, as a kid. Still did, now and again, especially at work. It helped me to focus on the task I was doing somehow - or, at least, that was how I justified it to Amy and Ruth.

Still, with Jessica, it was occurring a lot, and she did seem to be lost in a fantasy world, more often than not, which she disliked sharing with anyone else. She didn't appear to have any friends of her own: just Jade, and Carys and Becky, the two girls *she* was always knocking around with.

At that moment, I caught the name Jessica was using in her one-way conversation, and it was as if I'd been smacked in the face, with what we'd all been missing, but should surely have realised.

It all fell into place, and I felt hot tears, descending my cheeks. It made sense, didn't it? Jessica *would* turn to the only true friend she'd ever had: her sister, Bonita.

I made a mental note to have a word with Jess - after I'd hopefully had a much-needed night's sleep myself.

Chapter Thirty-Two

"I'm presuming that wasn't good news?" I said, as my brother replaced the receiver. I'd arrived home after work, to find Matthew dealing with a, clearly stressful, phone call. "Jade, I take it? What's she done this time?"

It was May 1986, by this point. I couldn't believe that, in less than a month, it would be the first anniversary of Bonita's death.

"Not Jade, although I wouldn't mind guessing she knows something about this. I thought she'd been suspiciously quiet. Luce, you wouldn't mind picking Jade up from Becky's, would you? You know where the Fishers live? Seventeen Walnut Drive - a few doors down from Danny's mate, Ivor."

"Yes, I know - and of course I don't mind, but what-?"

"I need to go to Perrin's, the newsagent's, and speak to the store manager. They've caught Jessica shoplifting." My brother looked pale, and frankly, exhausted.

"*Jessica*? Are you sure? It couldn't be that Jade gave her sister's name instead, could it? She's done that before." I'd find out soon enough, based upon whether Jade was actually *at* Becky's, of course.

"No, the guy said he even wondered that himself, for a moment, but then he remembered that Jade's the one with short hair. Unless she's got hold of a wig, which admittedly I wouldn't put past her, this is definitely Jess. He also told me that she hadn't stopped crying. Doesn't exactly sound like Jade, does it? I've got to go, Lucy."

Next thing I knew, the front door was slamming, and Matt was gone.

And I tried to make sense of yet another turn of events, as I walked briskly in the direction of Jade's friend's place.

Chapter Thirty-Three

"You have no faith in us, Matthew Ryman," I said.

"It's not that. I do. But this is the twins we're talking about. Well, let's face it: Jade. This is *Jade* we're talking about. Even Mum can't handle her."

"Yeah, well - Mum's a nervous wreck half the time. Has been since..." I didn't want to say "since Dad left", even though we both knew full well what I meant. "She's often been dealing with Sarah too, which hasn't been easy, in recent years."

"Sarah's doing better, isn't she - now that she's got rid of that loser, Farooq?"

"Yeah. Him, and Kirsty Bryant. I think she's starting to make friends with Tracy again, which is good to see."

"Yes, I always liked Tracy and Fiona. Sarah's much better off with friends like that."

"Well, I'm not sure she's made it up with Fiona," I said. "She put them through a lot, and I got the impression Fiona was reluctant to be friends with her again - but she should come around eventually, now that Tracy has. But going back to Jade - don't worry, okay? Even if you don't trust me and Charlotte, remember James is coming along, too. He's got a kid of his own."

"That's true enough, although Erica does seem to do most of the hands-on stuff, from what I've seen. Plus, Primrose is such a sweet, quiet girl - hardly comparable to our Jade. Still, I suppose he does at least have some experience. We'll just have to see how it goes."

"Matt, we're only taking two seven-year-old girls to a garden centre, and I'm sure, between the three of us, we can keep them out of trouble, for long enough for you to look at a few shrubs, or whatever it is you want to look at."

"I might quote you on that later, sis."

"Feel free. I'm sure it will turn out fine."

It was a couple of weeks since Jessica's shoplifting incident. It had transpired that the twins, along with Carys and Becky, had decided to start up their own "business", selling stationery items, nicked from local shops, to their classmates. Of course, the whole thing had been Jade's idea - and, just as predictably, Jess had ended up doing most of the actual stealing.

Anyway, daily life had settled down since then, as much as it ever did, and Matthew had taken the responsibility of maintaining our fair-sized back garden from Mum, who had enough to deal with. And Matt really enjoyed gardening - found it therapeutic, and he certainly needed some outlet.

He wanted to go to this huge garden centre, located about ten miles away, and that was where Charlotte, James, and I came in. Matt had vaguely mentioned wanting to go there, but clearly written it off, on the grounds of - well, past experience of taking the girls there: Enough said.

Hence, today's planned excursion. It would certainly be a challenge, keeping our eyes on Jade and Jess, but in many respects, I was looking forward to our afternoon out.

**

"It's great to see you, James," I said.

James had met Charlotte and myself, along with the twins, in the reception area, as arranged. He looked well, and more relaxed than usual, wearing a turquoise T-shirt, and jeans. More often than not, of late, I'd seen him in the suits he wore every day to work.

"Matt's looking at some shrubs, and we thought we'd start with the aviaries. You don't know whereabouts they are, do you? Me and Charlotte haven't been here before."

James shook his head. "Sorry, no: My first time, too. I really should take Erica and Primmy out more, to places like this. That said, Matt *did* give me some sort of map." He pulled a crumpled leaflet out of one of his jean pockets, and opened it up, to reveal a vibrant illustrated map.

"Those are out of date. They move things around all the time," announced Jade.

"We'll show you," said Jessica, taking my hand.

And James, Charlotte, and I let the girls lead us straight to said aviaries - which, admittedly, *were* impressive. There were three: one containing cockatiels and lovebirds; one, budgies; the third, canaries and finches.

The twins raced each other to the first aviary, and the rest of us followed.

Jessica was wide-eyed. "Are these parrots? They're beautiful."

"They're cockatiels and lovebirds, darling," I told her.

"Dad said we couldn't have them, because they're too noisy and it would annoy the neighbours," said Jade. "I reckon that would be the best part. The people next door play loud music anyway, so noisy birds would serve them right."

"They're not too noisy," said Jess. "I like them. Dad said he might let us have a budgie or canary, but Nan doesn't agree, and neither did Mum, and that's why we haven't got them before. We're not supposed to know that, but they must think we never hear anything."

"The walls have ears, right?" I remarked. "I'm sure your parents and Nan have their reasons, Jessica, and taking on a pet is a big responsibility."

"I know that. Let's look at the next cage. That one has budgies in."

James and Charlotte had moved on to the second aviary already.

"Look, Luce - that olive-green one, at the back: the image of Sparky, don't you think?" James's face lit up, as he spoke about one of Elizabeth and Stanley's pet budgies.

"Definitely. Sparky was a little plumper though, as far as I remember. Are Sparky and Ruben still around?"

"Yes, getting on a bit now, but they're both doing great."

"Oh, look at that white one," said Charlotte. "There are so many colours, aren't there? When Tara showed me around her dad's aviaries, I fell in love with these birds - and the canaries and finches."

I remembered that my uncle, Mike, did have a couple of aviaries, in his back garden.

Jade and Jessica were moving on to the canaries and finches, so I started to head in that direction myself, and James and Charlotte followed.

"What type of finches are these?" asked James. "Mostly Zebras, right?"

"Yes, they're Zebras, Bengalese - and a couple of Star Finches, too." I replied.

"The Stars are the tiny ones," said Charlotte. "We should visit Lucy's uncle some time. Tara wanted to have our own aviary, but chance would be a fine thing, living in a second floor flat. I suggested having a canary or a couple of budgies, but she wasn't into the idea - said they should really live in flocks. It probably isn't ideal anyway, with the cats."

"Didn't your family have a canary at one time, Luce?" said James.

"Yeah, we did - called Caspian. He sang beautifully, and woke us all up every morning. He actually came from one of Mike's aviaries. Only lived for six months though, poor thing. Cath cried so much, Mum wouldn't let us get another."

"Cath?" said Charlotte. "Don't you mean Sarah?"

"No, definitely Catherine." I was actually surprised Charlotte didn't remember. "I mean, Sarah was upset, of course - as we all were - but Cath was heartbroken. I've never seen her cry so much."

Not even the day she'd moved out. Strange how I hadn't thought about that canary for years, or the impact that his death had had upon my elder sister.

James nudged me. "Lucy, where are the girls?"

I tumbled back to reality, and looked around me, in all directions, feeling somewhat nauseous.

"All right, stay calm. We'll find them. You and Charlotte head in that direction." James was pointing. "According to my map, that path leads to the play area. I'll go the other way, and try to find the sheds and summer houses. Matthew did mention beforehand, that those are the most likely places for them to disappear to."

After a few minutes of walking around with Charlotte, in a state of pure panic, the two of us bumped into Matt. My friend shot me a glance, that instructed me to remain calm and act normal. To that end, she began to make casual enquiries about the pot plants and shrubs, on his trolley.

Matt replied briefly, and then, of course, added: "Where are the twins?"

"With James," said Charlotte, possibly a little too quickly.

Holy shit, what was the point in lying?

"But I've just spoken to James," said Matt. "He told me the girls were with you two."

I burst into tears. "Matt, I'm so sorry. It was all my fault."

Matthew put his arm around me. "Charlotte, can you carry on looking? I need to talk to my sister."

"Yes, of course - no problem." As upset as I was, I didn't miss the fact that my friend still couldn't talk to Matt without blushing.

"Come on, Luce. I'll buy you a coffee, okay?"

"Coffee? But I don't understand. We've lost your daughters. What if they've been kidnapped or something?"

"Would *you* kidnap Jade? She'll drive the 'kidnappers' up the wall, in the space of ten minutes."

"I'm serious. These things happen, Matthew. You know they do. How can you joke about something like that?"

"No more arguments. I'm buying you coffee, whether you like it or not."

And so my brother and I headed back towards the same reception area, where Charlotte and I had met up with James. The coffee shop was located to the right of reception.

***

"You okay now?" asked Matt, once we were seated in a quiet corner of the moderately busy coffee shop - which, undoubtedly, had been packed an hour or so earlier, during the lunch-time peak.

"Yeah, I'm fine - but why are you worried about me? The twins-"

"Will be fine. They always do this. That's why a whole group of us came along - in anticipation of the part where we would need to send out a search party. This *is* a large garden centre, but there are only so many places they can hide. If James and Charlotte don't come back with the pair of them, by the time we've finished our drinks, we'll go and help them." Matt could see I was dubious. "I'm not saying I don't worry. Of course I do. But this is the twins, and it's what they do. I'm more concerned about what trouble they might get into - overturning pot plants and the like. I dread to think."

I nodded, hastily brushing away fresh tears, but Matt wasn't fooled. He reached across the table, and took my hand. "Hey, come on. Luce, you're doing great. This is *not* down to you."

"Then why does it feel like it *is*? I always mess up."

"No, you don't. You've been amazing since..." Matt's own voice was starting to crack. "I miss her, Lucy - so bloody much. If Bonnie was here, she would, more than likely, have kept Jade and Jess in line. Bonita liked her pranks, but she wasn't like Jade - always taking things too far."

"I know. We all miss her every day. I only cope myself because I still don't really accept it. It's never entirely felt real."

"I don't think I'll ever believe or accept it. I can't. If I did, I'd fall apart, and then who would look after the twins? Maybe the fact that they're so demanding has helped, in a weird way. And Clare broke down, which was her luxury. I didn't have much choice but to keep going. Still, I couldn't have done it without Mum, and all of you."

"Thanks, Matt."

"By the way, did I mention that Edwina won't have the girls any more? Well, not unless her husband's around, but you know the hours Alan works."

"That *does* surprise me. I thought she adored the kids."

"Well, she does, of course - but Jade's behaviour *has* been getting worse. Apparently, she 'can't risk Edmund and Lenora's safety'. It sounds a bit dramatic, but then again, there *have* been a couple of incidents."

"And you're convinced that's the whole reason? You don't think it has more to do with what's happened between you and Clare?"

"Oh, I'm sure there are multiple factors. I still refuse to say I don't blame Clare for the accident, when I partially do. If her sister holds that against me, that's *her* problem. I blame myself too, just for not being there."

"Matt, it was *not* your fault, and it wasn't Clare's, either. I wasn't her biggest fan, but it's not fair for you to..."

But I left my sentence hanging. James and Charlotte had appeared, with two extremely wet seven-year-olds, and a bizarre and convoluted tale, which culminated in a grand chase, and the twins jumping into some lake, full of remote control ducks. It was hard not to laugh, in the end - and we all did, including my brother.

It was the first time I'd seen Matt laugh since Bonnie's death.

Chapter Thirty-Four

"Luce, it's Danny. You doing much tomorrow night?" So began the slightly bizarre telephone conversation with my brother. I'd only got home from work about five minutes earlier, and was caught off guard.

"I hadn't really thought about it. It's Friday night, so the Lion's a strong possibility. Why?"

"Do you fancy coming for a meal, at Hannah's mum's?"

"Cynthia's? That's a bit out of the blue. Is this in aid of anything specific?"

"Does it need to be?"

"I guess not," I said, hoping he would get to the point soon.

"Phil does happen to be in town," he admitted. "We thought this would be a good opportunity for you to meet him."

Hannah's brother, Phil, had lived in Blackpool with their dad, after their parents' divorce - whereas, Hannah had remained with their mum. When he'd rented his own flat, that had also been in Blackpool. But lately, Hannah had mentioned the possibility of him purchasing a flat, around the corner from Cynthia. He'd apparently been applying for jobs, in the local area.

I considered, for a moment. "Danny, I hope this isn't connected with those jokes we had before. At least, I hope they were jokes. Something about setting me up with Hannah's brother?"

"I don't remember that."

"You are *such* a liar," I said. "Well, if it's a family thing, then I'll bring Sarah along, okay?"

"Yeah, fine - if she wants to come. No problem. You'll be there, then?"

***

152

My sister and I were able to walk to Cynthia's, as her house wasn't far from Mum's. Sarah's peroxide blonde hair was currently shoulder-length, which length suited her. She wore a lemon-yellow dress, which I felt sure was new, and the garment in question actually reached her knees - an unusual thing for my younger sister, these days. With her amber pendant on a sterling silver chain, and matching bracelet, the outfit was exactly right.

"You look amazing, Sarah," I told her, as we stood on the porch, about to ring the doorbell.

"Thanks," she said, sounding unconvinced.

How could someone so beautiful lack self-confidence, to the extent that Sarah did? She honestly didn't consider herself pretty, and never had trusted anyone's compliments.

"I'm glad you came tonight. To be honest, I didn't think you would."

"Why not?" This with a defensive edge to her voice.

"No big reason - just that it's Friday night. I wasn't sure you'd fancy a family meal."

"It's not fair to imply that I go out partying, every weekend. Yes, I've been out with Tracy a few times lately, but I'm no worse than anyone else. I know I went crazy with Farooq and Kirsty, but you can't hold that against me forever."

"No - no, of course not. Forget I said anything, okay?" I rang the bell.

"Anyway, I want to meet Phil. He seemed like a really nice guy, when we spoke on the phone."

"You spoke to Hannah's brother? Why?"

"Why *not*? You treat me like a little kid. If you must know, it was ages ago. He called to speak to Mum, just before Danny and Hannah's wedding, but she wasn't at home, so we chatted instead. He was disappointed about not being able to make it, and he knew Hannah would be upset."

"Just a bit, and I can't say I blame her."

"Yeah, well - there were circumstances. Their dad wasn't well."

The door opened, and Cynthia, with her big hair, enormous gold hoop earrings, and voice even louder than her vibrant, floral dress, invited the two of us in, showing us through to the dining room.

Cynthia did the introductions, and Phil kind of mumbled, "Hi," to my sister and me, but I could tell he was painfully shy, as opposed to rude or indifferent.

He did bear a strong resemblance to his sister. It was the wide-set hazel eyes, and those thin, oval faces. Phil's hair was brown too, although slightly darker than Hannah's, and wavy, whereas hers was straight. He wore smart-casual clothes, which were fine in themselves, but didn't look quite right on him somehow. The sky-blue shirt must have been at least two sizes too large, and he looked uncomfortable, both in the clothes - items possibly borrowed from a friend or family member - and in himself.

"I've made vegetable curry," said Cynthia. "I hope that's fine with you all. What with Hannah being vegetarian, and Phil vegan, I thought it best to make something we could all enjoy. I'm as sure as I can be that everything's vegan."

Okay - so, as if his sister being veggie wasn't enough, Phil Jackson had to take *just bloody awkward* to new heights, and insist upon being vegan.

"I'd love to be vegetarian or vegan," said Sarah. "I've often thought of it."

I rolled my eyes. "You *have*? You surprise me, Sarah. I can't see you giving up your McDonald's - hamburger *or* milkshake."

"I hardly ever have McDonald's any more." My sister was blushing. I had to be right about this: Sarah liked Phil.

Well, he was an improvement on Farooq, at any rate.

Trouble was, Phil wasn't looking at Sarah. He couldn't take his eyes off me. And Danny and Hannah, for their part, couldn't stop looking hopefully, from one of us to the other. They clearly had their hearts set on a Phil and Lucy romance.

"Veggie curry is fine, Cynthia," I said.

Chapter Thirty-Five

I twisted the telephone cord. "But I don't fancy him, Charlotte."

"Lucy, how many guys have you been out with?"

"You know how many guys I've been out with. Two: James and Kev."

"And you fancied both of them?"

"Well, obviously - misguided as that may have been. I'm not sure where we're going with this."

"It's obvious, isn't it? You tried going out with guys you fancied, and that didn't work."

"So now I should go out with ones I don't fancy? That's just weird. So, I just go up to some random guy I don't fancy, and ask him out? Like, that is such a great plan."

"But Phil isn't a 'random guy'. You know him, and you get along. Maybe the other side will - you know, develop."

"If you say so. But I still wish I hadn't agreed to this. I'm going to have to make it really clear to him that I don't want to be more than friends."

"You'll just make it worse."

"Tell me about it. So, what *should* I do? It's all very well for you to say I should date a guy I don't fancy. It's me who has to actually go through with it. What happens when I have to kiss him - and the rest?"

"It's a first date, Luce. And Phil isn't Kev. He sounds like a really nice guy."

"I'm not sure I even like 'nice guys'."

"You liked James."

"Yeah, and look where that got me."

"You need to stop analysing. Have a good time. That's what you need right now."

"It *is*?"

"Of course."

"Well, I'm glad you're such an expert. I'm only relieved I convinced Danny and Hannah to come along. I can manage a 'double date', I suppose. Maybe if I stopped calling it a 'date', and thinking of it as a 'date', that would help. We're all going out together as a group, that's all: my brother and his wife, his wife's brother, and me. It's more of a family thing, when you think about it."

Charlotte laughed. "Think of it however you like, Lucy. He probably sees it as a date, though."

"I doubt if he's that bothered and, if he is, that's his problem. I ought to cancel the whole thing, but I guess I won't. It might be fun, and I sure need some of that in my life. I think you were right, in that respect."

"That's the spirit."

"Yeah, well - whatever. I'd better go, Charlie. Catch you later, okay?"

***

"Hannah, Mum does have some experience with kids, you know," reasoned Danny, exasperated, as ever, at his wife's reluctance to leave their son with anyone at all, even the boy's own grandmother. "She's raised five of us, and has been playing a pretty major role in bringing up Matt's girls, too."

I hoped that my slight sigh, at this point, had gone unnoticed. We went through this routine, each and every single time that Josh stayed with us, without exception.

I knew for a fact that it wasn't personal to Mum, as Hannah didn't like leaving him with her own mother, either. Seemed paranoid and nonsensical to me, but maybe I would have felt differently, had it been my own kid in question. I only hoped I never ended up like Hannah.

"Joshua will be fine, Hannah, dear," said Mum, giving her daughter-in-law a hug. "I do understand, though. It's never easy, leaving them. I felt the same way with mine."

Holy shit, why did Mum have to humour her - and even start to join in? The pair of them would be tearing up soon, and then we might never get out at all.

Then again, that was not without its advantages.

I couldn't believe I'd agreed to this *non-date/date*, but at least it was a double date - or not. That took the pressure off somewhat. And almost certainly, this would be a one-off. Even in the unlikely event that I ended up fancying Hannah's younger brother, it would take a lot to convince me that I wanted another bloke in my life, after James and Kev.

We finally left the house, and Danny drove us to our destination.

As the three of us walked through the car park, in the direction of the Italian restaurant, Hannah grabbed my arm. "I think Phil really likes you, Lucy," she told me, clearly working on the assumption that I would be desperate for reassurance on this point.

"See how it goes, Hannah, but don't get your hopes up. I'm not sure I'm into the idea of a new relationship right now."

"He's nothing like Kev Tanner, you know." Abruptly withdrawing her arm. "You could do a lot worse."

I exchanged glances with Danny, who shrugged.

None of us spoke again until we entered the restaurant. "There he is," announced Hannah, gesturing towards the bar.

Chapter Thirty-Six

The following evening, I was in the Lion, with Charlotte and Sarah.

"So, anyway - after he'd call me Louise about six times, I finally managed to get him to start calling me Lucy. That lasted for about the next half hour or so, and then, he suddenly decided to switch to Lucinda. Apparently, he got confused because he used to have a pet goldfish named Lucinda. Who the hell has a goldfish called Lucinda? And honestly, how hard is it to remember the name Lucy? Four letters, two syllables. Not exactly difficult, is it?"

Charlotte laughed. "But seriously, Luce - other than that, did you get on? I mean, it *is* pretty annoying, when someone spends half the night calling you by wrong names, but some people do that. My aunt calls me Charmaine, because one of her neighbours is Charmaine. I've more or less given up trying to correct her, as it doesn't make the slightest bit of difference."

"Yeah, well - it was okay. I'm glad that Danny and Hannah were there. I couldn't have got through it without them. He went on and on about country music. I thought he'd never shut up. He didn't seem to grasp the concept that none of us were remotely interested."

"My mum likes country music."

"Yeah, but she doesn't go on about it all night, to other people who don't. And Phil's into these 'theme nights', too. You dress up like cowboys, and act like idiots. He wants me to go to one in town."

"What did you say?"

"I couldn't say anything. I was biting the inside of my mouth at the time, trying not to laugh. Trouble is, I think he interpreted that as a, 'Yes.' He started talking as if it was all agreed, after that."

"You are such a bitch, Lucy," snapped Sarah, out of the blue. "Phil Jackson is a genuine guy. You don't even deserve him, and he doesn't deserve to be made fun of, by the two of you. If you can't see his value, that's your loss, but I don't think you should be using him, or hurting him more than you need to."

Charlotte and I exchanged glances. My sister hadn't been contributing much at all to the conversation, until that point.

"Sarah, I-"

"Save it. I have to meet Tracy, anyway." And, that said, my sister stormed off.

"What was *that* all about?" asked Charlotte.

"Sarah's got a crush on Phil," I replied. "She'll get over it, once she realises what a bore he is."

"I still don't entirely get it. No one's making you go out with him, and okay, Danny and Hannah are pushing for it, but it's not as if you've ever listened to their advice, in the past. Look at you and Kev, and the level of family support for that relationship - not that I blame them."

"I know where you're coming from, and it isn't easy to explain. Maybe dealing with all that disapproval for so long has taken its toll, and I'm liking the feeling of pleasing my family, for once - liking it, but resenting it, too."

"Yeah, I guess so," said Charlotte, still sounding unconvinced.

We then resumed where we had left off, relentlessly making fun of Phil Jackson: his clothes, musical taste, general awkwardness, and obsession with veganism and environmental issues. It was ages since the two of us had laughed so much and, even though we both knew full well that we were being mean, it felt therapeutic to do the whole *giggling girls, best friends* routine. It wasn't even *about* Phil any more.

The instant my friend kicked me under the table, I should have realised that her expression had changed. I did eventually twig, and looked into Phil's wounded puppy eyes.

"I'd better be getting back, actually. I promised Tara I'd cook tonight. Catch you later, Lucy - Phil."

Thanks a lot, Charlotte. And yet, she was right. I had to take responsibility for what I'd just been saying.

"Listen, Phil - I'm sorry," I said, forcing myself to look him in the eye. "Me and Charlotte were messing around, that's all. It didn't mean anything. Can I buy you a drink?"

"It's okay. You were talking to Charlotte. None of my business. And I'll buy you one. I'm meeting my sister here in about an hour, but I did come early, on the off chance." *The "off chance" of seeing me?*

"So, we're okay, then? No hard feelings?"

"We're fine - and of course not."

"I'll understand, if you want to cancel. Friday night, I mean."

Phil actually looked me in the eye. "Do *you* want to cancel?"

"No." I was surprised to realise that this was true.

"That's good. I've been looking forward to it."

Which I hadn't been, of course. We both knew that. And yet now, I honestly was.

Chapter Thirty-Seven

Phil kicked things off by insisting that we walked almost fifty percent of the journey into town. Apparently, he wanted to save the Planet - not to mention, some money on the bus ride, by cutting out a couple of fare stages.

By the time we arrived, I was sweaty and grumpy, neither of which seemed to bother my companion. The softening in my heart, experienced on Wednesday night, was replaced by the usual feelings of irritation, which Phil Jackson had brought out in me from the start.

I wanted to like him. I actually *did* like him. It was just that he wound me up - and added fuel to the fire, by trying too hard to be nice to me. He had, at least, got to the stage of remembering my name, which was *something*.

"The Ship?" he suggested.

I hesitated.

"It's not where the event's taking place. I know you don't like country music."

"Phil, I don't really mind..." But I left it, seeing the expression in his eyes.

"So, The Ship, then?"

"The Ship's fine."

***

It was a comparatively quiet pub, even on a Friday night, and the low volume of the, mainly dated, music played there, would have had the advantage of making conversation easier - had the conversation been flowing, which it was not. Phil and I were making small talk. If only Danny and Hannah had come along. Double dating had been so much easier, and more enjoyable.

I lit a cigarette from the one before, and tried to concentrate on what Phil was saying. He tended to mumble, which make the task that much harder.

Our table was located next to the ladies', and I watched as drunken girls passed, in pairs or small groups. Found myself missing Charlotte.

Probably about twenty, long and painful, minutes later, he suggested that we step outside for some air. It was finally getting busier, and somewhat stifling.

This is it, Lucy. He's going to kiss you.

Time to stop wishing he was Kev or James, because honestly, neither of them had treated me well, as a girlfriend. James, at least, had turned out to be a good friend, whilst Kev had treated me like shit, pretty much from the start.

Phil, meanwhile - he was lovely.

So, what the hell was wrong with me, right?

We slipped into the cool evening air. It was lightly raining, and I wondered whether Phil would expect to walk most of the way back? Surely not?

But that was the least of my concerns, wasn't it?

Phil took my hands in his own, and looked me in the eye. "It's okay," he said. "I understand."

"Understand what?"

"Look, Lucy - I like you a lot, and I know my sister and Danny think...Anyway, I can tell you're not interested. I kept hoping you might change your mind, but it's not going to happen, is it?"

So, I had my opening: my moment. Phil was making this as painless for me as it could be.

Yet, in that instant, everything became clear, in my mind. I grabbed Phil, and kissed him as passionately as I ever had Kev or James.

When we came up for air, Phil looked at me, with such a strange combination of shyness, bewilderment, and awe, that I couldn't help laughing.

"Well, I wasn't expecting *that*."

"You're not complaining, though?"

"Of course not. Can I ask you something, Luce?"

"Ask away."

"That kiss - it means we're together now? As in, boyfriend and girlfriend?"

"Yeah, it does."

"I thought you still loved Kev Tanner - or maybe James. It seemed as if-"

"Phil?"

"Yes?"

"Shut up, okay?"

And we kissed again. I wasn't in love with Phil, but I liked him, and wanted what he was offering.

Security - and to feel appreciated. After everything I'd been through, that was what I craved, more than anything else. And Phil Jackson made me feel more secure, more needed, than Kev or James ever had. That was enough for me.

Chapter Thirty-Eight

"We have to do *something*, Lucy. I still can't believe you've put up with me for a whole year."

Yeah, well - I could hardly believe it myself. Then again, I was more surprised that Phil had put up with my moods for so long.

It was Friday night, and we were in the Red Lion, with Matt, Danny, Sarah, and Tracy.

Predictably, Sarah reacted, the moment Phil's hand touched mine. Raced off in the direction of the loos, followed by Tracy.

"Do you have to wind her up like that? She *is* my sister."

"You don't still think - you know, what you were saying the other day?" He actually looked kind of cute, when he got all flustered and bemused.

"Yes, Phil. I told you ages ago that Sarah fancies you."

"Just a bit, mate," said Matthew. "Poor girl - got to feel for her. Broken hearts seem to run in the family."

"Speak for yourself," said Danny. "Me and Hannah are doing great, thanks."

"Is my sister coming tonight?"

"Probably not. She still doesn't like leaving Josh with anyone."

"It's bloody ridiculous," I said. "She needs to get over it."

"It's understandable," said Matt. "I've stayed in a few times myself, because I haven't wanted to leave the girls."

"Yeah, a *few* times - and probably ones where there was some sort of logical reason. Anyway, Hannah's a full-time mum, so she's literally at home with that kid most of the day."

"Lucky her, having the option."

"Matt, get real. You'd go up the wall, if you couldn't work. Anyway, Jess is one thing, but no one could deal with Jade for twenty-four hours, and stay sane."

"Who said anything about *sanity*, Luce? I don't think that's part of the deal."

Sarah and Tracy were back. Sarah had been crying, of course.

"Are you okay, Sarah?" asked Phil.

I shot him a look. Did he always have to try so bloody hard to *do the right thing*?

Sarah blushed, her expression reflecting conflicting emotions: embarrassment, verging on mortification - and ecstasy that Phil had noticed her, and shown concern. She toyed with a strand of her shoulder-length, blonde hair. "Fine, thank you."

It was then that I spotted that woman - the moment after Matt did. And my brother looked about as happy as Sarah had, a few minutes earlier.

Clare marched up to our table - as well as she *could* march, in six inch heels. To say that her low-cut, scarlet sweater and black miniskirt didn't leave much to the imagination was an understatement.

"Hello, Matt," she said, ignoring the rest of us. "I think we need to talk."

"What the hell are you doing here?"

"You really know how to make a girl feel welcome. I'd rather not be here myself, but you weren't returning my calls. I didn't have much choice. Let's go outside, shall we?"

"Anything you want to say, Clare, you can say in front of my family."

"If you think I'm yelling over this music, when it concerns my daughters, you've got another thing coming. I've got more class than that, even if you haven't."

"Class isn't a quality I associate with you, as it goes. As for *your* daughters, you've got a nerve. Did Mum tell you where to find us?"

"She said you weren't at home, and I took an educated guess."

"'Educated' *and* 'class'? Really think you're something, don't you? Now you're screwing that dirty old man, no doubt with his bank balance in mind! Know about Parker, does he?"

"Me and Steven aren't together any more. I'm marrying Malcolm, as if it's any of your business. And we're having the girls!"

So much for not yelling. Were Matt and Clare even capable of holding a conversation, without it ending up as a screaming match?

"Over my dead body!"

"Yeah, well, let's hope it doesn't come to that. Me and Malcolm are in a much better position to look after the twins. From what I've heard, you're not exactly coping. You insisted on having this out in public, so fine. You're an unfit father. You don't have a clue how to deal with Jade, and you're neglecting Jessica, whilst failing to control her sister. Your mum's too old and incompetent to cope with them, to the extent you're expecting her to. That covers it, for now. You'll be hearing from our solicitor."

At which point, she turned on her red, patent leather stilettos, and made her exit, leaving the rest of us stunned. Perfect execution, on her part.

Phil made his excuses first, hastily followed by Sarah and Tracy, leaving my brothers and me.

Matt grabbed his pint glass, and knocked back the contents, with a vengeance.

"Go easy on that, bruv," said Danny. "You're giving her ammunition."

"Ammunition? After everything *she's* done? Including walking out on those kids, when they needed her most? She called *me* an 'unfit father'. And did you hear what she said - after I said 'over my dead body'? She threatened me."

"The two of you are going to have to talk about the situation, in a calm and rational manner, at some point," I said. "I'm sure you can sort something out about access."

"Whose side are you both on? Clare isn't after *access*. She wants to take my kids away, and let some old bloke take my place, and get Jade and Jessica to call him 'Daddy'. Well, I'm not having it."

"You seriously think Jade will agree to call Malcolm 'Daddy'?" I said.

"Are you saying Jess *might*?"

"Matthew, you have to stop jumping down our throats," said Danny. "We *are* on your side, although by rights, shouldn't it be the girls' side? Surely they're the priority here?"

"They've been mine all along. Jade and Jessica were *the* reason I didn't top myself, after Bonnie died. It was Clare who left *us*, and made herself the priority."

"She pretty much had a nervous breakdown, Matt," I said.

"Nervous fucking breakdown." He slammed down his pint glass. "Chance would be a fine thing. You think I don't want to opt out, and put it down to a 'nervous breakdown'? I'm sure I've had a dozen. I pick myself up and carry on, because *someone* has to."

"You don't have to tell us what you've been through, or how strong you've been. We've been there with you," said Danny. "Lucy's right, though. You're going to have to talk to Clare, sooner or later. I can't see her letting this go."

"I don't want to talk to her, and to be honest, I don't want to discuss this any more tonight. I'm heading home. You coming, Luce?"

"Danny's taxi is due in about half an hour. I'll keep him company until then."

"Okay, fine. I'll see you at home, then. See you, Dan."

Chapter Thirty-Nine

"It seems suspiciously quiet around here. Where *is* everyone?"

I'd arrived home from work, to find my brother, sitting there, staring at the TV.

He didn't reply. Continued to stare at the meaningless image. Looked like some sort of medical drama. Volume was muted.

I grabbed the remote, and switched off. "Matt, what's happened?"

He finally looked up at me. "Mum's got the twins. They're at her sister's. Sarah's out with Tracy. Lucy, Jade might be expelled."

"You're kidding?" I sat down next to him, on the sofa. "Do they even expel kids from primary school? I've never heard of it. What the hell did she...?"

I noticed the cherryade stain, on Mum's, once immaculate, velvet sofa. Jade had been determined to blame her twin for that, even though Sarah and I had both witnessed Jade deliberately pouring the contents of Jessica's glass, on to the piece of furniture.

"Bunked off, with Carys and Becky," answered Matt. "It seems they walked it to Lakefield Comp, waited around until Gemma Tanner and her friend came out, and proceeded to kick the shit out of them both. Jade slashed Gemma's leather jacket off her back with a pen knife. And, no - I've got no idea where she got a knife."

"A knife?" My heart hammered. "Shit, Matt - is Gemma okay?"

"Yeah, she's okay - a few cuts and bruises, but nothing serious. In a state though, as you can imagine. Apparently, Jade held the knife in her face, at one point, but didn't actually use it - so her coat was the only casualty." I noticed the lines around my brother's eyes, as he spoke. "Jade passed it to Jessica afterwards, who was then conveniently holding it, when they were caught. Of course, she tried to blame Jess, but no one's buying that one - not any more. Jade thumped Gemma, while her friends had Lila pinned to someone's garden wall."

"But surely Jade couldn't have hit her *that* hard? I mean, Gem and Lila are twelve, and Gemma's no fighter, but she can hold her own."

"I thought the same at first. Then I remembered how bad Jade's been lately. She regularly bites me and Mum, and does draw blood. And those fights she gets into at school - those go beyond spitting and hair pulling. She fights like me and Danny did - not the way you and Cath used to."

"I know she sometimes fights boys, as well as girls but, still - boys her own age, right? If Jade really *is* beating up kids Gemma's age, this has reached a whole different level."

"That's exactly what I'm telling you. It *has*."

"And this incident - it took place right outside Lakefield? In which case, there must be plenty of witnesses."

"It wasn't directly outside. They'd managed to get Gemma and Lila down an alleyway, but it was still pretty near, and there were quite a few locals who saw enough."

"Poor Gemma. She can be a self-centred cow at times, but she doesn't deserve this. What *is* wrong with Jade?"

"I wish I knew. Mum and the girls will probably stay with Sylvia, for a couple of days. I'm not sure what the next stage is. This has gone beyond even whether she can stay at St. Andrew's. It's a criminal case now, and there could be psychiatrists and social workers involved. I had to tell Clare, and of course, she's blaming me, and determined to use it against me."

"Yeah, well, we need to focus on Jade, Jessica, and Gemma - what to do for the best. You and Clare having a go at each other isn't going to help."

"I know. Luce, there's something else - well, a couple of things, really. The first is that I spoke to Deborah. She's coming over, probably within the next half hour or so. She wants to talk things through."

I nodded. "How did she sound?"

"Exhausted - close to breaking point - about how you'd expect. Anyway, she apparently had to talk Kev out of coming straight over, and punching my lights out. Talking to Deborah sounds like the safest option, doesn't it?"

"Definitely. Matt, listen, I'm serious, okay? If you do speak to Kev, at any point, please don't wind him up, because he's capable of anything, where Gemma's concerned."

"I'm hardly likely to go out of my way to speak to Kev Tanner, and Deb said we could deal with this through her, so that's that, as far as I'm concerned. There *is* more, though. One of the specific grudges Jade had against Gemma was that her and Lila have been slagging you off, writing graffiti about you, and generally spreading rumours."

"Are you sure? I mean, Gem and Lila actually *did* that? It's not just Jade stirring?"

"Oh, Jade *is* stirring. Her suddenly valuing 'family loyalty' is questionable, in my view. It's any excuse to pick a fight. But yeah, it's true about the graffiti. I saw some of it myself."

"It's just, I was getting on so much better with Gem, before..." I choked back the tears. This wasn't *about* me. "No, it's okay. I think I understand. Kev did tell me Gemma hadn't handled it well, when I left him. She felt I'd abandoned her and Toby, in the process. In fairness, I suppose I did."

"None of this is your fault. I'm not telling you so that you'll blame yourself - just so that you'll know, especially since Deborah might mention it."

"Do you think I should go out? My being here won't exactly make matters easier, will it?"

"It's up to you, but I could do with your support, to be honest. I'd prefer it if you did stay, as long as Deborah's okay with it." It was there in his eyes: the extent to which my brother wanted me to be there.

"Of course I'll stay, if you think it will help."

The doorbell rang.

"That's probably her. I'll get it, Luce, and you put the kettle on."

***

Deborah had been at my mum's for roughly ten minutes, and my role, thus far, had been to make the drinks, and not interfere.

She and Matt were sitting on the sofa, much closer to one another than they ideally needed to be. Or my imagination? Yeah, well, whatever - as long as they were working things out, about Jade and Gemma, and that whole mess.

I paused for a moment, before bringing through the biscuit tin.

"As I said, I really am sorry. I can't stress that enough - or that we won't be letting Jade get away with it. "

"By 'we' - do you include Clare in this? I know you're not together any more, and it's none of my business, but to me, she *is* the twins' mother, and she might be able to help."

"I mean, myself and Mum, Dan, and my sisters - and yes, Clare, as much as I wish I could pretend the woman never existed. Listen, are you going to take this to the police, Deborah? I wouldn't blame you, if you wanted to, and I know it might be out of all of our hands, in any case, but I'd really appreciate it if we could try to sort it out between us."

"I understand what you're saying. I'm not planning to take it further, as it stands, but staff from St. Andrew's and Lakefield are involved now, and I don't know what they'll want to do. I don't want Jade anywhere near Gemma - or Toby, for that matter. Same goes for Jessica, and those other girls - Rebecca and Carys, I believe. Jade was obviously the ringleader, but right now, I don't want any of them hanging around, upsetting my kids. I spoke to Lila's mum, and she feels the same. Keep the twins under lock and key, if that's what it takes, because I won't be as understanding, if anything like this ever happens again. But no, in answer to your question, I won't go to the police."

"Thank you."

"I must admit, Gemma put herself at risk, to a certain extent, by wearing that leather jacket to school, although Jade's attack was obviously more personal. I did tell Mum not to buy her it. And, you know, I *am* here for you. I can't begin to imagine what it must have been like, losing Bonnie. That must have had an impact on the twins, too."

"Yeah, they witnessed the accident."

I offered the biscuits, feeling less convinced than ever that I was doing the right thing, by being there. But then again, maybe it would have been too much for Matt - answering questions about Bonita's death, on top of everything else.

Or maybe talking to someone like Deborah would have been exactly what he needed.

Deborah took a Custard Cream, and Matt, a Jammy Dodger.

And that was when the doorbell rang again.

"Oh, great timing," said Matt. "If it's the bloody Mormons again..."

But Deborah and I exchanged glances, and then the banging started. Not the Mormons. And Matt had worked it out, too.

"I'll get it, okay?" Spoken whilst already heading for the door, making my words more statement than question.

I should have used the chain, but in my confusion, I didn't, and Kev naturally barged straight past me.

"Kev, you can't just..."

"Oh, very cosy. I can see now why you didn't want me to come."

"I'm sorry, Matt. He just pushed past me."

"I thought we agreed," said Deborah. "I told you I was dealing with this. This is Mrs. Ryman's house, and you weren't invited in, so I think you should leave."

"And this is your idea of 'dealing with' it - flirting with Jade Ryman's dad, after she's just beaten up our daughter? That kid had a knife. She's out of control."

"Well, you're the expert on 'out of control' - I'll give you that," said Deborah.

"Right, that's enough," said Matthew, getting to his feet. "I'm showing our 'guest' out. As Deborah pointed out, Tanner, this is my mum's house, and you can't walk in off the street, and start throwing your weight around. The situation regarding our daughters is in hand."

Kev grabbed my brother. "You think you're fucking hard, Matt Ryman? Everyone knows your psycho brother's the one you hide behind. That and Daddy's rep, of course. You're fuck all on your own. I don't like that you're flirting with my wife, and neither of you seem to give a crap about the state Gemma's in."

"Let him go, Kev," I told him.

He looked at me. "Thanks for taking my calls, Luce. I really appreciate it. Nice to know our relationship meant anything at all to you." He released Matt anyway, with a violent shove that sent him crashing into the sofa, where Deborah was sitting.

Deb went to help him up, but Matt insisted he was fine, and proceeded to get up, of his own volition.

"If it helps," said Matt, once he'd caught his breath, "Deborah and I *were* getting somewhere - and, no, we weren't 'flirting'. You'll believe what you want to anyway, but that's the truth - take it or leave it. Relationships are the last thing on my mind, right now."

"Not that it's any of your business," said Deborah. "Also, I'm not your wife any more. Ex-wife, remember? As you yourself pointed out, you were living with Lucy, which I don't have a problem with, but you can't then call me your 'wife', and tell me who I can and can't talk to. It's nothing to do with you any more."

"You can do what you want. I wouldn't want to see my kids' mother make a fool of herself, that's all. And I don't understand how you can all sit around, having fucking tea and biscuits. I'm the only one who cares that Gemma..." He broke down.

Of course, Kev *would* be in pieces. He loved Gemma so much. What had Deborah said, when I'd first met her? "More than he ever did me, or ever will you."

I went to him, instinctively. He'd collapsed into the armchair by the window: the floral one, which didn't match the rest of Mum's three-piece suite. A present from Dad's parents. She'd always hated it.

I knelt down by him - held him and stroked his hair, the way I'd always used to. I couldn't just leave him to it.

"Well, you've got Lucy where you want her," said Deborah. "It always has to be about you, doesn't it?"

"Deborah, just leave it, okay? You can see he's upset."

"He's manipulating you. I've seen it all before. This isn't about Gemma."

"It wasn't before I showed up, that's for sure. Oh yeah, and only women are allowed to cry, right, Deb? Gemma's my daughter. Am I supposed to see her broken like that, and not have feelings?"

"I actually agree with that," said Matt. "Blokes have feelings too, and we're not expected to."

"That's nonsense," said Deborah. "When did I say that men can't have feelings? I've got feelings about what happened too, but I'm trying to actually deal with the situation. Are you going to tell Lucy and Matt about the day we broke up, Kev? Oh, I'm sure you gave Lucy your version, but I doubt if you mentioned that, after you'd lashed out at me and then Toby, you hit your precious daughter, too. Tell you that, did he, Luce?"

"This isn't helping," I said, endeavouring to conceal my shock. No, he hadn't told me. "Matt, would you take Deborah to the Lion? Me and Kev need some space."

"I'm not leaving you alone with that psycho."

"The compassion didn't last long, did it? You're hardly in a position to be talking about 'psychos', when your eight-year-old daughter's behaving like one."

Matt looked at Deborah. "Would you be okay with that? A quick drink at the Lion?"

"Yes - yes, I suppose so, if it's what Lucy wants. At least we might actually get somewhere, away from all this drama." She turned to Kev. "You lay a finger on Lucy, and you'll never see either of your kids again. I'll make sure of that."

"She's such a bitch sometimes," said Kev, as the front door slammed.

So, it seemed we were over the emotional part now. Back to sarcasm and cold indifference, laced with an undercurrent of resentment.

"Yeah, well, you're jealous enough, about her even talking to my brother. Maybe Deborah has feelings, too."

"'Talking'? Yeah, right."

"See? You're jealous."

"So you're jealous that you think I'm jealous? Almost worth being jealous, just for that."

"Jealous that you're jealous? I can't keep up here."

"Yeah, you can - and Matt's welcome to her, okay? You didn't return my calls. Your mum slammed the phone down on me, and Matt told me to fuck off, in those exact words, but Sarah said she'd pass on my message."

"Yeah, she told me."

"I miss you, Luce. I'm nothing without you."

"Roxy's been keeping you company though, by all accounts. Roxy - or is it Sasha? Why screw one barmaid when you can have two, right?"

"I didn't say I'd joined a fucking monastery. How's it going with Phil Jackson, anyway?"

"Okay. Phil's a nice person."

"Not going great, though?"

"No, not really."

"How about McIntyre? He still sniffing around?"

"Kev, we've been here so many times. James is married with a kid. He's not interested in me, beyond friendship."

"Jury's out, if you ask me, but you're still into him."

I rolled my eyes. "I don't have to answer to you about my feelings for Phil, James, or anyone else - and you don't have to answer to me about Roxy or Sasha, or why you're so jealous about my brother talking to your ex-wife. Let's leave it there, okay?"

"It hit Gemma hard, when you left."

"Is that why she started having a go about me? You know that was part of the reason why Jade went for her, don't you?"

"Hardly justifies what your niece did - her and her gang."

"Of course it doesn't, but you have to realise that Gemma isn't a saint."

"My daughter could have been scarred for life, if Jade had decided to slash her face, as well as her jacket. And that's just physically - never mind the emotional scars. You know what really does my head in, though? Knowing I could have done anything. The moment I saw the state of Gem, I wanted to kill Jade. I wanted her dead, and I didn't give a toss that she was only eight." He broke down again.

I held him - let him cry it out.

Deborah was wrong. Oh, she was right, in general. Kev was manipulative and, yeah, he would fake tears, if that was what it took to get his own way. But he was broken, and that was real. There was a point at which no one could fake broken, not like that.

"It's okay," I said, at length. "We've *all* wanted to kill Jade."

He pulled away. "No, I mean, literally. If she'd been here when I arrived...I'm sorry, Luce. I don't want you to hate me."

"Mum took her and Jess to my aunt's. And I could never hate you, okay?"

Kev glanced at his watch. "I need to head off soon. Will you call me, Lucy? Don't just say you will. I want to talk some more, but I have to know where I stand."

"Well, I'm here right now, and ready to talk. Where do you have to be that's so urgent? The King's Head, right?"

"Yeah. I'm not meeting Roxy or Sasha - just Jake, Farooq, and Farooq's brother, Abdul."

"I'm not sure that's much of an improvement. Can you really not see that that's exactly why I broke up with you - because of what you do, and that whole lifestyle - your behaviour and your attitude?"

"None of that was any different when we got together."

"I thought I could deal with it then. I can't, or maybe I just don't want to any more."

"I wish it was as easy as you think. I wouldn't show up. I can't stand the Bryants or Farooq, or any of that lot, down the King's Head."

"It doesn't matter. Just go, okay?"

"So I take it you're not going to call me?"

"Is there any point?"

"You tell me. If you're happy being unhappy with Phil Jackson for the rest of your life, I guess not."

"I'm happier with Phil than I was with you."

"You don't love him." He lightly brushed my hair. I'd forgotten how he could make me feel, with the tiniest touch. Not something Phil had ever been able to do.

"You'd know that, would you? It's not about Phil, anyway. Even if I wasn't going out with him, I wouldn't get back with you."

Kev's expression said it all. That I was talking crap, and denying my true feelings.

But he was wrong. I knew how I felt. But I would never forget how fucked up our lives had been, existing in that bedsit. All the yelling and screaming, and casual acts of violence - day in and day out. I was never going back to that.

"Sarah thought I should get back to you - reckoned I was wrong to ignore your calls. It might be partly because she likes Phil herself, but I think it was more than that. She said you were 'lovely'. You'd better not have tried it on with her, that's all I can say."

"Is that really what you think of me?"

"Well, you've been with Cath. I did think you might be hoping for the full set. I only thought it for a moment, though. I know you wouldn't touch Sarah - but something changed her mind about you."

"I talked to her one morning, at the house. She was in the kitchen, making breakfast, and I could tell she'd been crying." He touched my arm, lightly. "She'd probably be good with Phil. I wouldn't let that Farooq anywhere near her, if she was my kid sister. Take care, Luce."

"Yeah - yeah, you too."

And then, we kissed, anyway.

"Come home, babe," said Kev. "I won't go, okay? I mean it. I'll go cold turkey - the drugs, drink, everything. I can't see the likes of the Bryants letting it go, but we'll deal with it. I feel like crap most of the time, and I've fucked up everything - hurt everyone I care about. I'll do whatever it takes to get you back, and make it up to my kids and Deb."

"I want that for you more than anything, Kev. I'm here for you, as a friend, but we're not getting back together, and I won't move in with you again."

"You're screwing with my head. I don't buy the 'as a friend' crap. You kiss Charlotte and Amy the way you just kissed me, do you? Then again, who knows with Lyndhurst?"

"You've always been jealous of Charlotte," I said. "That's even more ridiculous than your paranoia about James. You're right, though. I shouldn't have kissed you."

"I didn't say you *shouldn't* have."

"Well, *I'm* saying it. I shouldn't have."

"I need you, Lucy. I can't do this without you."

"You'll have to. We're not together any more. You *are* strong enough. I know you are. Just do it for yourself, okay? Not for me - or even the kids, or Deborah. You have to do it for you. It won't work otherwise."

"But I don't care about me. I'm only strong enough if I've got you with me. There's no point without you."

"That's not true. I believe in you. I'll talk to Deborah and my brothers - get you professional help."

"Doctors, counsellors, and the like?" Spoken with pure contempt. "Forget it. They can't be bothered with the likes of me, and you're living in a fantasy, if you think they'll be able to 'cure' me. Oh yeah, and what Deborah said - it was true, okay? The day we broke up - the day she took the kids to her parents' - I hit Gemma. She was the one person I thought I could never hurt, and I did. Gem's never said a word about it. Maybe she's blanked it out or something. It's what you do, isn't it? Anyway, you were probably right, to want out. You're better off with Phil or James."

I couldn't think of an instant response, and Kev was already slamming the front door, before I could say a word.

Chapter Forty

The clashing vibrant decor in Cynthia Jackson's living room, combined with Matt and Danny's disco lights, recently recovered from Mum's loft, left my head spinning. The Special Brew, admittedly, might also have played a role in this.

I had retreated to the kitchen, where the colour scheme was scarcely less hideous, but at least I could hear myself think, and escape from the flashing lights.

And yes, I was avoiding Phil. We were still together, but barely. I couldn't even think about doing anything about that until we'd at least made it through this evening: Phil Jackson's twenty-first.

He was making a huge deal out of it being a celebration of our "anniversary". He was doing it on purpose, of course. Had to be - trying to make me feel guilty. Swig of Special Brew. I bloody well didn't, though. I had nothing to feel guilty *about*.

Jade and Jessica were living with Clare now, at her mum and dad's. Matt hadn't discussed his decision with any of us - simply announced that it was the way things were going to be. But Mum had overheard a couple of phone calls, and apparently, he was trying to talk Clare out of taking them to Durham, to be with her and Malcolm.

As for the twins themselves, Jade hadn't been suspended or expelled, but her behaviour wasn't improving, to put it mildly. And Jess was more withdrawn than ever.

Matt could have come along, without the kids to look after, and I *had* suggested it, but he'd insisted he wasn't "in the mood". He never *was* any more. All he did was work: increasing his hours progressively, week by week.

I hadn't spoken to Kev since that evening, but had heard enough, via my brothers, to know that nothing had changed. He'd never said anything remotely along those lines before - about quitting drugs and booze. But, whatever, right? They were only words, without any follow through. Why should I feel bad? What had Deborah said, about him manipulating me? Sounded about right. Bloody emotional blackmail.

I drained the last drop of Special Brew, crushed the can, and perched it on the top of the, already overflowing, bin. Reached out and grabbed my next.

"Don't you think you've had enough, as it is?"

I turned around to see Charlotte. Who grabbed my arm, and practically dragged me away from the table.

"They're playing Madonna again," I said. "I'm sure they've been playing her half the night. I wouldn't mind, but Kirsty got Sarah into her, as in - I must have heard every track on every album at least eighty times."

Pretending not to notice that my friend was pissed off with me. Great tactic, Lucy. Like that would work.

"You need to take it easy, you know. Why do you have to drink Special Brew, anyway? It's vile."

"Habit, I guess. I'm Kev Tanner's ex, remember? Special Brew, Tennent's Super - par for the course."

"You always go on about Kev and James, when you're drunk. I feel sorry for Phil."

"Steady on, Charlie. Sarah will get jealous, if you feel too sorry for Phil. She's madly in love with my boyfriend, you know. My sisters always try to nick my blokes. Have you noticed that?"

Of course, my timing was spot on, as always. I glanced around in time to witness my kid sister turn on her heels.

"You bitch, Lucy Ryman," said Tracy. "Sarah - hold on..."

"Don't look at me like that," I told Charlotte. "She's the one trying to steal my boyfriend."

"She isn't trying to 'steal' him, and what you just said was bloody cruel. I'm through with trying to stop you making a fool of yourself.

I'm going to find Tara, and ask her if we can leave. You're on your own."

"Charlotte...Oh, you know what - forget it. Just fuck off, if that's the way you want it."

What happened after that was a blur, but the upshot was that Phil eventually hunted me down. Encouraged me to come back into the lounge, and dance with him.

I was a dead weight in his arms, and it was easier that way. Endurable, at least.

Unusually, Phil was pissed, too. It took me a while to realise, because I was so far gone.

He took my hand, as Spandau's "True" finished. They were certainly playing all of Sarah's favourites.

I didn't realise what was happening at first. Phil got Danny's attention, and the music stopped. He then called for silence, and began that stupid speech, which served as the finishing touch, on the masterpiece that was our screwed up mess of a relationship.

It's knife-twistingly ironic, looking back on that incident, so many years later. As I declared to Phil that night - "nobody owned" the Lucy Ryman I was, in those days. And she certainly didn't take ownership of her own actions and reactions.

I can't even remember the specifics - what exactly Phil said. He went on and on about how much I meant to him, and how grateful he was that I'd put up with him for over a year. I think I actually got scared that he was going to propose or something - right there, in front of everyone.

And yet, it was surreal, because it was obvious that he knew. Knew it was over. That it had been, before it had even started. My heart had never been in it, and Phil had never been able to make me fall in love with him. Even though, at times, I'd wanted that to happen almost as much as he did.

I mean, I'd wanted to want something rational. Something real, and pure, and uncomplicated, and mine. I should have wanted it, and I did, but didn't. And the didn't part won.

"Are you planning to go after him, Lucy? Because, if you're not, I'll have to," said Hannah.

Phil had stormed out, through the patio doors, and we could just about see him, sitting on the bench, under the oak tree.

"Maybe we should leave him to it," said Danny. "He obviously needs space."

"He doesn't need space. My brother's upset. He needs to know that we give a damn and, since Lucy clearly doesn't, it's down to me."

Hannah was already moving towards the door, but I grabbed her by the arm. "I didn't say I wouldn't do it, did I?"

But Sarah shoved us both out of the way. "Don't you think you've done enough already, Lucy? I'll talk to him."

"Like hell. Where do you get off, acting as if Phil's *your* boyfriend? I'm going, so mind your own bloody business - and that includes all of you."

But Sarah wasn't about to do that, and chased me down the path. As well as she *could* chase, in her long, coral dress, and ridiculously high heels.

"Do you seriously not realise how stupid you look, dressed like that? It's obvious you're trying to impress him, and it's not going to work. Phil doesn't fancy you."

"That's for you to say, is it? You don't care about him. And he isn't your boyfriend any more, either. You just chucked him, in front of everyone."

"Only after he humiliated me, in front of everyone. Anyway, that's why I need to talk to him, isn't it? So, how is this anything to do with you? Just go back to the house."

"We'll ask Phil if that's what he wants."

"Oh, whatever. He's hardly likely to want you hanging around."

We'd made it to our destination, by this point. And Phil must, realistically, have heard at least some of our exchange. He continued to stare into the little fish pond, at the bottom of the garden.

"Phil, are you okay?" asked Sarah.

"Look, Sarah, this is between me and my boyfriend. Get lost, right?" And I shoved my sister, who lost her balance and ended up falling backwards, into the hedge - just as Tracy came along, to help her up.

And, of course, Sarah's best mate had to give me a mouthful of abuse.

"Just leave it, Trace," warned Sarah. "I said I was fine."

Finally, Phil stood up, and turned to face the three of us. "Right, girls - you have my attention. Clearly, a few moments to myself was too much to hope for. What can I do for you all?"

"We just want to know if you're okay," said Sarah, her eyes duly filling with tears.

"Oh, yeah - never better, Sarah. I love being dumped and humiliated by the love of my life, and then poked and prodded by my ex and her little sister, until I respond. I guess, as far as unforgettable twenty-first birthday parties go, this one's a roaring success. Tracy, if you want to help, can you escort your friend back to the house?"

Tracy nodded. "Yeah, okay. Come on, Sarah. It's bloody freezing out here."

"I want to say something first," said Sarah. "I take it you're getting rid of me and Tracy so that you can talk to my sister, Phil?"

"Yes, that's right. I want to talk to Lucy."

"He isn't worth it," said Tracy.

"Yeah, well, that's not the way I see it," said Sarah. "I wish it was. The thing is, I really care about you, Phil Jackson. And it hasn't done me any good, but I like you, anyway." The tears were flowing steadily, by this point. "I'd have done anything for you, but all you want to do is keep chasing after my sister. I don't get you, and you've missed out on someone who actually gives a damn about you. If you want Lucy, after everything she's put you through, it's your problem. I'm not going to hang around, making a fool of myself, any more."

Tracy put her arm around Sarah. "Let's get you inside."

Sarah nodded, and they walked away. Like, *finally*.

"Thanks, Phil. She's such a drama queen."

"Maybe. At least she cares, though. I've been pretty mean to her. Anyway, it's not Sarah I wanted to talk about."

"I know. Listen, Phil - I'm sorry." I realised how deeply I meant it. Tears moistened my cheeks, almost before I knew I was crying. "We *are* okay, aren't we?"

"You really need to ask that? No, Lucy - just to clarify, we're not 'okay', and there is no *us*."

"But we're still friends, surely?"

"No, we're not. Because, you see, Lucy, friends don't treat each other like that - the way you've treated me. And they don't put up with the level of abuse I have, either. I have to take some of the blame."

"Danny and Hannah are married. We won't be able to ignore one another entirely."

"No, there *is* that. I don't know how things will work out, long-term. All I know is, for now, I think we need to cut off contact. I can't deal with being around you. I want you to go and find my sister, and ask her to take you home. She's about the only one who's sober enough to drive."

"Matt's picking me and Sarah up anyway, in an hour or so."

"You're not understanding me, Lucy. I want you to leave now - as soon as possible. You're not welcome here any more. Maybe I'm not going off my head and breaking things, including you, and I'm sure that's what Kev Tanner would do. Maybe that's my failure. But, believe me, if you consider me capable of feeling anything, I have all those feelings right now - of wanting to break things."

"Including me?"

"Especially you, Lucy. Now, get the hell out of my life. I can't even look at you."

No way was I begging Hannah for a lift, of course. I slipped out, by the gate at the side of the house, not even considering how I would get back home from here.

After I'd thrown up in someone's forsythia, I gave in to the impulse to sit down in the middle of the street. A case of sit down before I fell down, pretty much.

And then, the next stage: I let myself cry. Screw restraint. I just sat there and bawled, at the top of my lungs, because it didn't matter any more, and I was all out of logical solutions to my lousy predicament. There was nothing left, as far as I was concerned. Self-pity? Oh, one hundred percent. Drink-induced, and unapologetic. So, I cried relentlessly, not giving a crap about whose sleep I might potentially be disturbing.

And, when I was done with tears, I lay down and started to drift. *Just need to sleep - just to sleep...*

"Lucy, it *is* you. I thought it was."

"What the...?"

But Deborah was dragging me to my feet. "You can't stay here, in this state. Who got you into this mess? If it was Kev, I swear I'll kill him."

I took a moment to register my surroundings, and test my ability to stand without falling. So far, so good, although I was still on the shaky side.

"I've parked on double yellow lines, so we'll have to get you to the car, before I'm nicked. Just take it steady. Hold on to my arm, if it helps."

"Okay. And, no, I haven't seen Kev. I was at Phil's twenty-first. We broke up, and he chucked me out. Well, kind of. He said to ask Hannah to take me home, but I didn't fancy it."

"So, who else was at this party? Matt and Danny? Sarah? Charlotte? Because, honestly, I can't see how they could leave you to walk the streets, in such a vulnerable state."

"Danny, Hannah, and Sarah were all there. I guess they still are. Matt didn't go. He was supposed to give me a lift home, but Phil wouldn't let me stay. We're finished. I said that, didn't I? I did chuck him, but I didn't mean it. But then, he wouldn't have me back, or even talk to me."

"He should have made sure you were safe, no matter what. It's only chance that I came by, when I did. I've been out with my friends, Brenda and Yvonne. It was Bren's birthday, and we went for drinks, except that I wasn't in the mood, and I had to drive back, in any case. If you think you might be sick, I can give you a paper bag? I always keep a supply, in case Toby gets travel sick."

I had my best attempt at alienating Deborah - literally the only person who had bothered with me that night - by going on about being "in love with your husband", for practically the entire journey. She spent most of the time emphasizing that she needed to "focus on the road".

As we rounded a corner, that was familiar to even my muddled brain, and I realised that we had almost reached Mum's, she finally looked across at me. "Talk to Kev when you're sober, Lucy. If you can also find a time when he's not drunk or stoned, you might get somewhere. I've been pretty much where you are now - only with two kids, as well."

"So, you don't love him any more?"

"I care. I'm not in love with him, no."

"The thing is, when I'm sober, I might not want to talk to him. I might not think it's a good idea. That's why I want to talk to him now. I love him when I'm sober, but I don't tell him then."

"Lucy, we're here. Will anyone be in?" Deborah opened the car door, and I got out, still a little unsteady on my feet.

"Mum's staying the weekend with her sister. Sarah's still at the party, flirting with my so-called 'boyfriend', and I guess Danny and Hannah will still be there, too. But Matt should be home. You like him. Kev thought you fancied Matt. You do, don't you? You're blushing."

"Come on, Luce. Keep hold of my arm, and we might just about get you there in one piece."

Chapter Forty-One

Sarah sat down next to me, on my bed. "Lucy, I need to talk to you."

"Really? You *do* surprise me. You've barely said a word to me, for the past fortnight. I can only apologise so many times, you know - and I can't tell Phil I'm sorry in person, if he won't meet up or take my calls."

Sarah put her arm around me. "I've been hard on you, haven't I? Phil knows you're sorry. He just needs some space."

"You've seen him?"

Sarah nodded. "Yesterday lunch-time. We went for coffee."

"Is he okay?"

"He will be," she said. "From what I could make out, he knew, in his heart, that the relationship was ending. He just didn't expect it to happen the way it did, and it's left him pretty stunned. Anyway, it isn't Phil I wanted to talk about."

"Something's wrong, isn't it?" I fiddled with my gold creole earrings.

"Well, it actually could be a good thing." Sarah hesitated. "Cath's coming to visit, with little George. Mum invited her." She was rushing her words, knowing I was highly unlikely to view a visit from Catherine as "a good thing".

"What the hell did she do that for?"

"Cath *is* her daughter, and this is Mum's house."

"Dad's, actually. Mum checked with him, I take it?"

Sarah rolled her eyes. "I don't think he knows, but it's only for a couple of days. Surely even you want to see her, after all this time? And our nephew. I know I want to see them both."

"Dad would chuck her out on the street, if he knew - with or without the kid. You and Mum both know that. I've a good mind to tell him."

"Don't you dare." Holding my gaze.

"Oh, relax. I'll keep your little secret. Just don't expect me to hang around much, while she's under this roof."

"She's still our sister."

"Yours, you mean."

"Don't be ridiculous. We're all sisters, whether any of us like the fact or not. Anyway, for your information, Mum *did* ask Cath to stay here, but she isn't. She knew you'd be like this. She's staying with Tara and Charlotte."

"My best friend? That's loyalty for you."

"Don't blame Charlotte. Catherine approached our cousin, and she'd already more or less agreed. It seemed like the best option. Danny and Hannah don't really have the space."

"Whatever. At least this way, I don't have to see her."

"She's coming over Monday night. And don't tell me you're going out on a Monday night." Sarah stood, and headed for the door.

"I am, as it goes - with Amy and Ruth."

She faced me, even as she opened the bedroom door. "Oh, how convenient. Just try to be here, Luce. Seven, seven-thirty. It isn't much to ask."

***

I'd arrived home early, specifically in order to "miss" my sister. But there it was, in the drive. That familiar red Talbot Horizon, with all the same lousy car stickers, and a couple of new ones. And half of Toys 'R' Us, on the back seat.

I took a deep breath, and reached into my bag, for my key. So, she'd come early, to catch me out. Fine. If Catherine Ryman wanted a showdown, she could bloody well have one.

It was George I noticed first. He was sitting on Mum's living room floor, surrounded by Lego. The larger bricks, that Matt's girls had played with, when they were little - hadn't seen those for years. And Sarah was down there with him.

"Hello, Lucy," said Catherine.

My elder sister was perched on the edge of the sofa. Hair back to its natural dark brown, and she'd let the perm grow out, too. She wore minimal make-up, and a small pair of silver creoles was all, in the way of jewellery.

Yeah, well - whatever. She could change her image as much as she liked. It didn't change anything, or make her less of a slag than she'd always been.

"Is this a set-up? You weren't supposed to come until tonight."

"Of course it's not. Sarah doesn't work Mondays, so we thought we'd have some extra quality time together: the two of us and George. I take it you weren't going to be here later, then?"

"What do *you* think?"

George caught my eye again. It was impossible to ignore him.

"Sarah, can you take George for a walk or something?" suggested Catherine.

"Yes, okay." She got to her feet. "Come on, George. We'll go to the park again. Would you like that?" She held out her hand, for her nephew.

"Can I play on the swings? *And* the slide? *And* the climbing frame?"

"Of course you can, darling," said Sarah.

Having negotiated terms, George accepted her hand. "Are you coming, Mummy?"

"No, sweetheart - just you and Aunt Sarah this time. You have fun, and tell me all about it, when you get back. I need to speak to Aunt Lucy."

"This is my Aunt Lucy? So, why can't she come, too? I want Aunt Lucy to come!" He started to cry, and kicked a pile of Lego.

"George, be a good boy, and go with Aunt Sarah," said Catherine, but her son was having none of it, and turned up the volume on his bawling.

It took maybe ten minutes or so, to pacify George. Eventually, he did calm down, and off he went with Sarah - all smiles and excitement again.

"He's always known he has an aunt called Lucy," said Catherine. "He drew a picture of you once. You had green hair."

"He looks like his dad."

"I know." She adjusted a hair grip. Was obviously growing her fringe out, and had reached the irritating, in-between stage.

"Has Kev seen him?"

"No, he hasn't. At first, I didn't want him anywhere near my child but, when George was about six months old - well, I guess it was my hormones. I felt really emotional, and that I wanted his dad to see him. I'd heard that you'd moved in with Kev, and I didn't want to cause any trouble, so I called him at the pub."

"'Didn't want to cause trouble'? Pull the other one. You just didn't have the guts to ring, in case I answered."

"Lucy, please - hear me out, okay? I'm trying to be honest here."

"Honest - you? Okay, so - when George was first born, you reckon you didn't want Kev 'anywhere near'? What's your kid's name, Cath?"

"George Ryman."

"Not Tanner Ryman, then? Because Danny told me it was."

"Tanner's his middle name, that's all. He goes by George Ryman. He was never going to take his dad's surname as his own, but I thought my son deserved something. I thought you'd have been more upset if I called him George Kevin."

"If you gave a toss about upsetting me, you wouldn't have used any of Kev's names. It completely contradicts what you said about not wanting him 'anywhere near.'"

"Think what you want, but I didn't want Kev involved, at that stage. I just didn't want to deny that George *had* a father. But, as I said, my feelings changed, and I tried to get Kev to at least acknowledge George's existence. Maybe he didn't believe I wasn't after money, but he didn't want to know, and told me so, in his usual charming style. So, that was that. I gave up, and got on with my life, and raising my kid."

"It goes to show you don't know much about Kev. Truth is, he barely even bothers with Toby. Ask Deborah. Your mistake was having a boy. Kev's only interested in daughters. He's completely obsessed with Gemma."

"What are you saying? That Kev's a pervert, who's 'into' his daughter?"

"I'll slap you so hard, if you say anything like that again. He would never do anything to harm Gemma, and he'd kill anyone who violated her - or Toby, for that matter." I took an essential deep breath. "Kev has issues, and I don't fully understand, but he's been damaged by his own childhood. He can't love sons, the way he loves his daughter. Even if I knew more, I wouldn't tell you."

"You really love him."

"It didn't do either of us much good, but yeah, I do."

"I'm not a threat to you, Lucy. If it helps, I'm with someone."

"Sarah did say something. He's black, right? I can see Dad loving that. The only reason Farooq can still walk down the street is because he's in with the Bryants."

Catherine fiddled with her hair grips again, this time with shaking hands. "Dad can go to hell. Delroy has connections too and, believe me, Dad and the Bryants, and all the guys like Kev Tanner and that Farooq - they're small fry."

"If that's true, you shouldn't be letting this Delroy bloke near you and your kid."

"Oh, so suddenly, you *do* care? Look, Luce - there's a difference between having contacts you could call in, if push came to shove, and...What I'm saying is, me and Del, we're engaged, and he's a decent bloke. George is in no danger, and none of us are in danger from Dad and his gangster mates, okay?"

"It's your life. So, you're engaged, but no ring?"

"Delroy only asked me a couple of days ago, and he wanted me to choose my own ring."

"You're pregnant again. You're getting married because you have to."

"One out of two. Yes, I'm pregnant. But I hardly need to get married, because of that. I'm an unmarried mum already. What's the difference, to do the same thing again?"

"Well, I hope it works out for you, but I do need to get ready. I'm going out with Amy and Ruth."

I would have felt better if my workmates had actually agreed to my last minute suggestion. That way, I wouldn't have been lying, and I wouldn't have had to lose myself for the evening. As it was, I would have to get drunk by myself, at some pub where nobody knew me - and hope that nobody who *did*, made a random decision to pop in.

It would almost have been easier to deal with Catherine and George. But only *almost*.

Chapter Forty-Two

As is often the case, I felt much better, once I'd finally thrown up. My head still hurt like hell, and the room wouldn't remain still for five seconds together, but at least my tummy had settled somewhat.

I had tried to piece together the confused kaleidoscope of events from the previous evening, and come to the conclusion that I didn't need to know.

I was as satisfied as I could be that I hadn't engaged in sexual activities, with any of the random blokes I'd flirted with. Beyond that, the precise details of my own drunken behaviour were what they were, and I was sure paying for my stupidity now, with bells on.

I glanced at my watch, as I slammed the front door behind me. Cath always *had* been better at mornings than me, and Charlotte and Tara both had to be up early for work.

Anyway, I didn't have much choice. I had to be at my own place of work by eight-thirty, and the partners were increasingly strict, with regard to punctuality, of late.

If there was an easy and a hard way, I was going to do things in Lucy Ryman style. It was time to resolve things with my sister, and I couldn't possibly have admitted that last night.

I took the bus to Tara and Charlotte's. I'd, to date, visited them both there, on a grand total of six occasions. Even now, it seemed weird, to think of my best friend living anywhere other than with her mum, within easy walking distance of my own family home.

It was still not yet 8am when I pressed the intercom.

"Lucy, I was literally on my way out. I'll buzz you in, but then it's a case of letting you in and heading off myself, okay? I take it you're here to see Cath?"

Charlotte buzzed me in, and I took the stairs. I was beginning to see Amy's point about lifts, of late. The whole feeling trapped thing.

"Go through. They're in the kitchen, having breakfast."

"I take it that slice of toast is yours." Reference the half-eaten slice that Charlotte was juggling, whilst shoving her left arm into the sleeve of her jacket. "Do you and Tara both drive yourselves in? Your offices are across the street from each other, aren't they?"

"Yeah, they are. And, no - we go in her car normally. But she had to get in even earlier than usual - so she reckoned. Bloody impatient cow, if you ask me, but I love her, anyway. Catch you later, Luce."

And she was out of the door, before I could reply.

I went through to the kitchen, where Catherine was trying to negotiate with her son: "George, can you at least *aim* for your mouth? I don't want to be cleaning Coco Pops off the ceiling, as well as the carpet."

I couldn't help smiling. "You need any help?"

My sister looked up at me. "Is this *Round Two*, or are you ready to talk?"

"Ready to talk. Well, apart from the fact that I have to be at work by half-eight, but minor details, and it's only round the corner."

"Surely it would have been better to come after work, then?"

"I thought I might change my mind, and I didn't want to."

"George, can you go to your room, please?"

"I don't have a room. I'm sleeping in the same room as you. I slept in the bed, and you slept on the floor - remember?"

"Go to that room then, and play with your toys. It's not as if you didn't bring half of them with you."

"But, Mummy, why-?"

"George, I'll lose my temper in a minute. Just do as you're told."

George knocked his breakfast bowl off the table, and slammed the door behind him.

"He gets it from his dad," I told her, as I retrieved the bowl. "Get me a cloth or something."

"Thanks. They keep the cloths in that drawer, right behind you. And, yeah - maybe. Reminds me of his aunt, as it goes."

"I take it you mean Sarah?"

"Which of us would you say threw the most tantrums?"

"No comment." Having cleaned up her son's mess, I sat down next to my sister. "Listen, Catherine, I'm not saying we're fine, because we're not. It's not just that you slept with my boyfriend, is it? You had his kid."

"Yeah, well, one of those was a direct result of the other. We both know the facts of life."

"But you didn't even consider not having the baby?"

She regarded me, an intensity in her eyes. "You're saying I should have aborted George? You can *say* that, having seen him?"

"It's not fair to phrase it that way. He wasn't George then, was he? It was just some fetus."

"You're wrong. George was always George. You saw what a mess it made of Sarah, Mum forcing her to get rid of her baby. And I don't believe you'd ever consider an abortion, either."

"Probably not. But it isn't the only option, is it? You could have had him adopted."

"I didn't want to. Lucy, how do you feel about Deborah Tanner?"

"Deborah? Why? What's this got to do with her?"

"You like her, right? Consider her a friend, even?"

"She's not exactly a friend. She's known Matt and Danny longer than me. But yeah, I like her. Where's this going?"

"It shows you're not exactly that jealous of anyone who's ever been with Kev. And she was his wife. Me and Kev only had a one night stand."

"Only? You're my bloody sister. And you had his kid, so I'd say it amounted to a bit more than a 'one night stand', wouldn't you?"

Catherine frowned. "It was an excuse. We both know it. Yeah, what I did hurt you, but it also gave you a reason to get rid of me. You know about Dad - what he did to me."

I wiped the sweat from my face. What was it with the air conditioning, in this place?

Holy shit, can't breathe. Got to get out of here. Escape. Can't breathe. Get out of here.

"Lucy, are you okay? Let me get you a glass of water." Catherine was on her feet already.

"No," I said, recollecting myself. "No, I don't need anything from you. I just need to get out of here."

Catherine grabbed my arm. "Sit down, Lucy. Please. Take a few deep breaths, and you'll be fine. You can't keep running away forever."

"I thought we'd got past all this. I never liked that Dad favoured Sarah, but you really couldn't deal with it, could you?" The words were spilling, almost as rapidly as the thoughts themselves. "That you weren't his favourite daughter. You weren't even his second favourite daughter, because that was me. How could Daddy not love little Cathy best, when she was so clearly the pretty one?"

"You know I hate being called Cathy. No one's ever called me that, other than him." She was actually crying.

"Oh, please - not the waterworks. Go ahead, then. Let's hear your lies again. Get it over with."

"I'm not lying, Lucy. And you're the one person who knows that, for sure."

I didn't comment. It was enough to breathe. Just breathe. Make it through the moment.

"You walked in on us, that afternoon - and walked straight out again. You saw Dad raping me, and you didn't understand, because you were two, at the time. And I was four. Four years old, Lucy. A little kid, like George is now."

"You're lying. What's wrong with you, Catherine? Who would make up something like that about their own dad? I know he was never the world's best father, but-"

"Not 'the world's best father'? He's scum. And you know what he's capable of, because he touched you, too."

"You can't say things like that! Why are you doing this? You're making the whole thing up!"

"So, why are you crying, if it isn't true? Why are we both crying? Tell me that, Lucy!"

I was. I hadn't even noticed I was crying. "I'm crying because of what you're doing. You're crying because you're an attention-seeking drama queen."

"He touched you, Lucy. When you were five. He had his hand down your knickers. That sick bastard beat up his sons, and abused his daughters. The one thing we always told ourselves was that at least Sarah was okay - at least he would never touch her."

"He *did* though, didn't he?" The realisation was an internal scream, refusing to be silenced any longer. "In the end. Once she was 'damaged goods', anyway."

"Did she tell you?"

"No, I just knew. Same as you did. Sarah's rape - did that have anything to do with...?"

"Not sure, but something Danny said - well, made me think it was some sort of revenge. Someone getting their own back on Dad, by defiling his 'angel'. He used to call her that, remember?"

"Yeah, I remember." I glanced at my watch, aware that my arm was trembling. Along with the rest of me. "Shit - the time. I'll be late for work." Going through the motions of panicking about my job, even though I couldn't give a crap.

"I'll phone them for you - say you're sick. You can't go in now."

"I'll be okay."

"Of course you can't go in. You're shaking, Lucy. Do you want to lie down? I'm sure Charlotte and Tara wouldn't mind."

"No, I want to go home."

"I'll give you a lift. And don't tell me you can get the bus. I'm driving you home, and that's that, okay? I'll go and get George, and we'll be off."

I went over to my sister, and hugged her - one of the few times I ever had.

"Where are we going, Mummy?" Voice from the doorway. George clutched a little blue teddy, with a pastel yellow bow.

"George, I thought I told you to go to your - to *the* room?"

"I heard you and Aunt Lucy shouting. Why were you both crying? Has somebody died?"

"Of course no one's died, darling. But we need to take Aunt Lucy back to Nan's. Be a good boy, and find your shoes for me. I never have a clue where you've hidden them."

"If somebody hasn't died, it must be something else big. Grown-ups only cry over serious things." *Serious, pronounced see-ruzz.*

"Okay, that's enough questions, young man. Shoes: Now. I'm not going to tell you again. You ready, Luce?"

Chapter Forty-Three

"I didn't know Matt had the day off," said Catherine.

I looked up from my routine task, of fumbling around for my key, which was supposed to reside in a zip compartment of my bag - except that I was forever forgetting to fasten the zip.

Sure enough, Matt's blue Escort was on the drive. I didn't think he even *did* days off any more.

It couldn't be something bad. No way. I couldn't deal with anything else going wrong.

Get a grip, Lucy. So, Matt's got a day off work, and didn't tell you, or did tell you, and you just don't remember.

The main thing, in practical terms, was to quickly say, "Hi," and then disappear to my room, before he noticed the state I was in. If Matthew questioned me too much, I'd burst into tears all over again, and then he'd want to know why.

And I'd be forced to lie to him, since the truth definitely wasn't an option.

"I didn't know, either. I guess he had some annual leave to use or lose. Thanks for the lift, Cath. 'Bye, George."

"You sure you're okay, Lucy?"

"As okay as I'm going to be. I'll give you a call in a day or so."

"Take a couple of days off work, if you need to."

"Nice idea, but I can't afford to. I've let Amy and Ruth down, as it is. The partners had a ton of meetings scheduled. But they don't need me, making a mess of things, putting salt in the tea instead of sugar. I'm rubbish at that job already, let alone...But anyway, I'll go back in tomorrow morning. Take care, okay?"

I slammed the car door. Headed towards the house. Past every familiar shrub, in that familiar front garden. Reached the familiar purple front door. Everything so bloody familiar, and yet all appeared as if within a sepia-toned dream sequence.

And then, I heard a familiar female voice, trying to alert my brother, even as I swung open the lounge door.

They made a frantic effort to extricate themselves, but not fast enough. Deborah's hair was dishevelled, and she was still sorting out her bra straps.

So, my workaholic brother could drag himself away from work, when he wanted to. I'd just found out about our old man, sexually abusing my sisters and me. And Matt was more bothered about getting off with Deborah Tanner.

"Luce, I wasn't expecting you," he said.

"Clearly not. Sorry to have interrupted. I was going to my room, anyway."

"I take it things didn't go well with Cath, then? Sarah said you'd probably go and see her this morning."

"Like you care. But good guess, Sarah - full marks. Now, as I said, I'm going to my room."

I made it just in time. Crawled under the covers, and sobbed my heart out. It felt as if I'd never stop.

But there came a point where I couldn't cry any more, and I sat up in bed, staring at the ceiling. I grabbed a tissue from my bedside cabinet, and blew my nose noisily.

There was a tap on the door. I tried to ignore it, even though I knew that wouldn't work.

"Lucy, it's me," said Deborah. "I left Matt downstairs, watching telly. Can I come in - please?"

"Yeah, okay."

Deborah came over, and sat on the edge of my bed. She stroked my hair, the way Sarah might have, and the fact that it didn't feel weird, was its own kind of weird.

And what had I told Cath? That Deborah wasn't "exactly a friend"? Yeah, although I'd obviously been right about her knowing Matt better than she did me.

"So, are you going to tell me what's wrong?" asked Deborah. "Has something happened?"

"Everything's wrong."

"Can we narrow it down a bit? You don't have to tell me, Luce, but we get on, don't we?" Her face looked even thinner than usual - even more pale.

I didn't know what to say to her. I mean, where do you start?

"I can't believe you're upset about me and Matt, or even particularly surprised, because you knew I liked him. You weren't shy about mentioning it before, and I realise the drink was talking, but you were still right. You *are* okay about it, aren't you?"

"Of course I'm 'okay about' you and Matthew. It's not for me to be 'okay' or not, in any case - but don't worry. If you can put up with my brother, it's fine by me. I'd rather see him with you than Clare, any day, and if you can make him happy - well, it's not like he doesn't deserve it, after everything he's been through."

"Thank you. That means a lot. You deserve to be happy, too. You really can't tell me what's wrong? Is it to do with Catherine? Matthew mentioned that she was back."

"As I said, I went to see her, just now." Which, I knew, wasn't much of an answer.

"I take it she brought the little boy? George, right?"

"Yeah, she did. And yes, George. She's called him George Tanner Ryman. You haven't seen him, I take it?"

"No."

"He looks like Kev. So, that's that. No chance she was lying about the father. But, before you start thinking that's what I'm upset about, it isn't. It's not one thing. Just everything, like I said. I mean, I *did* break up with my boyfriend, of over a year."

"Phil?" Her expression said it all.

"See? That reaction was practically worthy of Sarah. I *was* going out with Phil. Do you think I had no feelings at all about our relationship ending?"

"I don't think that, no. But *you* finished with *Phil*, didn't you?"

"Debatable, really. Anyway, who cares whether I dumped him or he dumped me? I *did* care. I wouldn't have been with him otherwise."

"So, you're saying you're heartbroken over Phil Jackson? That you were lying in bed, sobbing your heart out, over an ex-boyfriend you kind of liked?"

"How do you know I...? Oh, look, forget it, okay? I didn't say I was *only* upset about Phil. Things got pretty emotional with Cath, but it's not what you think - about her and George, and him being Kev's. There's something else - something she said."

"You can't tell me, can you?"

"I can't tell anyone - not yet. I don't even know if I believe..." I broke down again.

Deborah hugged me. "Hey, it's okay. Lucy, it's going to be okay."

"It's not, though. Everything's messed up. I honestly can't take much more."

When I was done crying, I turned to Deborah: "So, does Kev know about you and Matt yet?"

"Not yet."

"Yeah, well - he'll hit the roof, when he does find out. He suspected before, and went off on one, remember?"

"He'll be okay about me and Matthew, but he's going through a lot right now. Telling him about my new relationship can wait. Listen, Luce - I told Kev I'd talk to you, so I'm going to say this."

But she didn't get the chance, because the door swung open, and my brother was standing there, complexion beetroot.

"I *knew* it. What did I tell you, Deborah? I don't want you passing messages from your psycho ex-husband to my sister." Matt clenched and unclenched his fist, as he spoke. "Maybe you can't or won't cut Tanner out of your life, because of the kids, but Lucy has no obligation to deal with him. You can see how upset she is already - and, most probably, your mutual ex has something to do with that. I don't want him anywhere near Lucy and, if he even *thinks about* hassling Catherine and George..."

"You *finished*? Only I thought we agreed, Matt?" said Deborah. "I'm talking to Lucy. She doesn't need everyone going on at her."

"I'm not 'everyone'. I'm her brother. I should have been able to trust you to talk to Lucy, without bringing Tanner into this, but clearly I was right not to, wasn't I? Whose side are you on?"

"'Side'? This is about 'sides'? You claim to dislike Kev so much, but you're as paranoid as he is. Lucy's not a little kid any more, and I think she's capable of making her own decisions, don't you? She doesn't need you eavesdropping on her conversations."

I threw off the covers, and sat up. "Right, that's enough - both of you. I am *here*, you know. I do appreciate your concern, Matt, but Deborah's right. We were having a private conversation, and you should be able to respect that. Now, please - can you give us a minute?"

"Whatever. Just don't expect any sympathy from me, when Kev Tanner fucks up everything for you, all over again."

"Matt? Please stop working on the assumption that I'm going to get back with Kev, just because I'm willing to hear Deborah out. You worry too much, and it's not that I don't want you to care, but have some faith in me too, okay?"

"It's not *you* I don't have faith in." He barely left the door on its hinges.

"Thank you, Lucy. And Matthew will be okay. I'll talk to him later, when he's calmed down a bit."

"Yeah, well - he's got a point about Kev. He's hurt me, over and over again. Hurt you too, for that matter. I shouldn't even want to hear what he has to say."

"But you do, don't you? You care. I can see that. You know, Kev told me he'd do anything to have you back, and I can't believe I'm saying this, but I really think he means it. He's gone cold turkey on drugs, drink, everything. I'm not saying that's all down to you, but I'd say you're one of the main incentives."

"He says he's given up drugs, and you believe him?"

"Lucy, have you ever *seen* anyone go through heroin withdrawal?"

I considered her question. Danny had been messed up on pretty much every drug out there, as a teenager - but he'd got sent away, when he'd hit rock bottom. Some recovery centre. Matt did see more of that side, but my sisters and I had been so young, at the time. Mum had kept us sheltered, for the most part.

"No, not really," I replied.

"Well, I have, and it isn't pretty. And that's what Kev's going through, as we speak. He begged me not to call a doctor, but I'm still not sure if I'm right to go along with that. Two of my uncles had to be 'persuasive' with Farooq, to get him to move out, and I don't even want to know precisely what *that* involved."

I didn't want to know what it would have involved, either. "If Kev really has given up drugs, that's great news - if it lasts. But what has it got to do with me? I don't want him back, Deb - not after all we've been through. And if you, of all people, are saying I should, that has to be the ultimate irony."

"I know."

"You said yourself - you've seen the drug withdrawal thing before. I take it that was with Kev, too?"

"My dad as well," she said, "but you're right. Kev has tried to quit a couple of times."

"I had no idea about your dad - sorry, Deborah. As for Kev, though - you can see what I mean, right? Even if he does get clean, is it really going to last?"

"There are no guarantees in life, not with anyone."

"Oh, I agree - but that means we have to weigh up the odds, and decide if it's worth the risk."

"And you don't think Kev's worth the risk?"

"No, I don't. That might be harsh, but it's how it is. You can't blame me. You felt the same way, in the end, and you were married with kids."

"It wasn't the same for me. He never loved me, the way he does you. And, even now, it does actually cut me up inside, to admit it."

"Screw that. You can't romanticise drug addiction. Like, Kev's giving up drugs because he's so in love with me? Sorry, it doesn't work that way. This is real life. How much does he love his daughter? And he still never gave up drugs - not and stayed off."

"Of course I'm not romanticising drug addiction, but love is powerful. And yes, okay - I can hear it in the way Kev talks about you - that he loves you. And, think about that from my point of view - because, yes, I'm with Matt now, but I was in love with Kev once. You think it's easy for me to admit he was never in love with me? That he would change for you, out of loving you, when he never bothered for me? And I can't answer you for sure about why he couldn't or wouldn't quit drink and drugs before, even for Gem. It's different though, isn't it? She's his daughter, and we're supposed to protect our kids, and be strong for them."

"It's more mind games. I don't want to be anyone's reason to live," I told her. "I've listened to you, and what you're saying Kev's saying, and I don't want to hear any more, okay?"

"All I'm asking is, come with me to see him. I need the support too, you know. He hasn't exactly got many people."

"Yeah, well - the way he's treated everyone around him, what does he expect?"

"So, what do I tell him - that you won't come?"

"Yeah, that's right. Tell him I love him, but I don't want to see him again. He needs to let me go."

Deborah hesitated. "Yes, okay - I'll tell him," she said. "And, if I was wrong to mention any of this, I'm sorry. Are we still friends?"

Had I seriously told Catherine that Deborah was "not exactly a friend"? And after she had been the one to bring me back safely, after Phil's party, too.

"Of course we are. You don't ever need to ask that. Deborah, the truth is - I can't deal with Kev's problems right now. Can you check my brother isn't listening in this time? I need to tell you what Catherine told me, and I can't risk him overhearing."

Chapter Forty-Four

It was June 1988 - eleven months since I'd broken up with Phil. And things had moved on, to the extent that Phil, Sarah, and I now regularly went out for coffee together, or met up at the Lion for a drink.

Sarah and I were in our room, chatting, whilst my sister got ready for an evening out with Tracy.

"So, did Fiona say why she wasn't coming, after all?" The original plan had been for the three of them to go out for pizza, and then on to a pub or two, and possibly a nightclub.

"Not sure," said Sarah, continuing to apply her mascara. "She cancelled this morning. Reckoned she was tired. She does work pretty long hours."

"At Sunshine Insurance, right? Is she in the same department as Matt?"

"Yeah, Sunshine Insurance. But, no - she's in Accounts. Rather her than me." She held up two lipsticks: "Which one?"

"The dusky pink looks pretty, and it matches your dress. You don't believe her, I take it - about being too tired? You think she's making excuses?"

"Yes. I think Fi's moved on. She's in with Tiffany and Aisha now." Sarah brushed away a couple of tears. "At least there are no bad feelings, though - or, at least, I hope not. I don't want her hating me."

"Of course Fiona doesn't hate you. It was only ever Kirsty she had a problem with."

"Who *hasn't* got a problem with Kirsty? Apart from Delroy Walker, of course."

"Oh, don't. I can't believe he actually married her. I assumed he was stringing her along, like he did Cath."

"Apparently not. And I would guess Courtney's going to have a half-brother or sister, too. Not that Kirsty said, but she definitely looked pregnant to me, and Tracy agreed. How do you think Catherine will take it?"

"Honestly? At this point, I don't think she'll care. She's devoted to George and Courtney. Being a mum really seems to bring out the best in her. Last time I saw her, she looked radiant, and she assured me that wasn't down to some bloke."

"I think you could be right. Cath's better off focusing on herself and the kids. Last night was a laugh, wasn't it? It's amazing how we can all go out as friends - you, me, and Phil. I'd never have believed it."

"Me and Phil were always meant to be friends, not a couple. But are you guys getting together, or what? It's obvious you still fancy him, Sarah, and I can tell he's interested."

Sarah's expression darkened instantly. "Leave it, Lucy. Me and Phil are just friends."

"But Danny thought-"

"Danny needs to mind his own business, and so do you. I've made a fool of myself over Phil before, and I'm not going down that road again."

I didn't like to mention that, if she really saw Phil as "just a friend", she wouldn't be getting so agitated. But I opted to follow my sister's advice, and "leave it". They would get together, sooner or later.

"I must admit, I do kind of envy the way you end up being friends with your exes," said Sarah. "I mean, both Phil and James. You seem to end up getting on with your ex-boyfriends better as friends, once your relationships finish, than you ever did as boyfriend and girlfriend."

"Is that a good thing? I guess it is from the point of view of making male friends, but it's not ideal for finding a life partner. And it puts off any potential new boyfriends, too - not that I'm bothered right now, but I'm not sure I'd recommend it, in general."

"I never hear from Farooq any more - not that I particularly want to. But it would be nicer if we could be civil, and I didn't have to feel weird about seeing him in the street."

"I heard he's married with a kid now."

"Yeah, Danny said. He asked me if the marriage was 'arranged'. I said all weddings needed some sort of arrangement. Surely he remembered that much, from his own? He couldn't be bothered to push the point - just gave me one of his looks."

"That's Danny, doing his overprotective brother thing, that's all."

"I know. It's annoying though, all the same."

"Anyway, I don't always end up being friends with my exes. Me and Kev didn't end up friends," I reminded her.

"You did end up being friends with his other ex, though."

"True. Just as well I do get on with Deborah, too - what with her and Matt."

"Do you think those two are serious?"

"Serious enough. Put it this way - I wasn't surprised Matt moved back into the Newton Lane house. I think Deb plans to join him soon."

"With Gemma and Toby? I can see that going down well - especially when the twins come to stay."

"Yeah, well - it's how it is, and they either want to be together or they don't."

Sarah looked reflective. "Kev's stayed clean, hasn't he?"

"As far as I know."

"It seems sad to me, that you can't be friends, in that case. I mean, since you're friends with James and Phil."

"I hear how he is via Deborah, now and again. That's enough for me."

"Yes, I suppose so."

The doorbell rang, and I was glad of it. I wasn't keen on the direction our conversation was taking.

"Can one of you get that?" Mum called, from downstairs.

"What did her last slave die of, anyway? I'll go, Luce. It will most probably be Tracy. A bit early, mind. She'll have to wait, while I sort out my hair."

But I'd also got to my feet, and I touched Sarah's arm, as I passed her. "You're okay. I'll get it. You finish getting ready."

That said, I raced downstairs, and answered the door.

To Kev Tanner.

Chapter Forty-Five

"Aren't you going to say something? Invite me in or something?"

"I hardly think that would be appropriate, do you?"

"Well, maybe not, but you haven't slammed the door in my face, so do you want to go for a walk? We need to talk, Luce." Holy shit, he looked amazing. And I'd missed him, so much more than I'd dared to consider.

"We *do*?"

"I think so."

I grabbed my denim jacket. "Just popping out, Mum!"

"Lucy, who is it? Where are you...?" But I was out of the door, before the interrogation could commence. Mum had appeared in the hallway, in time to see Kev - but not soon enough to say anything, or prevent me from going with him.

I would face up to my mother, and Sarah, and anyone else who might care to express an interest, opinion, or objection of any kind, in due course.

"So, where are we heading? Not the pub, right? I mean, if there's any truth to what Deborah's been telling me."

"No pubs. And yeah, it's true. I'm clean. How far are you up to walking?"

"Where did you have in mind?"

"This way." He indicated. Down Auden Road?

Which wasn't much of an answer, but since it didn't make much odds where we walked to, I went along with it.

"By the way, how did you know I'd be home?" I glanced at my watch. "It's ten to four." I'd taken Friday and the following Monday off work, which was the only reason I was around.

"Sarah mentioned that you had some annual leave. We bumped into each other in town, a couple of weeks ago."

Interesting. She hadn't mentioned that to me, but was suddenly asking questions about why I wasn't friends with Kev. I made a mental note to follow up on this later, with my sister.

***

We'd passed Newton Lane, Greenfield Road, and the school. That felt like ages ago. I was liable to end up with blisters, if we didn't stop walking soon.

"You've lost weight," said Kev. Finally. Not sure how long, or far, we'd walked, without exchanging a solitary word.

"Maybe. Not as much as you."

"Yeah, well - that's what happens when you spend weeks throwing up one end, and having diarrhoea the other. And not necessarily one at a time. I've regained some weight, but whatever, right?"

"Deborah did say it 'wasn't pretty'. She never really got why I wouldn't come and see you - reckoned I was a selfish bitch."

"She *said* that?"

"Not in so many words. She didn't have to."

"I think you're wrong. Deborah understood. It was me who didn't, but I do now, and I'm glad you didn't come. It wouldn't have done either of us any good - you seeing me in that state."

"You should have let Deborah get professional help. Even if you didn't want it, you should have accepted help, for Deb's sake."

"Are you ever going to give me a break, Lucy? Do you have a fucking clue what I went through? And, before you ask - yeah, I do know I put you through hell - you and Deb, Gem, Toby - all of you."

"Toby, as well as Gemma? That's progress, at least. Where *are* we going, anyway? We've been walking for ages. I wouldn't have worn these heels, if I'd known. I guess at least you're fitter than I thought. I'm struggling to keep up here."

"I'm not really. You just get used to pushing yourself, in the end. We're almost there, in any case."

"Glad to hear it. Where's 'there'?"

He grinned. "Here. Turn right, and it's straight ahead: Malory Precinct. And it's Friday afternoon, so the shops will actually be open this time. The cafe, too. I take it you're needing refreshments, after I made you walk all that way?"

I could feel the tears, stinging my eyes. "Yeah, but I need to take a moment first - get myself together."

"Same bench?"

I nodded. Safer than speaking. Kev put his arm around me.

I could answer Sarah's question, after all. Some people can't be *just friends*, and shouldn't be more.

In retrospect, I did hear the sirens - whilst we were in the cafe. I barely even registered, at the time.

When I arrived home, a couple of hours later, I was prepared to be cross-examined by both Sarah and Mum. But no cross-examination occurred.

Chapter Forty-Six

"Okay, so are you going to tell me what's going on, Sarah? What happened to Tracy?"

"She phoned to cancel, after she heard."

"Heard what?" I couldn't take much more of this. "You're scaring me now. And where's Mum?"

"She's with Elizabeth."

"Elizabeth? As in, Eliza McIntyre?" I didn't think Mum and Elizabeth McIntyre got along particularly well but, for the life of me, couldn't think of any other Elizabeth my mum was likely to know.

"Yes, Elizabeth McIntyre. Listen to me, Lucy. I'm trying to tell you something. And you have to promise you won't go off the deep end. You're to stay here, because you can't do any good by...Anyway, there's been an accident."

I felt a familiar crashing feeling. The world crashing in around me. Like Bonnie all over again, and yet, not like Bonnie. But every bit as horrific.

"James." I almost whispered his name. "It *is* James, isn't it? He isn't...?"

"No, James is okay. Or, at least, he isn't dead, or badly injured. But he *has* been in an accident. A car crash."

I only then allowed myself to breathe. "I must see him - check he really is okay." I was on my feet already.

"Sit down," said Sarah. "What did I tell you? And you didn't even ask about the passengers, let alone the other vehicle." She took a deep breath. "Erica and Primrose are both dead, Lucy. And they think the other car was stolen, by a couple of kids. Literal kids - maybe thirteen or fourteen. Nothing's official yet, but it seems as if one of them was Richard Bryant, Jake's eldest."

I could barely take it all in. *Erica and Primrose are both dead, Lucy.* "Please, Sarah - tell me where James is. Is he in hospital?"

"No, not any more. They had him in, to look him over, but he had nothing more than a few cuts and bruises. The doctors discharged him."

"And he went to his mum and dad's?"

"Yes. They didn't want him going back to his own house. I don't think he would have been allowed to go, if his parents hadn't said he could stay with them. And Elizabeth had a go at the police, who wanted to question him. Said he wasn't up to it, and they could speak to him once he'd rested."

"I can't stay around here, doing nothing." I got to my feet and headed for the door.

But Sarah was ready for my attempt, and barred my way, restraining me with a strength I didn't know my sister had. "You promised."

"I didn't, as it goes. I don't want to hurt you, Sarah, but I will."

"If you're that determined to go, I won't be able to stop you. I know that. But I'm asking you not to be so bloody selfish and thoughtless. Your going over there now isn't what's best for James or his family, and it isn't really best for you, either. And our brother *does* need you."

"Matt. Yeah, of course - I'll stop by there first. I'm glad you mentioned it." This would have brought everything back, about Bonita's death. The anniversary of which was next week. Three years. How *could* it be?

"He's staying with us overnight. The only reason he agreed to be here was you. Apparently, you're the one who got through to him, after Bonnie died."

I nodded. Sarah relaxed her grip on my two arms, knowing that she'd finally got through to me. I wasn't going anywhere that night.

"He's in his old room?"

"Yes. And thank you, Lucy."

Chapter Forty-Seven

I didn't end up going to the McIntyres' until Monday morning.

I had a day off anyway, which I'd planned to spend with Charlotte. We'd been looking forward for ages to a trip to London Zoo. Of course, we weren't going, in the circumstances, and my friend had cancelled her own annual leave.

But the partners seldom authorised such last minute adjustments, and it had suited me, in any case, to have the day's holiday, as arranged.

I left the house early, to avoid questioning. Just as well Mondays were Sarah's regular day off, from her job at a local supermarket, and she tended to get up comparatively late. It was up to me to judge whether I should or shouldn't visit James, and I could do without hearing her moan about my decision. She'd probably had a point, that going over there that first night would have been too much. But it was Monday now, and I wasn't leaving it any longer.

Elizabeth's pink and yellow roses, and those splendid sunflowers, continued to bloom. A peacock butterfly landed on the lavender bush, right beside the front porch, joining numerous other butterflies and bees.

After ringing the doorbell intermittently for several minutes, I had to leave it, and go for a walk. Found myself heading for Malory Precinct.

Cursing the heat, I unbuttoned my scarlet blazer. Until, finally - took the jacket off, and shoved it into my bag: the navy-blue shoulder bag I generally used for work. Not much point in neatly folding the thing, as per the Amys of this world. Given that I was myself, and not Amy, it would only end up with a bottle of orange juice spilt on it, or something along those lines.

Of course, Erica had been one of those glamorous, "perfect" types, too. She'd probably never left work with a hair out of place, in her life - never even put the bins out without full make-up.

Yeah, well - wouldn't do her much good now, would it? I brushed away the first tears I'd shed, since Sarah had given me the news. I'd been worried sick about James, concerned about Matt - but had barely even considered Erica, or even Primrose. What the hell was wrong with me?

I reached the precinct. Dived straight into the little cafe, and walked past the table where Kev and I had sat - currently occupied by a young mother, with a boy of about three, and a baby.

The older child had spilt strawberry milkshake all over the table, and he and his younger sibling were apparently holding a *who can cry loudest* contest. I felt like competing, aware that I could beat them both, hands down.

"Are you going to join me, Lucy?" His voice jolted me out of my daydream.

And I turned to see the Reverend Stanley McIntyre. He was on his own, and put down the newspaper he had either been reading, or pretending to. *The Guardian*, naturally.

I sat opposite to James's dad, whom I had always liked. He had less hair than when I'd last seen him, and the majority of what he did have was now grey, but the kindness in his wide-set blue eyes was familiar and comforting.

Stanley caught the eye of the waitress, and ordered coffee for us both. I knew he wouldn't let me pay.

"Have you been to the house yet?" he enquired.

"I did call around, but there was no reply."

"It isn't you, Lucy. James practically threw me out, and threatened to go back to his own house, if we didn't give him some space. I promised Elizabeth I wouldn't leave him, until she returned. I don't feel happy that I had to break my word on that, particularly as I'm as terrified as she is." His hand shook, as he raised his cup of coffee. "Are you going to try again?"

"Yes, I was hoping to. Is that okay?"

"It's very much appreciated, dear. Don't be too upset, if he won't talk to you. In all probability, he won't, but if there's any chance that you could get through to him...Well, you know what I mean."

"Yes - yes, I know," I said. "Sarah told me I should leave well alone."

"Eliza would probably agree with your sister, but we must each form our own judgements, as to what to do for the best. How *is* Sarah? She stopped coming to church."

"She's doing much better lately. She went through a bad patch, but I'm sure you must know something of that. Stanley, about the accident - how did it happen? Was Richard Bryant the other driver?" Even as I asked the last question, I knew Stanley wouldn't comment specifically about Richard Bryant, and whether he'd been involved, even if he knew.

"The other vehicle - a Ford Escort - came around the corner at probably ninety miles an hour, according to witnesses. This is strictly off the record, at present - but apparently, the driver was heavily intoxicated, and heading the wrong way down a one-way street. He was also underage, as were his two passengers. All three are in critical conditions, I believe."

"Where did it happen?"

"Tyler Street. I'm not sure whether I ought to be divulging this, but they'd been to the doctors'. That's why James left work early - so that he could accompany Erica." Stanley's shaking voice and haunted expression were almost too much for me.

"Erica was sick?"

"No - no, not at all. It was actually wonderful news. They'd been trying for a second child, and it hadn't been happening. The doctor had just confirmed that Erica was pregnant. James lost his wife and both of their children, in that accident. If you've ever wondered whether there are moments, however brief, when a vicar questions his own faith - I can assure you that such moments exist. I couldn't be more thankful that my son survived, Lucy, but I had to listen to him say that he didn't share my feelings - that he should have been the one to die."

"But it wasn't his fault, was it? That other car..."

"No, it wasn't his fault, but that isn't how James sees it. He's particularly occupied by the fact that Erica wanted Primrose to stay with Elizabeth. He insisted they attend the appointment together, as a family." He glanced at his watch. "I shall have to leave you, Lucy. It's ironic, but I have a wedding, this afternoon. Highly unusual, as well as ironic, with this being a Monday. I'm only grateful that it isn't a funeral. I really don't think I could have dealt with that."

"You're still working, then?"

"Yes. I couldn't be of use to James at home. Reverend Cook had been prepared to step in and help, but it seemed more appropriate for me to work. I'm neither brave nor heartless. I carry on because, to be honest, I don't know what else to do, and I do have duties."

"I understand. I'll finish my coffee, and then I'll be off myself."

"You'll try the house again?"

"Yes, of course I will. Thank you for the coffee."

"You're very welcome, dear. Thank you for your company. Give my love to your family, particularly Sarah. Tell her she's always welcome at church."

He was definitely *not* heartless. But I couldn't agree with Stanley McIntyre, that he wasn't brave.

My vision was blurring, in that familiar way, but I wouldn't let myself cry - at least, not yet. I had to keep it together, if I was hoping to be of any help at all to James.

***

It was Rachel who opened the front door, in the end. Always on the pale side, she appeared more so than ever. "Hi, Lucy. I was hoping you might come. I don't know if James will see you, but I'll do my best. Come in anyway, and I'll make you a cup of tea."

"How about your mum?"

"She's taken my sister to our aunt's, for a couple of hours. Tina's really upset. James can't deal with her, crying all the time, and she can't handle the way he's reacting, either. Mum won't object to you visiting, under the circumstances - and, if she does, she'll have me to answer to, because I want you here. You're the one person James might actually talk to."

She led me into the familiar kitchen, the decor pastel blue and turquoise, as it had always been.

Rachel wore her navy and grey Lewis Palmer's uniform, suggesting that she *had* been into school. Either that, or she wanted her parents to believe she had. Anyway, I wouldn't be the one to ask whether or not she planned to attend the afternoon session.

"Do you take sugar?" she asked, whilst filling the kettle. "I should remember, I suppose."

"No, thank you - and you couldn't know, because I actually *did* take sugar. I gave it up a couple of months ago."

But, judging by her vacant expression, she wasn't registering a word I said. I watched as she added three heaped spoonfuls of sugar - into a mug of coffee, as opposed to the tea she'd offered. Organised, competent Rachel McIntyre - as pedantic as her mother. She resembled a malfunctioning robot now, as she stirred the sugary concoction.

Her hand shook, as she handed me the large, turquoise mug. Rachel sat down opposite me, at the kitchen table. She started to cry, and I instinctively went to her, and hugged her, as if she were my own sister.

Well, she almost could have been. Sister-in-law, at any rate.

I felt sick at myself. But, for so long, I'd trained myself to think along those lines. It had become automatic.

I stroked Rachel's thick, brown hair. Let her cry, until the sobs finally subsided.

"Thanks, Lucy," she said. "I'll go and see if James..."

But James was there already, wearing the ancient grey-blue dressing gown, that he must have owned since he was about fifteen. I'd never seen him wearing it before - only ever seen it hanging on that rusty copper hook, on his bedroom door. His vacant expression brought back memories of Matt, right after Bonnie's accident.

"I'm so sorry, James," I said, breaking that agonising initial silence.

"You and everyone else - especially me. Won't bring my family back though, will it?"

"No - no, it won't, but if there's anything I can do - apart from saying all the wrong things, because that's all I'm doing here, isn't it?" I turned to James's sister. "Thank you for the coffee, Rachel. I should probably go."

"Please don't," said Rachel, fresh tears streaming. "Tell her to stay, James."

"It's up to Lucy whether she stays or not."

"Do you want me to?"

"Of course I do. Luce, you're not saying the wrong things, okay? There aren't any right ones. There *is* something you can do for me. Wait here with Rachel, and I'll get dressed. Mum and Dad said not to, but I don't care. I want to go back to the house. Come with me - please? I can't face being there on my own."

I glanced at Rachel, who nodded. Then, I turned back to James. "Of course I'll come, if that's what you want."

***

Given that James and Erica had lived around the corner from his family home - and I mean, literally - there was scarcely time to register what I'd agreed to, before James was turning the key. I followed him inside.

I'd been twice to the house, when Tara had lived there. The beige hall carpet hadn't changed, although it had acquired a couple of stains, bearing testimony to this as a family home.

According to Sarah, Erica's death had hit our cousin hard. I'd intended to call, and speak to Charlotte, if not Tara herself. Other than our brief exchange, regarding today's cancelled trip, we'd not been in touch. I would rectify that, as soon as possible. But James had to be my priority, for the time being.

He was already in the lounge, and I caught him up. All was pink and peach, and floral designs - much more Erica than James, and definitely more pink than Tara had ever tolerated.

"I told Mum not to touch anything, but she's tidied up. Primmy left her dolls all over the living room floor, and there wasn't time to do anything about it. I *told* her, the stupid woman. I said to leave it."

James opened a cupboard door, and slammed it shut. And another. And a drawer.

"James, calm down," I pleaded. "I'm sure your mum was only trying to help."

"She should have respected my wishes." James was paler even than Rachel. "I can't find Prim's dolls, or the Lego. She's thrown them out, Luce. I know her - interfering and justifying her own actions, with pathetic 'for the best' excuses. My mum has basically thrown my daughter in the bin."

"You're not thinking straight. If they were Primrose's toys, they're probably in her bedroom, if that's where they were normally kept. Your mum was trying to help, by tidying up. There's no way she would have chucked them out."

James had one foot on the stairs, but stopped. Sat down, on the second lowest stair, and broke down.

I sat next to him, and put my arm around him.

***

"Have you eaten anything?"

It was half past four, and I was still with James. He'd slammed the door in his mum's face, and was insisting we ignore the phone.

"Mum made dinner last night, and tried to shove a bowl of Cornflakes at me this morning. The thought of eating makes me feel sick."

"I had a look, when I made coffee, and you haven't got much in."

"There isn't much here, because Erica and I were supposed to be picking up some shopping, on the way back." His voice cracked again. "I'm sorry."

"Don't be. You're going to feel like this, and it gets better, and honestly, also never does."

"I don't know how Matt got through. I guess maybe because he still had Clare and the twins."

"His relationship with Clare ended the moment Bonnie died. As for the twins - well, they witnessed everything, and they're both traumatised. Those girls *are* the reason he carried on - and Matt would tell you that himself - but losing Bonnie destroyed that family."

"At least he had something to live for - that's all I'm saying. What have I got? A well-paid job I probably can't even handle any more. A family home, but no family. I think we've got some baked beans, but not much else."

"Baked beans on toast, hold the bread?"

"Well, there *is* the corner shop, if you like overpriced, stale, white loaves."

"Better than nothing, I guess. Come with me, okay?"

"You think I'm going to do something stupid?" This, with a sardonic edge that chilled me. So unlike the James I'd known since childhood.

"Of course not, but I'd feel better if you came with me."

"Just in case I *do*."

"James, please."

"It's okay, and yes, I'll come. It makes no odds. I had enough with my parents and sisters before, that's all. It's not like I haven't had those thoughts - the *throw myself under a bus* variety. It would be logical, in many respects."

"Please don't talk like that."

"It's only the truth."

"So, then - how can you say we're all wrong, not to leave you to it?"

"If someone's going to kill themselves, Lucy - they will, okay?" Words spoken in a tone that was beyond weary - almost bored. "They'll get the chance, sooner or later. I'm not going to, but I won't say I don't feel like it, when the idea that I could, at any moment, is all that's getting me through."

***

"James, you've got to answer that, or at least let me. You owe it to your parents and sisters, to let them know you're okay." The incessant ringing of the wall-mounted phone was becoming unbearable.

"'Okay'? How the hell am I supposed to be 'okay', after what's happened?"

I reached and grabbed the receiver, regardless.

"Lucy, it's Sarah. Mum was worried, but I told her you'd be here."

"Fine - so now you know, and you can tell Mum I'm okay. If you want to make yourself useful, you could give Elizabeth and Stanley a ring - tell them James is okay, but he needs some space."

"You shouldn't be there, Lucy," she said. "It's wrong."

"It's none of your business. James needs me, and I'm here for him. That's all there is to it."

"When will you be back?"

"I don't know. As I said, James needs me. I'll stay as long as it takes."

"Kev called earlier. What am I supposed to tell him? I got the impression he'd guessed. He knew about the accident."

"Sarah, I can't deal with this. Tell Kev what you like, but if he comes around here, making trouble, I'll call the police. James doesn't need it right now, and neither do I. If that's everything, we'll leave it there, okay? Tell Mum I'm fine, and I'll be home when I'm home."

***

I glanced at my watch, at the point when I could barely keep my eyes open. 3am. Holy shit.

James noticed the gesture. "You need to go, don't you?"

I considered for a moment. "I *do* have work tomorrow - or, more accurately, today. I won't leave you, if you need me - but won't you consider going back to your mum and dad's?"

"Not at this hour. I'll go and see them all later, but I want to stay in this house. I don't live with my parents and kid sisters any more, and it doesn't help me, being there. They keep trying to help, and they can't." He looked at me, at that moment, with an intensity that terrified me, and said: "Stay, Lucy. Stay here tonight."

In reality, of course, I'd stayed for half of it already. That had happened, but without planning. But to officially be "staying the night"?

"Of course I'll stay. But we're both going to have to get some sleep. I'm happy with the sofa."

"I haven't slept since the accident, even though I spent practically my entire time in bed, at Mum and Dad's. You can have our bed." 'Our bed'. His and Erica's.

"No, James - that's not right. You need to at least rest, even if you can't sleep. You have the bed. A few hours on the sofa won't do me any harm."

But James grabbed my arm. "I'll sleep in the bed, but I want you with me. I can't be on my own. Please, Lucy - I'm begging you."

"You're not making sense. You don't know what you're saying."

"I can't be on my own," he repeated.

"You can't be saying you want us to sleep together?"

"Yes, that's exactly what I'm saying." There was a determination in his voice that shook me to my core.

I went along with it. I'll never know why, but I did. I assumed, initially, that James wanted us to lie together. When he wanted to hold on to me, somehow that felt natural - in the weird, surreal atmosphere, and the extreme circumstances.

I was in my T-shirt and knickers. Until James started to peel off my clothes, and I let him. We were kissing, and I felt hot and moist for the first guy I'd ever loved.

I pulled away, and sat up in bed. "We can't do this. I need to go home."

"No, you don't. Life can be over in a moment, Lucy. We both know that. You're the one person I can be with now. I want to hold on to you - know that you're still alive."

But somehow, the holding on, the kissing and cuddling, was never going to suffice. It could only end in the inevitable.

James and I hadn't actually had sex, when we were going out together. There had been a couple of fumbling attempts: venue, *The Field*. But we had been kids, and not ready, and James had been raised to be a good boy, and had a head stuffed full of religion. And I'd had my own issues.

So, we made love for the first - to each other - time: frantic, passionate moves, and I don't think either of us was entirely present, or had a clue what we were doing, or why.

And the ending, when it came, was abrupt, and left me broken.

James had popped to the loo. Except that he hadn't returned. I waited, and nearly dozed off at one point, and finally, sat up abruptly. He still wasn't back, and I was scared. I put my T-shirt and knickers back on, and started searching.

Found him eventually, in Primmy's bedroom. Sitting on the floor, next to her bed. He clutched a little pink teddy. Hadn't even seemed to register my being in the room.

"James," I said, "are you okay?"

He looked at me, but didn't reply.

"Come back to bed. Please?"

He stood suddenly, and flung the cuddly toy across the room.

James looked me directly in the eye, and said, in a flat, mechanical tone: "You must be glad my wife and kids are dead. You wanted them out of the way, and you got your wish, Lucy."

I felt sick inside. "How can you say something so awful? I've been trying to help. You insisted I stay."

"You didn't take much convincing."

I started to cry. "If I was wrong, I'm sorry. I care about you, and no, of course I'm not 'glad' about Erica and Primrose and the baby. How can you think that of me? All I wanted was to be here for you."

"Get dressed, and get out. I never want to see you again. You're a slag."

I'd never heard James use a term like "slag" before. He had to be going out of his mind.

I'd give his parents a call later - ask them to keep an eye on him. But, as for helping him myself, I was done. I couldn't take any more, and I wasn't prepared to.

So, Sarah had been right, after all. I shouldn't have got involved.

Yeah, well - I'd learnt my lesson now. I was through with James - and with Kev Tanner, and blokes in general, for that matter. I wouldn't let any of them hurt and humiliate me again.

Chapter Forty-Eight

A full year since Erica and Primrose had died, and James and I had barely spoken. I didn't know how he'd survived, except that he apparently had. Charlotte reckoned he'd become a workaholic - like Matt, only ten times worse.

There hadn't been any reason for our respective families to interact much at all. Well, apart from polite day to day interactions between Matt and Deborah, and James's family, on account of their being neighbours. Gemma and Toby lived with my brother and Deb, although invariably, one or both of them would stay with Deborah's parents, whenever the twins were there.

I'd gone to Matt and Deb's, straight from work, hoping for a comparatively quiet night. Even though she seldom looked after Jade and Jess any more, Mum was continually babysitting for either her cousin, Vivian, who had three sons under the age of five, or her friend, Freda, who'd had a surprise baby girl, at forty-nine. As for quiet: Some chance, given that Clare had come over. And she and my brother were definitely on form.

"I could hear you both shouting two streets away," I told them. "What have they done this time?"

I had heard the twins' names, but even if I hadn't, would have guessed the row was about them. When *wasn't* it?

"Graffiti," replied Matthew.

"Again? Not more bus shelters? Smashed glass into the bargain?"

"No bus shelters. A church this time."

"Your ex-boyfriend's dad's church, to be exact," added Clare, relishing the look of horror on my face.

I thought about the Methodist church, where Stanley McIntyre worked. Remembered Stanley's kindness on our last meeting, at that cafe. But then, James's dad had always been lovely.

"It was mostly about Tina," said Matthew, "and her friend, Julie."

"There was something about Gemma, too," said Clare, apparently not sufficiently upset by the incident, in and of itself, to prevent her from taking the opportunity to wind me up.

"Same grudges. Jade really doesn't let things go, does she? Where *is* Gemma, anyway? And Deb, and Toby?"

"Gem's at Lila's. They've got ballet tonight, and Gemma's spending the night at Lila's. Toby's out with his mate, Oliver. Deborah's at her mum and dad's."

Clare's look was priceless: one of feigned boredom. Jealous, of course. It was okay for her to screw Steven Parker for years, and go off with Malcolm Astley, but Matt finding someone else had thrown her. Yeah, well - what did she expect?

"Miss Harding wants us to go in and see her tomorrow afternoon, at half-three," said Matt. "What world does the woman live in? Teachers might finish work mid-afternoon. Some of us have real jobs."

"Yeah, and work is so much more important than what's going on with your own daughters."

"Don't make me laugh. *Our* daughters, remember? And the reason you apparently can't go down the school is also work, so you're not in a position to judge."

"Short-term temping is different. I can hardly ask for time off, when I'm only working there for a fortnight in total."

"If you're only there for a fortnight, it doesn't make much odds, does it?"

"Of course it does. The agency aren't going to find me work in the future, if I let them down. Then again, I'll have to take the chance, because you obviously don't want the inconvenience."

"Be reasonable. Your boss could find someone else to do the filing. I've got a busy department to manage."

"You bother more about Deborah Tanner's kids than you do about ours. That spoilt brat Gemma, who thinks she's going to become a ballerina. Just imagine, her old man, showing up for her *Swan Lake* debut, smashed out of his skull." She turned to me. "Oh, sorry, Luce - how insensitive of me."

"Are you finished, Clare?" demanded Matt. "It's obvious where Jade gets her venom from!"

"Yeah, and she gets the violent tendencies from your side!"

I stood. "Right, that's enough. I'm off home. Mum couldn't fill that house with enough screaming kids to compete with you two. If either of you had shut up for long enough to let me get a word in, I'd have told you this before: I've got the day off work already, and I don't mind going up the school about my nieces. I'll give you a call later, Matt. If it helps, I'll do it, okay?"

Chapter Forty-Nine

"Miss Harding? I understand you wanted to talk about Jade and Jessica Ryman."

"Yes, that's right. You must be Mrs. Ryman." Miss Harding was a thin woman, aged about forty-five, with fine, grey hair, and silver-rimmed spectacles.

I felt momentarily confused. Why did she think I was my mum?

Then, the penny dropped. "The twins' mother is Clare Smith," I explained.

She'd addressed the letter to Miss Smith, hadn't she? I wondered whether the teacher had made a genuine mistake, in that respect, or whether, in reality, it was simply her way of pushing the point.

But, either way, I wasn't Clare, and we had to get that detail out of the way. "I'm Lucy Ryman, Jade and Jessica's aunt," I told her. "My brother, Matthew, is the girls' dad."

This was the same primary school we'd all attended - my siblings and myself. The place hadn't changed much, but everything seemed smaller somehow, and almost disappointingly unimpressive.

"Oh, I see," said Miss Harding, adjusting her glasses. "I would ideally prefer to speak to either Miss Smith or Mr. Ryman. We wouldn't generally discuss issues, concerning pupils at this school, with anyone other than a parent or guardian."

"I appreciate that, but you didn't give much notice, and my brother and Clare both had work commitments. You did seem to think that the matter was urgent. Will you talk to me or not?"

"It *is* urgent." She rustled a pile of papers on what had once been Mr. Patterson's desk - random, and currently irrelevant, fact. "I would still prefer to see one or both parents. This is most irregular. However, given the circumstances, I think the priority is to speak to someone."

And I would do? "Thank you, Miss Harding. So, what's the problem?" Although I had a feeling that it would be more a case of short and long lists.

More adjustment of glasses. "We should probably start with Jessica."

"Okay." I knew why, of course. Jade's problems had the more serious implications. To a significant extent, they were also the source of Jessica's.

"Of course, the death of the twins' elder sister must have been devastating. I taught Bonita for a year. Such a sweet child, and very intelligent. Her loss must have been a tremendous shock to your whole family. I *am* sorry." I detected a slight crack in the teacher's, previously steady, voice - and the change of subject and mood threw me somewhat.

"Thank you - and yes, it was. Jade and Jessica were there, you know? They witnessed Bonnie's accident."

"Yes, I'm aware of that. Miss Ryman, Jessica is increasingly withdrawn. She always *has* been prone to daydreaming, but it has reached the stage where I'm becoming concerned, and other members of the teaching staff have noticed. The one person who seems able to reach, and communicate with, her is, unfortunately, Jade. Hardly surprising, given that they're identical twins. However, Jade's influence upon Jessica is not a positive one. Rebecca Fisher and Carys Ilsley have been encouraged to be more selective about the company they keep, and this has benefited them, but also increased the pressure upon Jessica. I'm going to recommend that she is assessed by an Educational Psychologist."

"Jessica? I do see your point in general, but surely, if anything, it should be Jade, going to see a psychologist?"

"Yes, I was coming to that. Jade is going to be referred, as well - probably, in fact, to a psychiatrist."

"A psychiatrist? That's more serious than a psychologist, right?"

"It's different. At this stage, it's more important that you, and the girls' parents, are fully aware of what's going on with Jade. This has gone far beyond fighting, and general bad behaviour. We're talking about bullying, of a severe, and highly targeted, nature."

Miss Harding unlocked her desk drawer, and pulled out a bulging paper folder. Large, decisive letters, in black marker pen: *Jade Ryman.* She extracted a single piece of paper from Jade's file. Lined paper, evidently torn from one of Jade's exercise books. Or maybe Jessica's, judging by the crooked red margin. Jade could draw her margins much better than that - to the point where I couldn't tell the difference between her margins, and printed ones. Holy shit, my mind was full of lined paper and hand-drawn margins. I focused upon what Jade had written, in large, bold handwriting: *Jade Helena Ryman's Official Hit List.* And in smaller letters, like a subheading: *Revenge Attacks Executed by Jade Helena Ryman and Assistant/Slave Jessica Clare Ryman.*

There were twenty-seven names on the numbered list. Right at the top, predictably, was the name Julie Rollins. Two: Doreen Rollins. Julie's *mum?* So the list wasn't entirely restricted to children, although the majority of these were kids from this school, and I recognised several as names of kids in Jade and Jessica's class. Tina McIntyre was at Number Three. Gemma Tanner: Six. Toby Tanner: Nine. What the hell was Toby supposed to have done?

"The tally charts next to each name are of particular concern," observed Miss Harding.

I noticed that there were, indeed, marks beside many of the names, and some actually had multiple five bar gates. I began to take the teacher's meaning. The names weren't being crossed or ticked off, to indicate a "revenge" carried out. Jade was inflicting multiple punishments on many of her chosen victims.

"These 'revenges' - how serious are they?" I wasn't sure I wanted to know, but the question couldn't be avoided.

"Physical violence is certainly one type. Stealing, and often planting stolen items, to give the appearance of some particular person being responsible. Personal belongings have been hidden, thrown from windows or into toilet pans, smashed, graffitied upon, and even set fire to."

The last one particularly chilled me. I had distant memories of Jade setting fire to Bonita and Jessica's toys, and of the panic, and extreme distress, the incident had caused.

"How about Doreen Rollins? You do realise that's Julie's *mother*? She must be at least thirty. How has Jade achieved fifteen 'revenges' on her?" I pointed to the name on my niece's list, with three five bar gates next to it. "She can't have been throwing Doreen's textbooks or pencil case out of a classroom window."

"No, indeed," said Miss Harding. "Mrs. Rollins came in to see me, a couple of weeks ago. It's not overstating the case to say that she's on the verge of a nervous breakdown."

"You're telling me that's because of Jade?"

"Not entirely, no. But Jade harassment, often assisted by her sister, is a significant factor: probably the most significant. Hoax telephone calls. Threatening letters. Unpleasant 'offerings' through the letterbox. Ringing the doorbell and running away. It's been relentless."

To be fair, we'd all done that last one, hadn't we? Maybe not Miss Harding here, but certainly, Charlotte, James, and I had. Maybe the occasional hoax call as well, although I wasn't sure precisely what that would entail, with Jade involved. Jade and Jessica, because Jess *was* part of this, and couldn't be considered blameless. "Threatening letters" and "unpleasant offerings" - that sounded serious.

"You probably noticed that Jade's file contains much more than this one piece of paper. However, I don't feel justified in...The fact is that I discovered some extremely disturbing images in Jade's drawer.

The papers were wedged in so tightly that I'm surprised she managed to find room for her exercise books."

"You don't want to share them with me, because I'm not a parent or guardian." It was a statement, not a question. "How 'disturbing' are we talking?"

"In my twenty years of teaching...They're *disturbing*. Horrific."

Miss Harding proceeded to mention her suspicions about the deaths of various school hamsters and gerbils. That was when I realised I was out of my depth. I was that close to breaking down in tears, right there in that classroom - as a twenty-three-year-old woman, and not one of Miss Harding's naughty kids.

There were reasons why Jessica had never got a second pet rabbit. Why Matt and Clare had seriously considered, but decided against, acquiring a budgie or canary. Suspicions - only suspicions. In the same way as Miss Harding couldn't know for sure.

I would tell both Matt and Clare what I thought, in no uncertain terms. If they could have quit point scoring over whose job mattered most, and which of them could more easily justify being absent from work - well, maybe then, both of them would be here, taking responsibility.

"You were right, Miss Harding," I admitted. "I was wrong to come here. This is something my brother and Miss Smith should be talking to you about."

"Yes, it is." Her tone was as firm as ever, and yet, kinder. Further adjustment of glasses. "Could you perhaps have a word, to that effect?"

"Yes, naturally. I'll pass on what you've told me, and both my brother and Miss Smith *will* arrange to come in."

Chapter Fifty

"So Clare's moved to Durham, with the twins? On a permanent basis?" said Phil, his arm around my younger sister.

It was Friday night, and Phil, Sarah, Danny, and I were in an, unusually quiet, Red Lion.

"Indefinite, think that was the term - but yes, pretty much," I confirmed.

Phil frowned. "Is Matt okay with that?"

"Not really, but he wasn't given a great deal of choice."

"I heard that Steven Parker was hanging around again," said Danny.

He didn't *say*, right? I shot my brother a look. "When *hasn't* he been?"

"I'd like to punch his lights out, to be honest." Danny's expression added weight to the words.

"How would *that* help?" I said. "Anyway, Clare's a consenting adult. Takes two, and all that. Besides, it's Malcolm's problem now, if she ends up treating him like shit. What did he expect?"

"I just feel for Matt," said Sarah. "He must be heartbroken. Is he coming tonight - and Deborah?

"Hopefully. They both said they were." I glanced at my watch. "It's nearly eight. They should be here any minute now."

***

As it happened, it was a further half hour, before Matt and Deborah actually arrived.

"Sorry we took so long," said Deborah.

"My fault, I'm afraid," added Matt. "I took Deborah out for lunch, and a quick drink afterwards. Except that the 'quick drink' didn't end up being as 'quick' as originally intended."

"I'm impressed, Deborah," said Danny. "You actually persuaded Matt to take half a day off work?"

"The entire day." Deb's grey eyes sparkled, as she placed a hand on Matt's shoulder. "He's not nearly as bad as you all make out, you know. You should have seen the tantrum Gem threw this morning, when I said her and Toby had to go to my mum and dad's tonight. You'd think she didn't love it there, and spend half her time moaning that she couldn't go back and live with her grandparents and Aunt Vanessa."

Deb didn't miss the look on my face, when she said that. I understood too well about her daughter's tantrums. She gave me a slight smile.

"Anyway," continued Deborah, "Matt was wonderful with her. He's ten times more patient with that girl than I've ever been."

Matt shrugged. "Yeah, well - I'm used to Jade. Believe me, Gemma's no trouble, by comparison. I'll get the next round."

It was after my brother had got the drinks in that my mum arrived. My mum, who hardly ever went near a pub. And who declined offers from both of her sons to buy her a drink.

"I haven't come in for a drink. Deborah, I've been speaking to your mum."

Deborah became instantly pale. "What's wrong? Is she okay? It's not Nan, is it? Has she-?"

"No, they're both fine, love. It's Gemma."

"Gemma?" There was an expression of pure horror on Deb's face, as she spoke her daughter's name. "What's happened, Helen?"

"She's disappeared. It looks as if Kev has taken her."

I believed, for an instant, that I was going to pass out, there and then. The spots danced in front of my eyes for a few seconds, but the sensation passed, and the world came into focus again.

"And where's Toby?" demanded Deborah, her voice almost a scream.

"Toby's fine. He's with your parents and sister. Your mum picked him up from school, as normal."

"Gemma had a dance class after school," said Deborah, slotting the pieces into place. "Kev knew that, and showed up to collect her. My mum sometimes gets there a few minutes late, to pick Gem up from after-school activities. She knows to wait, though. Lila always stays with her. Mum generally gives her a lift, too."

"Lila walked home by herself, apparently. It's not exactly that far, so she didn't mind. She was the one who told us about Kev taking Gemma. She didn't think it seemed strange. He didn't force or coerce her, and he *is* her dad."

"What are you saying, that it's okay for him to take her?"

"Calm down, Deborah. I'm not saying that at all. I'm only saying that's why Lila didn't suspect."

Deborah broke down, and Matt took her into his arms.

"Have you called the police, Mum?" asked Danny.

"Rita did that, yes. I'm sure they'll catch up with him soon."

"He might not be in his right mind, though," I pointed out, which clearly wasn't what Deborah wanted to hear, because her sobs intensified.

"Lucy, how's that helpful?" said Sarah. "My guess is, he'll bring Gemma back, of his own accord. But, in any case, the police are bound to find them soon."

"I agree with you," I told my sister. "But, when that neat little resolution occurs, and Gemma's back home, what happens to Kev? He so obviously needs more support and, if you must know, I blame myself, for not being there for him, okay? I'm leaving, before I say anything else that might not be 'helpful' enough for you."

Chapter Fifty-One

Matthew and Deborah, Danny, and myself, sat there, in the living room at Deborah's mum and dad's, where she had been living with the two kids, since walking out on Kev. It was Saturday night, by this point.

Rita Ware, Deborah's mother, a very thin woman, of roughly fifty-five, with shoulder-length, white-blonde hair, was in the process of making tea and coffee for us all.

Vanessa, Deborah's younger sister, talked to us a little, whilst at the same time, trying to calm Toby down. He'd been told to go to bed so many times now, but it clearly wasn't happening. He was too distressed about his sister going missing, poor kid.

Deborah was up again, and pacing, like a caged animal. "What's taking the police so long? He could have taken her anywhere by now."

"I know it's not easy," I said, "but at least we know she's with her dad. Whatever we might think about Kev, he adores Gemma. He would never do anything to harm her."

"He's flipped, Lucy. None of us know what he's capable of."

I felt slightly sick. He'd begged me to get back with him. And I'd turned him down. Now, this had happened. It was hard not to see the connection, but Kev wasn't my responsibility, and neither were his actions or choices.

"Lucy's right," said Matt. "Even Kev wouldn't harm his own kid. She'll be fine."

"That's all very well for you to say. It's not your daughter who's missing. You have no bloody idea how I'm feeling, any of you."

Matt's expression hardened. "My eldest daughter is dead. The twins are hundreds of miles away, and I don't know when I'll see them again. At the end of the day, Gemma's going to be okay. I've lost everything, so don't tell me I have 'no bloody idea', as if you do."

Danny, who was sitting next to Matt on the sofa, placed a hand on our brother's shoulder. "Take it easy, bruv. We're all feeling the strain here, but arguing amongst ourselves won't solve anything."

"You're right that we're not solving anything, Danny. That's why I'm going to look for her myself," announced Deborah, already heading for the door.

"Deborah, listen - I'm sorry I lost it, but I can't let you-"

"You can't stop me, Matt."

"I know, but if you'll let me finish - I can't let you go on your own, okay? I'm coming with you."

"I'll come, too," said Danny. "You'll need someone to drive. Neither of you are thinking straight."

"Fine," said Deborah. "I'm not waiting around any longer, though. We're leaving right away."

Deborah's mum, who had just brought the hot drinks through on a tray, looked confused: "Where are you all-?"

"Lucy will explain, Mum," said Deborah. "Just listen out for the phone, okay?"

***

It would be two full hours, before Deborah returned with my brothers, dejected and exhausted.

Approximately two minutes after Mum had hung up, having spoken to the police. They'd caught up with Kev and his daughter, in Brixham, Devon. They'd been staying with his cousin, Stuart Jordan, Mark's younger brother.

Chapter Fifty-Two

The following evening, we were in the Red Lion, celebrating Gemma's safe return: Matt and Deborah, Danny and Hannah, and myself. Sarah and Phil were due to arrive, any minute.

"I still don't know if I was right to leave her," said Deborah. "She hasn't been herself since she came back, and she still insists she wasn't kidnapped. She's saying she wants to live with her dad."

"Kev Tanner shouldn't be allowed within a ten mile radius of either of those kids," said Matt. "I still can't believe you told the police to let him go."

"We've been through this already, Matt. I know you don't like him, and to say I'm angry about what he did is an understatement, but Kev *is* still my children's dad."

"And you believe he isn't going to snatch Gemma again? Yet, you're not happy leaving her."

"I don't think he's got any intention of taking her again, and I hardly think your mum would give him the chance. The only reason I didn't want to leave her was because of how she's been."

"Well, we're all happy you did come," said Danny, "and I do want to know what you guys were on about earlier. You said you had some good news. Not that getting Gem back isn't cause enough to celebrate, but there *is* more, isn't there?"

Matt and Deborah exchanged glances, and I realised then what it was. I caught Hannah's eye, and she was thinking the same.

"We were going to wait until Sarah and Phil arrived," said Matt, "but maybe it's just as well to tell you guys now. I wouldn't want to steal their thunder." His eyes sought approval from Deborah, who smiled and nodded. "I proposed last night, and Deborah said, 'Yes.' Looks like I've finally found a woman crazy enough to marry me."

"Congratulations, bruv," said Danny.

"Welcome to the family, Deborah," added Hannah.

The steady flow of hugs and congratulations, from all of us, lasted for several minutes.

"By the way, Matt - what did you mean about 'stealing their thunder'?" I asked. "Were you hinting that Sarah and Phil might have an announcement of their own?"

"You can ask them yourself," said Deborah.

"Ask us what?" said Sarah, pulling up a chair, the diamond ring on her left hand unmissable.

My little sister. She looked radiant. And I only had to look at Phil to see how much he thought of his fiancee.

She moved her chair closer to mine. "Lucy, are you okay? You're not crying, are you?" She looked scared.

I hugged her, feeling that I'd never loved Sarah more, or felt more proud of her, than I did in that moment. "I'm crying because I love you, you idiot - not because I'm upset that you're marrying my ex, okay? Anyway, someone has to take care of my rejects for me, right?"

She shoved me, playfully. "You just have no taste, Lucy Ryman."

I played along for about ten minutes longer, but I wasn't there, not really. It became increasingly difficult to conceal my agitation, but everyone else was too busy celebrating to notice. That actually suited me. If I could simply have become invisible and faded away, I would have. Trouble was, it wasn't about not being there, at the Lion. It was more about where I should have been instead.

I finally cracked. Made my excuses, and practically ran out of there, without looking back. I could explain later. I'd acted weird so many times, in my twenty-three years. Once more couldn't make much odds.

I tried to pretend I hadn't heard Deborah, calling my name. But it was no use. Of course, she was the one person who *had* noticed how I'd been, and she knew why.

I slowed down, letting her catch up with me. Continued walking, but at a steadier pace. "Look, Deb - I'm sorry to leave early.

You know I'm thrilled for you and Matt, don't you? And for Sarah and Phil. My heart isn't in it, that's all, and I don't want to bring the mood down."

Deborah touched my arm. "It's okay. I sensed you withdrawing, and I know you're worried about Kev. Is that where you're going?"

"I was going to try phoning first. Hopefully, at least one of the phone boxes by the shops hasn't been vandalised."

"Surely it would be easier to pop home, and give him a call from there?"

"You *are* joking? With Mum listening in? Plus, the risk of one of the kids overhearing. I'll try the phone boxes first. If I do get through, and he needs me, I can catch a bus into town. I know how much stress Kev caused you, with what he did, but I can't just leave him to rot."

"It's okay," she said. "I agree with you. I've been scared too, but I didn't feel able to deal with him. So, honestly - I'm grateful. Have you got enough change for the phone?"

"Yes, I checked already. Thank you, Deb."

She smiled, faintly. "I'd better get back. I told Matt I was popping to the loo. Good luck, okay?"

***

My hand shook, as I stood inside that phone box, and grabbed the receiver. Shoved in my 10p and waited.

It rang for an extended period. Then, finally, Kev answered. I wasn't sure whether the line was okay. It sounded as if I were ringing Australia.

"Kev, are you okay?"

He didn't reply.

Panic closed in. *Breathe, Lucy.* "You still there?"

"Yeah. I miss you, Luce."

"You haven't-?"

"No, but I came close. You don't know *how* close. I don't know how to do this on my own."

"I'm coming over. Have you eaten?" I slammed in another coin, to ensure we didn't get cut off.

"I haven't got any food. How am I supposed to buy food with no money? Deborah was helping. I spent everything I had on the thing with Gem, petrol and feeding her."

"Didn't your cousin have food there? I thought you stayed at his place?"

"Stu's 'place' is a bedsit, like mine, not some five-star hotel. He let us stay overnight, that's all."

"Okay, look - don't worry. I'll pick up a takeaway, and we'll sort it out tomorrow. Deb isn't that angry, not really, and you won't lose her support, or access to Gemma and Toby. She probably won't trust you to have them on your own at first, but she won't stop you from seeing them. Just try to stay calm. I don't know how long I'll have to wait for a bus, but I'm on my way, and you're not alone."

***

"You were literally starving, weren't you?" Spoken after watching Kev devour the last fry.

McDonald's wasn't exactly health food, but it *was* food, and it seemed to have done its job, for now. I'd make sure he got something more nutritious tomorrow.

"I prioritised feeding my daughter. I'm aware I've screwed up being a dad, just like I do everything else, but I'm not going to let Gemma starve, am I?"

I touched his hand. "Why *did* you take her, Kev? And without letting any of us know where you'd gone? We were all worried sick, especially Deborah."

"It seemed to make sense at the time. I'd lost everything, including you. Gem was all I had left. And she told me she's terrified of going into school, knowing that one day, Jade will be waiting again." There wasn't a thing I could say to that, having witnessed my niece's "Hit List". "No kid should have to feel like that, day after day, Luce. I've been there."

"Have you? You were bullied?" I expected to be closed down the next moment, because that was how it always went with Kev and me.

He hesitated. "Yeah, it was relentless," he admitted. "Then, I got beaten all over again, when I got home. Fun, right? I blank it out, most of the time."

"That's why you started taking drugs?"

"I don't like to say that. Life's more complicated than one specific crap thing causing another crap thing."

"I know, and there are always choices. It was a factor, though?"

"I guess so. I basically had severe depression, but no one even noticed. The only way I could get through school was thinking of ways to end it all. Shit, Lucy - I don't *do* this - talking about myself. I don't need sympathy."

"I don't see it as you trying to get attention or sympathy. All I've ever wanted was for you to open up to me."

"I realise that. I'll do my best, okay?"

I nodded. "What happened at school, with the bullying?"

"There was this girl - Octavia, but she mainly went by Ava."

"Beautiful name, either way," I said.

"Yeah, well, she *was* beautiful. I'd had this group of mates since primary school. We got to, like, thirteen, fourteen, and I started to withdraw. They just left me to it - hardly bothered at all, once everyone decided I was 'weird' and 'mental'. Once I had no friends left, this gang started on me."

"And then you met Ava, right?"

"You're good. Well, I knew her already, in a vague way. Her best mate, Susan, thought she was really something, and Ava was always the quiet one, who tagged along. Neither of them were anything to me. Then, one day, I'd had enough. I won't have much left, once I tell you this part."

"It's okay. Take your time."

I gathered together the various boxes and bags we'd eaten from, which I duly deposited in the metal swing bin. Spooned coffee into a couple of mugs, and flicked the switch on the kettle, that I'd filled up earlier. It was hit or miss whether Kev had a kettle in his room, at any point in time, but I was glad he did, currently. I didn't fancy using the communal kitchen - part of why I'd taken the easy option, when it came to food.

I placed two coffees on the precarious, three-legged table, which was the only table in there. I didn't want to wonder what had happened to the writing desk I'd left, or the bookshelves. Gemma had done ballet, tap, and gymnastics for years, and she'd had to store everything at Deb's parents'.

"I couldn't take any more, and they were after me - Oscar and that whole gang. It was morning break, and I remember them chasing me, and I was that close to pissing myself, I dived into the girls' loos in the Science block, and locked myself in. After I'd been, I just sat there, crying. So much for my street cred, right? That psycho drug pusher down the King's Head, who no one messes with."

"You're not a 'psycho drug pusher'. You're not weak, either. So, what happened next?"

"Ava and Sue came in. Sue was giggling. She giggled at everything, silly cow. I froze and tried to stay quiet, but I could hear them discussing whether I'd gone in there. In the end, Ava persuaded her friend to go ahead without her, and once it was just the two of us, she talked to me through the toilet door, until I eventually came out. Pretty weird way to start a relationship, but that's how it was."

"So, how long did you go out together?"

"About three years. The first year or so was amazing. But then, I started hanging around with these mates, and I knew Ava didn't like

them. I don't have to tell *you* how it works. I can't believe she put
up with me for as long as she did. The mates I'm talking about, Luce
- well, a couple of them were in with the Bryants. Once Ava ended
things, I lost it. I couldn't even imagine a future without her."

I didn't want to push for any more details about Kev's ex.
Strange, how I could have become good friends with Deborah, but
somehow, didn't want to hear about Ava. She was Kev's childhood
sweetheart, in the same way James had been mine.

In many respects, I ought to have experienced compassion for
Ava, and her position. She would have felt emotionally blackmailed,
trapped and scared, and yet also, resentful. I could relate to that,
but it didn't matter. Jealousy formed a tight knot in my throat, that
would make me cry, unless the conversation shifted.

"How about your home life?" Too soon, perhaps, and I risked
having the subject closed down forever, if Kev wasn't ready. "You said
you were beaten at home, too. Your dad, or both parents?"

"You've been there too, Lucy. It's why you and Cath had
problems, long before I came along." I met his gaze. Of course, he'd
always known there was something.

"Yeah, but we'll discuss me another time," I said. "Just answer
me."

"My dad, but my mum and sister did nothing about it. Well,
Heather did try, to a point, but she was scared, too. I'm not shutting
you out, babe, but I can't talk any more about it, not right now. I've
had enough. I *do* trust you."

I kissed the top of his head. "I know you do. You look shattered.
I didn't mean to push you. Just keep talking to me, okay? You
shouldn't have to deal with everything on your own."

He hugged me, and then, inevitably, we kissed, and I heard the
alarm bells, except that they were more like sirens.

I pulled away. "Kev, I don't think we should rush things, okay?
I'm here for you, but we're not back together."

"You'll have to translate, because I'm lost here. Are you saying you only came because you felt sorry for me?"

I took a deep breath. "No. And, for the record, I don't 'feel sorry' for you. You're not some innocent victim. You did some appalling stuff, when we were together, and yes, you've been sick, but you made choices. And you've made some better ones lately - not the thing with Gem, but giving up drink and drugs. You're brave and amazing, and I respect you more than I can ever express." Shit, I'd kept my voice steady, but no easy task, right?

"Respect? But you don't love me any more?"

"You have to push that, don't you?"

"Yeah, because it means everything, and because I still love you."

"I'll always be your friend. I haven't got more to offer right now."

"Friend? What, as in - a friend like Charlotte? Or one like McIntyre?"

"Why do you have to bring James into everything?"

"Because you still have feelings for him. You always have."

"The guy has been through hell, Kev. You're not the only one. And, as it happens, me and James aren't even talking. You're jealous for no good reason."

"Well, you sure as hell don't have that problem, anyway - not with Deborah. She's practically your best mate, isn't she?"

"So, now you're having a go because I'm not jealous. You *want* me to be jealous?" I'd been jealous enough of that Octavia/Ava girl, but somehow, Kev hadn't appeared to notice, or care about, that. "Anyway, you know Deborah's in a relationship with my brother."

"Yeah, I know. It's not really about Deborah or James. I just want you to love me, the way I love you."

"You know I love you. You think I'm going through all this because of *not* loving you?"

"Stay the night, Luce."

"I wouldn't leave you. I'll give my mum a ring - let her know I'm okay."

"So, where are you sleeping, the knackered old armchair?"

"It would do me. I'll sleep on the floor, if I have to."

"I'll sleep in the chair," said Kev. "It makes no odds. And I'm sorry. Having you here - it's enough. It's more than I deserve. Friends, yeah?"

And somehow, it hurt even more, because I could tell he wasn't playing games, or trying to manipulate me into sleeping with him - that he'd started out with that intention, but he was exhausted, emotionally and physically. He was planning to sleep in the chair, and didn't want to make me feel guilty about it.

"And the rest," I replied. "You don't have to sleep in the chair."

When Kev kissed me that time, I didn't attempt to pull away.

***

When I woke up, in the early hours, I slipped out of bed, and attempted to dress without disturbing Kev.

He stirred, as I was extracting my knickers from the left leg of my jeans. Having to recycle yesterday's underwear made our last night's passionate lovemaking feel tackier than it deserved to. It had, in truth, been amazing. But how could I not feel cheap, when I had to pick the previous night's clothes off the floor, and acknowledge that I'd lost control, and had no idea what to do next?

"You're going back to your mum's, aren't you?"

"I have to, Kev. I need to change clothes for work, anyway - and I also need some space. You have to get help, apart from me."

He sat up in bed. "It hurts, Lucy. I need to know where I stand."

"I wanted us to be friends. That's what I said."

"Wanted? Past tense? So what do you want now - more than friends, or...?"

I didn't reply. Didn't know the answers myself, let alone how to convey them. I'd finished dressing, and grabbed a brush from my bag. Searched for a compact mirror in there, but given up. We'd definitely had a couple of mirrors in the room, when I'd lived there, but those had disappeared. They weren't exactly worth much. But then, maybe Kev hadn't sold them. Maybe he'd smashed them, in one of his rages. I dragged the brush through my tangled hair, without the luxury of my own reflection. That probably had its advantages, in any case - if I looked as exhausted, and thoroughly stressed out, as I felt.

"Lucy?"

"We're going around in circles. It's destroying us both."

"*You're* going in circles. I know what I want. Just leave, if you're leaving, and don't bother coming back. I'll be okay."

"Promise me you won't go back on drugs or drink. It would break my heart, after everything."

"You're telling me about broken hearts? You smashed mine up, and then smashed up all the broken pieces some more."

"Promise me."

"What good is a junkie's promise, anyway? It's not as if you trust me."

"It took you long enough to trust me."

"Yeah, and it was my mistake that I did, because you stabbed me in the back." But his expression softened, all the same. "Look, Lucy, I won't go back on drugs or booze. Okay?"

"I love you."

"Not enough. Not as much as I love you."

"Really? Love - or need, in a different way? I can't fix everything, any more than Deborah or Gemma can. You can't use people the way you used drugs."

Instantly, his expression became hard and cold, any trace of compassion gone. "And you *can*, I suppose? It's okay for you to use me, or Phil Jackson, or anyone else you feel like. What really happened with McIntyre? Tried to 'console' him, after his wife and kid died, did you? Don't talk to me about using or manipulating anyone, because you're not exactly perfect."

"Did I ever claim to be 'perfect'? And keep your opinions to yourself about me and James. You don't know anything about it. I can't do any more for you, Kev. You need professional help."

I left, without slamming any doors in the process.

Chapter Fifty-Three

The New Year's party, to celebrate not only a fresh year, but a new decade, was held at Matt and Deborah's. Almost everybody I could possibly think of appeared to be there, and by nine-thirty, nearly everyone present was drunk. Including both of James McIntyre's parents. Admittedly, Elizabeth was barely tipsy, but even *that* was so out of character, that Charlotte and I couldn't stop laughing.

"I think James is around somewhere," said Charlotte. "I saw him earlier, talking to Matt and Danny, and a couple of others."

"Sarah and Phil are going to formally announce her pregnancy," I told her. "You know, just for the benefit of anyone who might not have noticed her, somewhat obvious, bump."

"Or the fact that she's one of the few people here, who hasn't touched a drop of alcohol all night?"

"Exactly. To be fair, she didn't want to say anything sooner, in case...Well, anyway - I don't think she can hide it much longer. If it comes as a genuine surprise to anyone, I think they need a trip to the opticians."

"Well, I'm happy for Sarah and Phil, of course. It's good to see her settling down at last. But don't think I didn't notice you changing the subject, Lucy. You guys need to talk, you and James - clear the air."

"Maybe it's not me you need to convince. I'm not sure whether James wants to 'clear the air', Charlie."

"If you want to find out, he's in the kitchen, talking to Rachel and her boyfriend." This from Amy. "You look stunning, by the way."

My friend referred, of course, to my long, pastel pink dress. So unlike the majority of my wardrobe, but I'd somehow felt drawn to it. Having bought the thing, it seemed to deserve a decent debut.

"Hi, Amy - and thanks. So do you." Amy was one of the few people I knew who could have carried off a dress like that: glitter and sequin overload. "Hi, Rupert. I must admit, I didn't notice you guys were here. There are definitely too many people, in this house. The party should totally have been at my mum's."

"It *is* kind of crazy," admitted Amy. "We can't stay long, but we wanted to stop by. Are you going to talk to James, then?"

"Yeah, looks like it. I won't hear the last of it from Charlotte otherwise. Where *is* she, anyway?" Charlotte had apparently vanished. "Is the kitchen as crowded as this?"

"Pretty much," replied Amy.

"Yes, it is," added Rupert, pulling Amy even closer to him than was already inevitable, in that environment. "We really ought to be moving on, baby. My parents will be wondering where we are."

"Sure you're not just trying to avoid Lucy's sister? You were that jumpy, when she spoke to you earlier."

"Why would I want to avoid Sarah?"

"Like I mean Sarah."

My cue to leave them to it. Honestly, Amy and Rupert: Some things never changed. Catherine had a new bloke, apparently - but George and Courtney would always be her priority now. I hadn't actually seen Cath yet, and had an inkling she might have been and gone, but Amy and Rupert probably weren't the best people to ask about that.

***

I became sidetracked, and didn't get to speak to James until over an hour later. He was still in the kitchen, but no sign of Rachel, or her boyfriend, Zack, by this point.

"Charlotte thought we should 'clear the air,'" I told him.

"You and Charlotte?"

"No, of course not. You and me."

"And *Charlotte* thought we should talk?" He smiled, almost imperceptibly. "What do *you* think?"

"James, you know I'm sorry, don't you? For everything. For Jade and Jessica doing that graffiti, and for - for how things went with us. For how I behaved after Erica..."

"I'm sorry, too. Don't worry about it, Luce. We're good."

"Thank you. How've you been?"

"Okay. Or more accurately, functioning and acting 'okay'. Working a lot. My family tell me I'm overdoing it, but it helps, and not much else does."

I nodded. It probably wasn't healthy, but James didn't need one more person telling him that. We all cope in our own ways, right?

"How about you?" he asked.

"I'm fine," I said, even though we both knew neither of us were remotely "fine". But the fact that all we'd had was small talk didn't matter, because the words were irrelevant. We had something deeper: understanding. We really were good. We were friends again, of sorts - as much as we'd ever be.

James wasn't angry at me. He didn't seem like a man with much anger left - or much fight.

"Lucy, can I have a word?" It was Deborah, and she appeared distressed.

"Yes, of course. Is something wrong, Deb?"

"I actually *meant*...No offence, James."

James looked from Deborah to myself, slightly bemused, but started to move towards the door, all the same.

But not, apparently, soon enough to avoid the encounter that Deborah must have been making a last-ditch attempt to prevent. With Kev Tanner.

"You never *could* leave well alone, could you, McIntyre? You don't even want Lucy, not really."

"Have you completely lost it, Kev?" I demanded. "This is a private party. Who even invited you?"

"I did," admitted Deborah.

"Look, I don't want any trouble, okay?" said James. "Lucy and I were chatting, that's all. I need to find my sister, anyway. Catch you later, Luce - Deb."

I nodded. "Sorry about this," I said. "Take care, okay?"

"Don't worry. And you, too. It was good to see you." He turned to Kev. "She's all yours, mate."

But, having interrupted our conversation, Kev glanced at me for a moment, and then left the room himself.

"What the hell was that all about, Deborah?"

"I need to go after him," she told me.

I grabbed her arm. "No, you don't. You need to explain what's bloody well going on."

Deborah shook me off. "Later, Lucy. I need to make sure Kev's okay."

"Yeah, well, maybe you can also make sure he doesn't randomly decide to murder James, or anyone else here. He *is* your guest, after all."

I reached for a can of Special Brew. *Really, Lucy? You haven't been on the Special Brew for ages. Surely Stella's sufficient?*

It wasn't. I cracked open the Carlsberg Special, with a vengeance. And that was why we shouldn't be together. We brought out the worst in each other. Or, at least, Kev brought out the worst in me.

Not that it took much "bringing out". I kept thinking I was getting better, as I got older. But I totally wasn't. Day after day, I gripped the cliff's edge, clutching fragments of sanity, pretending nothing was wrong.

"Hi, Lucy. You haven't seen Sarah, have you?"

"Oh, hi, Phil. Last time I saw her, she was talking to Tracy and her sister, Dawn."

He noticed the Special Brew can. Studied my expression more closely. "Are you okay? Did James say something to upset you? I know it's none of my business, but I still care. As a friend, I mean." The unnecessary clarification made me wonder.

"James was fine. It's not him. Deborah invited Kev Tanner, that's all. He had a go at James, and then stormed off. Deb's trying to talk some sense into him."

Phil placed a hand on mine, briefly. "Go easy on the drink. Kev Tanner isn't worth it."

I nodded. "Thanks."

"I'd better find your sister. If she agrees, I'm hoping to take her home early. I know it's New Year, but Sarah *is* pregnant, and it's obvious she's shattered."

"She's lucky to have you," I said.

Deborah passed Phil, on his way out.

"Has Kev gone yet?" I asked, feeling an ache, as I said the words. What if he *had*? What then?

"No, and I think it's time you stopped playing games, and drinking yourself to oblivion. Just admit you still love him. You don't mind admitting it after you've consumed enough of that crap you're drinking right now. Lucy, Kev built himself up to come here tonight, and he couldn't take it, when he saw you there with James."

"So, where *is* he?"

"In our bedroom - mine and Matt's. I told him you'd go up and speak to him. You *do* want to, don't you?"

***

I tapped on the door, and then realised how bloody ridiculous that was. I was knocking on Matt and Deborah's door - for Kev's benefit? How did I work that one out? I threw the door open, and walked in.

Kev was sitting on the bed. "Hi," he said. "Sorry about just now. I overreacted, but when I saw you and James together...I'd been hoping to talk to you. I lost it, and I shouldn't have."

"So, tell me something new, right?" But my tone wasn't harsh any more. I sounded exactly how I felt, which was resigned.

"You going to sit down?"

I nodded, and sat next to him, on the grey-blue duvet. I wasn't sure whether it was one Matt had had since he'd been with Clare, or whether it would have been bought since. In any case, he'd had it a few years, so pre-Deborah.

"So, what *is* it, Kev? I thought we'd said everything."

"I didn't think so. You find it hard to trust me, and I get that, but I'm not taking drugs or drinking. Surely that counts for something?"

"Yes, of course it does, but I told you I don't want to get back with you." But I looked away, so that he couldn't see my eyes.

"It's hard to talk here," said Kev, shifting his position on Matt and Deborah's bed.

"Yeah, I know."

"Let's go for a walk."

I glanced at my watch. Almost eleven-thirty. "We'll have to be quick, or we might not be back for midnight."

"I haven't got a carriage to turn back into a pumpkin. I take it your dress won't turn into rags? You look beautiful, by the way."

"Thank you. And yes, okay - we'll go for a walk. Anywhere in mind?"

"How about *The Field*? If you're okay with that. It's convenient, and it *is* nice. But I know you have memories associated with it."

"It's fine." I was slightly surprised to hear him call the place by its unofficial name, though: *The Field*.

And I wondered, vaguely, whether there was an element of testing me, to see how highly I valued a spot, associated in my mind with James. But, whatever. If he was testing, it was his problem, not mine.

***

Kev had insisted upon lifting me, so that I wouldn't tear my long dress on the fence. And the fact that we sat together on that too-familiar bench felt strangely inevitable.

"I used to come here sometimes, with Deborah and the kids," he told me, which perhaps wasn't surprising, given that he'd so casually referred to it as *The Field*.

"I went to this school. It was our playing field."

"I guessed that. Some of the memories you talked about - well, you mentioned *The Field*, and I made the connection."

I'd never been here as late as this before. Ebony darkness was almost uninterrupted, apart from the occasional light from a neighbouring house. The hoot of an owl served to place further emphasis upon the lateness of the hour.

"I can't remember what I said about the place. But yes, I *do* have memories here associated with James. We had our first kiss here, and it's also where he dumped me. But there are plenty of other memories about the place. Probably at least as many relate to Charlotte as James. It isn't a problem for me, and hopefully it isn't for you."

"No, it's fine. Memories are what they are." He pulled me closer, and we kissed, creating a fresh batch of *Field Related Memories*.

"We can't keep doing this," I told him.

"We can't stop, Lucy. Or maybe we can, but we don't want to. I love you. How many times do I have to tell you that, to make you believe it?"

I pulled away. "It's not a case of whether I believe it or not. I can't trust you. I don't want to trust you."

"Listen, Luce - please? I've decided to move away. This town has been nothing but a series of nightmares for me. Aside from that, it's not safe. The Bryants, Farooq and Abdul - all those people I was involved with - they're not going to live and let live. You don't hand your *P45* to people like them, and walk away."

"But it's not only the King's Head gang here. There's Deborah and the kids, too. And me. Was I part of your 'nightmare'? One minute you're having a go at James for talking to me, and the next, you're kissing me, and saying you love me? And now, you're leaving, anyway?" Tears stung my eyes.

Kev pulled a little red box from his jacket pocket, and handed it to me. I held the box for a moment, feeling the velvet texture.

"Aren't you going to open it?"

"Is it...?"

"Yeah, it is."

I opened the box, and saw an emerald ring - a good-sized emerald, surrounded by diamonds.

"It's real, before you ask. And no, it isn't stolen."

"I wasn't thinking..." But, of course, I would have, once my mind had caught up with my emotions. "How did you afford something like this? Tell me you didn't buy it on a credit card."

"Like, I can just *see* them giving *me* a credit card. Deborah lent me the money. And, if that seems too weird for you, think of it as a gift from your brother. The money came from their joint account. I don't think they expect me to pay them back, but I will. Marry me, Lucy."

"What, and move away with you?"

"That's what I've been hoping for, yes. But, if you want to stay, we'll stay. As long as I have you, I can stand it."

"You shouldn't have done this," I said. "Deborah and Matthew shouldn't have got involved, either. It isn't fair to put this sort of pressure on."

"What are you saying?"

"I'm saying no. No, I won't marry you. We're not even going out together. How did you get from that to marriage, Kev? And all this stuff about leaving - is this some sort of emotional blackmail? Because I don't think it's fair. Is it even true?"

He didn't get to answer before the noise began. Shouting, screaming, cheering - from all directions, including that of the party we'd just left.

"Happy New Year, Lucy."

"New decade," I reminded him. "Not the best start ever, was it?"

We kissed again, more passionately than ever, as if to make up for the lousy start. Not that it made any practical difference. But, in the short-term, we both got to feel better about this, as a beginning to 1990.

"To answer your question - yeah, it's true," said Kev. "I'm going to stay with my cousin in Newcastle - Mark Jordan's brother."

"I thought Mark's brother lived in Brixham."

"That's Stuart, the youngest brother. Ray Jordan is Mark and Stu's older brother, and the only one who actually owns his own house. Anyway, I'll stay with him, until I sort out something more permanent. It would be easier to get a job and get back on my feet, if I had a fresh start, somewhere new. It all makes sense in theory, but it's not the same without you. I want you to come with me. We can do this, Lucy. I know we can."

"I don't want to. It's over." *Despite the kiss.*

He didn't reply. Only looked at me for a moment, and then away, into the distance.

"It isn't because of James or Phil, or anyone else. I want you to know that."

"Yeah, well, if it's over anyway, then it's none of my business."

I held out the box, to return it. "I can't take this."

"Keep it. There's nothing I can do with an engagement ring."

"You could always give it to Deborah, to make up for selling her last one."

"That was low."

"Yeah, I know," I admitted. "I'm sorry. I'm just all over the place. But Deborah and Matt *did* pay for it, so in a way, it's theirs. Maybe you could give it to Gemma?"

"I'm past caring. If you want to give it to Deborah, Gemma, Sarah, or anyone else, feel free, but I don't want it back. If you won't take it, I'll chuck the bloody thing into the nearest hedge, or else down a drain. Seems symbolically appropriate, don't you think?"

"Kev, listen..."

"Forget it, okay? It doesn't matter. But I chose that ring specifically. I remember you saying you loved emeralds, and I thought the colour would look perfect on you. You always look amazing in green, with your red hair."

"You actually like my red hair? I've always hated it."

"You shouldn't hate it. It's beautiful." Words that made me realise I couldn't dye it, which I'd been considering.

"It comes from Dad's side. His old man had red hair, and his brother, Mike." Dad himself, pre-silver-haired decade, had been blonde. Still, I'd always been conscious that I resembled him more closely than any of my siblings.

"You're nothing like Dave Ryman. We've never really talked about him, have we?"

"You've given me your opinions about him, but I doubt if you'd remember. There wasn't much I wouldn't agree with about dad himself, but the way you laid into me and my family...Anyway, it doesn't matter. You can't unsay the words, and I can't unhear them. It's true enough that we've lived in properties bought with his 'dirty money', and not exactly had to struggle financially, and maybe it's not right for me to judge you, the Farooqs and Abduls, and even the Bryants, when it was my dad...Yeah, well - I know, okay? We all do, especially Mum."

"Lucy, I don't know what to say. I didn't mean...I don't know exactly what I said, but you know I'm sorry, don't you? And what I meant, just now - I meant, we'd never talked about what he did to you and your sisters. The abuse. I love you for how brave you had to be, to survive everything that evil bastard put you through. Did he abuse Matt and Danny, too?"

"Physically. He physically abused the boys, and sexually abused us girls. Not exactly *Father of the Year*, right?"

"It makes me sick inside. My dad used me as a punchbag too, so I get what it must have been like for your brothers. The other stuff - I can't even go there, especially when I think about my Gemma."

"I live with the scars. I don't even know whether James or Charlotte ever suspected. Most of the people in my life don't have a clue. But honestly, it's better that way - at least for me. Kev - *about* the ring, yeah...?"

"Please keep the ring. It wasn't intended for Deborah or Gemma, or anyone else. I certainly don't want Gem wearing it to school, and I know she would, to show off to Lila and Co."

I nodded, aware that I was shaking. "Thank you." I couldn't have said more, without completely breaking down.

I glanced again, momentarily, at the emerald ring. Then, closed the small red jewellery box, and slipped it into one of my coat pockets, which luckily, did have a zip. It wasn't an engagement ring any more. But, in a sense, it was an eternity ring. It represented eternal love, even though the relationship was already over.

I'd barely considered what to do next - such as, whether to return to the party - when I saw it: that look of sudden, acute pain. A reflex action, hand to chest and away again, so rapid, and as rapidly - unsuccessfully - concealed.

My heartbeat accelerated. "Kev, what's wrong?"

"Nothing. Just a twinge, that's all. You ought to be getting back to the party."

"Don't tell me it was nothing. You're in pain. What was it - chest pains?"

"I'm okay. And I *have* seen the doctor, before you ask. I've got a few health issues, but it's not exactly unexpected, is it - after everything I put my body through? I didn't say anything, because I didn't want you staying with me, if you didn't really want to, which I suppose...Luce, listen, there's nothing to worry about, yeah?"

I put my arm around him, and remained with him, for maybe ten minutes or so. And he seemed okay.

I kissed the top of his head, as I stood. "Come back with me? Everyone will wonder where we've got to."

"You go, Lucy - please. I need some space. And honestly, I'm fine. But I need to be on my own, and you need to be around your family and friends."

I nearly choked on the tears I'd tried to keep inside. "I love you so much."

"Take care, Luce."

I nodded. Took a deep breath, to regain control of my emotions. Turned and walked away.

I raced upstairs, gasping for air between sobs.

"Lucy, what...?" But I pushed past Deborah.

I threw myself on to Matt and Deborah's bed, and let it all out. I could hear Deborah talking, but nothing registered. Nothing.

I eventually realised how hot I was. I was still wearing my coat and scarf, both of which I proceeded to remove.

Deborah sat down on the bed, next to me. She put her arm around me. "Kev asked you?"

"Yeah, and I turned him down."

"I guessed as much. I was wrong, wasn't I? I shouldn't have encouraged him to go ahead and ask you."

"It doesn't matter." And it really didn't. I remembered thinking, so recently, that Deb *had* been wrong. But now, all cried out, I was too numb to care.

Sarah waddled into the room - looking, in that moment, more like Mum than ever. A younger version of Helen Ryman, exactly as our mother must have looked, when pregnant herself. The resemblance was almost ridiculous, and I actually felt as if I wanted to laugh. But instead, I started to cry again. It was incredible to me, that I still had tears left to cry.

"Lucy, what is it? Tracy told me Kev was here. What's he done to you?"

"Listen, Sarah," said Deborah, "I'm talking to Lucy. The best thing you can do, for now, is go back to the party."

Sarah actually looked ready to slap Deborah. Then, my sister burst into tears instead. "She's my sister, not yours. How dare you tell me to go back to the party? Do you think you've got some sort of connection, because you've both been with Kev Tanner? In that case, maybe we should invite Cath to join the 'private party.'"

I was taken aback by Sarah's cruelty, and jealousy. What had happened to my sweet, loving younger sister?

But, of course, I knew the answer: *Life* had happened to Sarah, as it had happened to all of us.

"Technically, Deborah *is* my sister-in-law. *Our* sister-in-law, to be precise." I took a deep breath, endeavouring to keep my voice steady. So far, so good. "Look, I don't want to argue with you, Sarah. I don't need it. You're pregnant, and definitely don't need the stress."

"You're saying you really do want to be around her, not me? You do realise she helped to set up..." But she caught my expression, and stopped.

Phil came in. "What's going on?"

Sarah ran into his arms, and he hugged her.

"Please, can you take Sarah home, Phil?" asked Deborah. "For her sake, and the baby's, as well as Lucy's."

"Yes, of course I will," Phil assured her. "But, Lucy, are you okay?"

"Yes," I told him. "Don't worry. Just get my sister home, okay?"

Deborah shut the door behind Phil and Sarah, when they finally departed. The open door had evidently been too inviting. I dissolved into a tearful mess in her arms, and she held me for a while, not saying anything.

When I was sufficiently calm, we talked. I told her how things had gone. She asked questions, here and there, but left me to do most of the talking.

"How did Kev take it?" she asked, eventually.

"It was hard to tell. He didn't lose it instantly."

"He was quiet?"

"I suppose so." And we both knew that that could be good - or else, very bad.

I froze inside, realising. I had left him. "Did you know about the chest pains, Deborah?"

How *could* I have left him there? Was I *crazy*?

"Yes, I persuaded him to go to the doctor. I didn't think he'd tell you, to be honest."

I couldn't speak. But I didn't need to, because it must have been there, in my eyes, red-rimmed and sore as they surely were.

"Lucy, listen - I'm going to head over to *The Field* - just check he's okay. I've got a bad feeling. It's probably nothing, but I can't ignore it."

But I'd seen her expression. "It isn't 'nothing', Deb. I'm coming with you."

"There's no need for that. You're upset already."

"You're scared, Deborah. You really think something's happened to Kev, don't you? And of course I'm coming with you. Anyway, apart from anything else, Matt would go spare if I let you go on your own."

"Matt would insist on coming with us, but I don't want anyone else involved, unless...I think we should just go, before your brother, or anyone else, can stop us."

***

I knelt down beside him, on the muddy field, in my pale pink dress. He wasn't moving - wasn't breathing. I checked for a pulse, knowing there wouldn't be one. Deborah knew, as well. Probably already thinking about her kids. How to tell Toby - and, the worst part - how to tell Gemma.

"Is he dead?" I asked her - for some reason, needing to go through the motions.

Deborah knelt beside me, placing a hand gently on my right arm. "I don't know, love. I need to go back to the house, and call an ambulance. You'll be okay to stay with him? I'll get Matt to come back with me."

"Yeah, I'll stay." Stay. Go. What difference did it make?

I couldn't have said exactly how long I waited there, with Kev's lifeless body.

"Lucy?" I looked up, into James's eyes. "Deborah's phoned for an ambulance. She and Matt have had to go after Toby and his girlfriend. He and Rhiannon apparently overheard the call, and he was determined to go to Lila's, and find his sister. Matt asked me to come and wait with you."

"Thanks, James - but you don't have to, if you don't want to. It can't be much fun, and I'll be okay on my own."

"Of course I want to. There's no way I'm leaving you, after I promised your brother I'd stay with you. Shouldn't we sit on the bench? Your dress must be covered in mud."

"No, I'm staying here. You're welcome to sit on the bench, though."

But James sat down next to me, not bothering about his own suit becoming dirty.

I looked into familiar almond eyes, that had lost their spark. "You get it."

"Yes. You know, I never understood about Kev, and the whole drug addiction thing but, after Erica and Primmy died, I basically used work as a drug. Still do, really."

"I think Matt did pretty much the same - that and focusing on the twins. He told me it had actually helped, in a way, that Jade and Jess were so difficult."

"Yes, I can see that. And people would view those things as 'being strong'. It's certainly more socially acceptable than heroin. That doesn't make it okay or healthy, and it doesn't make me and Matt 'better'. At one time, I would have believed it did."

And so, here we were again: James and myself, at *The Field*. The same two people, but irrevocably altered. Not perhaps, on the outside, drastically different. And yet, both of us, deeply scarred inside.

Chapter Fifty-Four

I made it through the funeral service, knowing what I had to do next.

There had been no trace of alcohol or illegal drugs in Kev's system, at the time of his death. He'd died of a heart attack. Years of substance abuse had taken their toll.

Apparently, it wasn't my fault. But, when you're the one who's turned down a marriage proposal, and then the guy drops dead, and you're told it was heart failure...

Deborah introduced me to a tall, thin woman, with tightly curled, silver hair, and a girl, aged around seventeen, with long, blonde hair, in a high ponytail. Kev's sister, Heather, and her daughter, Natalia.

Deb referred to me as "Kev's partner", as I'd previously picked her up on "fiancee". I really hadn't been either, but it didn't matter much now, did it?

"Is Violet coming?" asked Deborah. "I'm assuming Archie won't be."

Heather's expression was as cold as her younger brother's body. "Kevin caused our parents a great deal of trouble, over the years. Dad disowned him years ago, so you're correct in your assumptions. He certainly *won't* be attending. I think you must also be aware, Deborah, that Mum is extremely frail, and confined to a wheelchair. She could hardly be expected to put her own health at risk, simply to make an appearance at this afternoon's fiasco. Natalia and I are here, on behalf of the family. Let that be sufficient."

"Mark's here, too," I pointed out, nodding in Mark Jordan's direction.

Kev's cousin was accompanied by his current girlfriend, a petite brunette named Cecily. Donna Mann was apparently old news. Poor, desperate Donna. The image of her, lying at the bottom of those stairs, would never leave me.

"Yes, well - that's not a side of the family we recognise, but I *was* aware of his presence."

Natalia looked uncomfortable, and it was obvious, from her swollen eyes, that she wasn't as unaffected by her uncle's death, as Heather either was, or pretended to be.

Gemma and Toby, who'd both been amazing, were welcoming guests, as they arrived - and were currently talking to James and his sister, Rachel. I excused myself, and joined them, by which time Sarah and Phil had arrived, bringing Catherine and George, as Sarah had told me they would. I'd passed the stage where anything like that could hurt me, more than I was already hurting.

Gemma thanked them all for coming, before turning to my elder sister: "Catherine, can I ask you a favour? If you don't like the idea, it's okay, but I'd really like George to stand with us for the service. By 'us', I mean Toby and me, and our cousin, Talia. We'll look after him, and he *is* our little brother - mine and Toby's - so, to me, he should be with us."

Cath glanced at me, and I nodded.

My sister touched Gemma's shoulder lightly. "Of course he can, Gemma, love. I don't know how much he understands right now, but it will mean a lot to him one day. That's why I had to come." She turned to her son: "You remember Gemma and Toby, darling? You met them at Uncle Matthew and Aunt Deborah's wedding."

George nodded, and let Gemma take his hand. They looked as natural together, as if they'd been conventional siblings, who'd grown up together.

I managed to speak briefly to James, Rachel, Sarah, and Phil.

After which, Mum, Danny, and Hannah arrived.

"Didn't Matt come with you?" I asked. "I told Deborah I thought he would be."

"He's on his way, darling," said Mum. "He had to drop Jessica off at Cynthia's."

"How long will she be staying with Matt and Deborah?"

"I'm not sure. I did speak to Clare, briefly. She and Malcolm need to find out what's happening with Jade, which is out of their hands now. It seems probable she'll have to go into some sort of youth offenders' place. For now, it's better and safer for your brother and Deborah to have Jessica."

"How about you, Luce? Are you okay?" asked Danny.

"I'm fine," I replied, almost without thinking.

***

"I'm not going to make this long, because it's all I can do to keep it together." Gemma took a deep breath, fighting to control her emotions. "I suppose I'm considered 'popular' at school, but not one of my many friends is here this afternoon. I'm mostly okay with that, but it's disappointing that even my best friend wouldn't support me. But, in the end, I'm glad, because everyone who really loved my dad is here. People can be unforgiving. I live with my mum and step-dad, and we got a brick through our window, and graffiti on our garage, not even two whole days after Dad's death. I just want to put the record straight, for the few here who might be in any doubt: He was not a 'junkie'. He gave up drugs and alcohol, and did that without any medical help. My dad was far from perfect, and those of us who loved him know that, more than anyone, and we don't needs thugs and vandals to remind us. But he did have another side, a loving side, and I'm so grateful to those of you who also saw it, especially my brother, Toby, my mum, and my dad's fiancee, Lucy." And she was done, because she couldn't get more words out for crying.

And somehow, I'd remained sufficiently detached, and wasn't crying. There would be time enough for that, after all.

***

It had all been meticulously planned. No *goodbyes*. Just slip away.

Charlotte and Tara would be waiting around the corner, in Charlotte's white-going-on-grey Ford Escort. And the bags had been packed, which hadn't taken long, given that we'd be travelling light.

As everyone began to disperse, Deborah caught my eye, and I knew I couldn't ignore her. Didn't have it in me.

I grabbed her arm, and pulled her to one side. "Deb, we need to talk."

She looked at me. "Sure. Are you okay? Why don't you come back with me and Matthew, and the kids? We've got room for one more, and I said before, you were welcome to come with us."

By "coming back", she meant to the reception, which was being held at Rita and Tim's. I realised I'd barely spoken two words, all afternoon, to Deborah's parents, or her sister, Vanessa.

I practically dragged her into the side street, where Charlotte and Tara were parked.

"Lucy, what's going on?"

"Give me a minute. I have to tell Charlotte and Tara to wait for me."

"Why don't you say you're coming back with me and your brother?"

"Just wait here, okay? I'll explain everything."

I raced across the road, and Tara wound down the passenger window.

"Let's sit down for a minute," I suggested, on rejoining Deborah, indicating a nearby bench.

Deborah complied. "Are you going to tell me what's going on? Matt will be wondering where we-"

"I'm leaving. A couple of days ago, Charlotte told me her and Tara were going to stay indefinitely with this friend in Bournemouth, and it made sense, all of a sudden. They're sick of this place and, frankly, being persecuted for being lesbians - and I've had enough too, for different reasons. If I stay here, after everything that happened, I'll go crazy. I've left my job, and the three of us are moving to Bournemouth."

Deborah's expression was incredulous. "This is ridiculous, Lucy. You decided a couple of days ago? You obviously haven't thought it through. Does your mum know? Sarah or Matthew, or anyone?"

"No, they don't. No one knows - only Charlotte and Tara, and now you."

"I can understand that you're grieving." Deborah adjusted her hair grips. The afternoon's breeze was becoming more like wind, and starting to play havoc with our styling efforts. "Maybe you *do* need a holiday or something, but this isn't the way to go about it. And you actually quit your job? What did the partners say about that?"

"They weren't thrilled. I was supposed to give notice. But I've never been especially happy there, and I can find another job." I took a deep breath. "I don't need a holiday, Deborah. It's more than that. I didn't tell anyone because I couldn't deal with them trying to talk me out of it: with Mum and Sarah crying, and Matt and Danny deliberately making me feel even more guilty than I do already."

"And where does this leave me? I get to tell Matt, Danny, Sarah, and Helen? Not to mention Gemma, Toby, and Jess, as if they haven't been through enough. And how about James?" Deborah might not be yelling, but she was, for all that, as quietly livid as I'd ever seen her.

"Tell Matt. He'll pass it on. And James doesn't need me. We never did each other much good, anyway."

"That's debatable, but you can't possibly say Matt doesn't need you, or Sarah. Or the kids. You heard what Gemma said." Deborah broke down. "Maybe I should just say it, right? *I* need you, Lucy. Not only for Matt, Gem, and Toby - for me. What Gem said about her friends not understanding - did you see any of *mine* this afternoon? I know Charlotte will always be your best friend, but you're mine. I want you to know that."

I hugged her then. "You don't mean less to me than Charlotte. You have to realise that, Deb. You're the one person I couldn't leave without saying goodbye to. If that doesn't tell you how much I love you..."

"I love you, too. Ring me as soon as you get there, okay?"

I was crying as much as Deborah, by this point. "Of course I will. Once I'm settled, you can visit - you and Matt, and the kids."

Really, Lucy? How vast would you imagine this house is, anyway? It was also not my house, or even Tara and Charlotte's.

"Do you think you'll ever come back?"

"I don't know. I can't think ahead right now. And it does seem like a big deal to me, because I've never lived anywhere else, but it's not exactly the opposite side of the Earth."

"In many respects, it might as well be. You'll miss the day to day contact with your family and close friends."

"Well, one of each will be there with me, so that should help. I'm twenty-three years old, so I suppose it's time. Take care of Matt for me, and Sarah, and everyone. Give my love to Gemma and Toby. And Jessica, and Josh."

Deborah nodded, releasing me. "You'd better go. Charlotte and Tara will wonder what's keeping you, and your brother might send out a search party."

I didn't look back, as I walked away - couldn't risk a single backward glance, as I headed for Charlotte's car, and an unfamiliar destination.

Epilogue

It was July 1993, when Charlotte and I returned. Both of us staying with my friend's mum, for a few days. Beyond that, I don't think either of us knew.

I glanced around me, at the familiar living room. Photos of Charlotte, at various stages of childhood, still decorated most of the wall space, and smiled out from mismatched, cheap frames, on almost every available surface.

And yet, my friend was focused upon the one picture, in which she didn't appear. Placed on the top of the telly: Val, with a tall, grey-haired man, with glasses.

Horace, Val's new bloke, was a major reason why I'd opted to stay with Valerie and Charlotte. I hadn't met the guy yet, and Charlie had only done so twice, but apparently, that had been enough, and she required moral support. At twenty-seven - like, *seriously*?

Then again, the arrangement suited me. I hadn't felt comfortable staying with Mum, or Sarah and Phil. I could have handled Matt and Deborah's, but they already had a full house - including a three-month-old daughter.

The beige carpet had been replaced by a green one. Same brown leather sofa. Same coffee table, on which Charlotte's mug of coffee was waiting.

"Lucy, are you sure I can't get you a tea or coffee, too?"

"No, thank you, Valerie. I was just saying to Charlotte, that I need to pop out. I shouldn't be long."

"Okay, love. Are you going across the road, to see your brother and Deborah?"

"Not yet, no. I'll head over there this afternoon."

"Yes, okay. So, I presume you're anxious to see your mum and Jessica. Helen did seem quite upset that you chose to stay here, instead of...Anyway, it's none of my business. Charlotte, can you move that suitcase that you left on the landing, please? I could barely get past it, to use the toilet."

"I said I would, Mum. I take it I'm actually allowed to finish my coffee first?"

I attempted to make my escape, whilst the two of them were *not quite bickering* - as they had been since my friend and I had arrived.

Which didn't work. Charlotte grabbed my arm, as I was heading for the front door. "Not so fast, Lucy. We *are* still best friends, aren't we?"

"Of course. Why wouldn't we be?"

"Good. Then, you can tell me which one you're meeting: Phil or James?"

Shit, she was good. "Later, Charlie - okay? I have to go."

***

I was out of breath, by the time I reached *The Field*.

"Sorry I'm late. Thank you for waiting."

"Hi, Lucy. You look well."

"So do you, James." And he did, although he hadn't lost the haunted look, in his eyes. He also looked tired, although that could have something to do with the kids.

Apparently, the McIntyre family also now included a lively apricot Standard Poodle, who greeted me with enthusiasm. "This is Ailsa," said James, by way of introduction, as I stroked the dog.

Finally, my mind registered my surroundings, and it hit me, with the impact of a Heavy Goods Vehicle. Bad analogy, of course - given what had happened to Bonita, and to Erica and Primmy. But, holy crap - this place.

"The bench has gone."

"Yes, a couple of years ago. It was continually being vandalised, more than just the graffiti of our days. I suppose the school funds couldn't cover the constant repairs." He hesitated. "Are you all right, with being here? I was surprised, when you suggested it."

"Yes, I'm okay. I wanted to come back. And honestly, it's fine. I've always loved *The Field*. You don't have to stop loving a place, because you don't love everything that happened there."

"True. Not easy though, is it?"

"No." I hesitated. "So, you're married, with a baby girl? Deborah told me how much she likes Claudia, and how gorgeous the baby is."

James nodded, and produced his wallet. Extracted a photo. A woman, of about twenty-five, with long, ash blonde hair, and glasses. A girl, aged about seven, with shoulder-length, auburn curls. And the mother holding a beautiful, brown-haired, blue-eyed baby. "My wife, Claudia, step-daughter, Amabel, and daughter, Delphine Primrose. Taken a couple of months ago, so Belle is taller now, and her hair twice the length - and, of course, Delphie has grown so much, it takes my breath away."

"Such a beautiful family. And you met Claudia at work?"

"Yes. It would have to be, in truth, since I don't go many other places."

Don't. Present tense. "So, it sounds as if things are going well."

"You know they're not, Lucy. Claudia and the girls are wonderful. I don't deserve them. Sarah said something, I take it?"

"She told me she's in love with you. And there I was, thinking she was happily married. She showed up, out of the blue, with Caleb, a couple of weeks ago."

"I know. I told her it wasn't a good idea, but she wouldn't listen. She isn't in love with me, Lucy. She's crazy about Phil, and little Caleb."

"You didn't kiss her, then? She's making the whole thing up?"

"Ailsa!" James called, conveniently switching his attention to the dog.

"Answer me, James."

"Yes, I kissed her, and it was more than a peck on the cheek. She'd been having problems with Phil, and I...I'd been having problems, too."

"With Claudia?"

"With everything. With life." His expression was vacant.

Then, Ailsa came bounding up to him, and her affection seemed to bring him back to reality. He stroked the dog, and I joined him.

"Sarah grabbed me, when I was about to throw myself in front of a lorry. Your sister saved my life. She didn't say anything, because I begged her not to tell anyone. Are you all right, Lucy?"

I nodded. In truth, I didn't know whether I was all right or not, or even what constituted "all right" any more. "You were suicidal. And you hadn't told anyone?"

"I hadn't told anyone, no. And Sarah helped me through. She's been there herself, and she got it."

Yeah, Sarah had been there. I remembered too well. "Are you okay now?"

"Yes, I'm fine. It all just got too much, right after Delphine was born. I felt I didn't deserve her, or Claudia, or Amabel."

"Claudia doesn't know any of this?"

"No." And his tone told me that the subject was closed. Closed, and double-locked.

"There's nothing between you and Sarah, then - beyond friendship, and the one kiss?"

"Not on my side and, as I was saying before, I don't think she's really in love with me, either. She thinks the world of Phil. I'm going to tell you this, Lucy, and if I'm wrong, I'm sorry."

"Tell me what?"

"Sarah found a pile of letters you'd sent him. I've no idea what was in them, but she's always been convinced it was you he really wanted. And, after she found those letters...I know it doesn't make sense, Luce. I mean, you and Phil - you were barely even interested in the guy, when you were seeing each other."

I didn't comment, and James didn't notice. "I'd better be getting back," I said.

"Yeah, same here." Putting Ailsa's lead back on, to seal the deal. "Luce, I'm not in love with Sarah. I'm not in love with Claudia, either."

For an instant, I honestly thought...

And James hadn't missed it. He actually smiled. "Relax, okay? I'm not about to make the romantic declaration you wanted to hear ten years ago, and definitely don't want to hear now." Which was spot on.

I returned the smile. "Just as well. I don't think either of us need any more complications, right?"

"I think we work better as friends. Same as you and Phil, I suppose."

"I suppose." Like, James knew so much about Phil and me. But, whatever, right?

"I'm not in love with Sarah or Claudia. I'm in love with Erica, and I always will be."

I touched his arm, lightly. "I know."

***

Delphine McIntyre wasn't the only new arrival. The moment finally arrived, when Deborah placed three-month-old Selina Bonnie into my arms.

"She's a mini Gemma, isn't she? Except with darker hair. And a Ryman nose, poor thing."

"Don't you dare. Her nose is one of the things I love most. But yes, she's a lot like Gemma. I got out Gem's baby photos, to compare Selina to how her sister was. But your big sister was a silly girl, wasn't she, Selina? Yes, she was."

"I've never seen you this soppy, Deb."

"I know. Sorry, Luce."

"Bless you - don't be. I think it's lovely. Anyway, who could blame you for being soppy over this little angel? She's perfect."

"Yes, she is."

"So, where's Matt?"

Selina started to bawl, and I handed her, in all her perfection, back to her mum. By the time Deb had soothed the baby, my question had hung there, suspended, for at least ten minutes.

"He's visiting Jade," replied Deborah, at length. "With Clare."

Selina slept in her carrycot, and now it was Deborah who cried, in my arms.

"Hey, it's okay. I'm here. Sarah told me everything."

"She was about to smash the baby's skull on a table, Lucy. And, if she'd done it herself, and not been so determined to bully her own twin into...I'm not sure we'd have got there in time."

I froze inside. To know the facts was one thing. To actually hear the words from Deborah, another matter entirely. How had our family come to this?

I remembered something else, that had come out recently. Sarah had told me.

About the fall, that resulted in Clare's miscarriage. There had been a rug on the landing, usually positioned between Matt and Clare's room, and Bonnie's, as was. It covered a stain, of some description, on the pale grey carpet they had, at the time. No way would that rug have been at the head of the staircase, unless someone had moved it.

But, even if that *had* been Jade's doing, she couldn't have known how dangerous her prank was. Not at four years old - right?

"So, Jade went back to the detention centre, and Jess is living with Mum now?"

But that was as far as we got, before the key turned in the lock. And, no - not my brother. It was Gemma.

Who marched straight up to me, and slapped me. A hard slap in the face, that stung, and brought tears to my eyes.

"Gemma, what do you think you're doing, young lady? You apologise to Lucy."

"No, Mum, I won't. I told you I'd slap her, if and when I ever saw her again." She turned to me. "You walked out on me and Toby, when we needed you most. Thanks a lot, Lucy."

"It's okay, Deb," I said. "Look, Gemma - you *are* right, and I'm sorry I let you and your brother down. But I'm only human, and I needed to get away, after your dad died."

"I know. I understand, to a point, but what you did really hurt. So, I had to hit you. And now we've got that out of the way, you can give me a hug. I bloody missed you."

So, I did. Classic Gemma, really. Slapping me, and then asking for a hug - and getting one, too.

Deborah had mentioned, during our comparatively few phone conversations, that Lila was now training to be a professional ballerina. Which we both knew had been Gemma's ultimate dream. Lila hadn't been sensitive, and Gemma, for her part, had been jealous and resentful, and not even attempted to fake the supportive best friend.

Then again, that was how Deb had told it. And, let's face it, she and her daughter...

"I take it your brother's still at Rhiannon's?" asked Deb.

"I'm not Toby's keeper, but I'd say it's a fair bet. It would almost be easier to admit he lives with the Farmers. He must spend, like, ninety-five percent of his time over there."

Deborah frowned. "We're still his family, Gemma. He could break up with Rhiannon tomorrow, and it would be us he'd turn to, to pick up the pieces."

"Not those two. Have you *seen* them? They're *seriously* in love. Speaking of which, did Matthew go off with his ex again?"

"Gemma! Sorry about this, Lucy."

"It's fine."

"Right, young lady - make yourself useful, and take your sister for a walk. I need to talk to Lucy."

"Can I have that new top? *And* the jeans?"

"Probably. Not that I should have to bribe you to look after your own sister, especially since you're working now, anyway."

"You do realise Lila and that bitch, Gloria, have been spreading it that Selina's *mine*? Those two ought to be back in primary school." This, whilst efficiently getting Selina ready, indicating no lack of practice.

Gemma slammed the front door behind them.

"Yes, Jade went back to the detention centre," Deborah said, once Gemma had departed. It made my head spin, to resume precisely where we'd left off. "And this time, it's a long-term arrangement. Hopefully, permanent."

I nodded. Yes, that was consistent with what Matt had told me by phone, the one time we'd discussed the subject. Jade had gone indefinitely.

"The night it happened, I wouldn't have either of the twins here, and Clare wouldn't have Jade either, because of Rory."

"Yes, that's right. Clare and Malcolm had a little boy."

"Yes, he's adorable," said Deborah. "Anyway, Clare drove down, and was ready to take Jessica, but Jess wouldn't go, and your mum stepped in. She's been there ever since, and will barely talk to me and Matt, or her mum. She occasionally stays with her other grandparents, to give your mum a break. Jessica isn't adjusting well, and still reverts to the idea of wanting to be with Jade. As if she thinks her twin is living in some sort of hotel or something."

"My brother visits Jade, of course. I know that must be hard to take, but he wouldn't turn his back on his own daughter. That's not Matt."

"Oh, really? He's not exactly attentive to Selina, and she's his daughter. And *she* hasn't tried to kill someone." I was taken aback by the bitterness in my sister-in-law's voice.

"That's not fair. I know my brother wouldn't neglect Selina. He adores her."

"You haven't been here, Lucy. And he's always talking to Clare. They don't only go together to visit Jade. They go for coffee or drinks together afterwards. To 'talk about Jade', naturally. And she's always phoning him, about her latest dramas. Yes, Matthew's your brother, but he's not a bloody saint, and I'm not going to pretend he's been there for me and our baby, when he hasn't. Sometimes, I think Hannah had the right idea, except that I'd take the kids with me, if I walked out."

"That was next on my list - to find out what's going on with Danny and Hannah," I admitted.

"Listen, that's none of my business. I shouldn't have said anything. It just gets too much sometimes, that's all."

"Yeah, I know. Try not to worry, Deb. Clare's with Malcolm now, anyway. And Matt loves you."

"He and Clare have a lot of history."

"True, but most of it isn't the sort of 'history' to inspire sweet nostalgia. My brother blamed her for Bonnie's death - felt she was negligent. There's no way they'd come back from that."

"If you say so. In the end, Matt can do whatever he wants, up to and including leaving me for Clare. I've dealt with worse, over the years."

"I know."

"The thing is, my kids will always come first. I was talking to Cath recently, and she said pretty much the same thing. Blokes do what they do. Matthew can let me down, and I'll be okay. But, if he lets Selina down, he'll have me to answer to."

"If he lets either of you down, he'll have me to answer to. I honestly don't think he will, though. Deb, *about* Danny and Hannah - you said she left him? Only I thought it was him who was supposed to have gone."

"Yes, she threw him out. She's in their flat on her own, and Cynthia has Josh. If you want to know any more, you'll have to speak to them directly. Matt has a number for wherever Danny's been staying." She hesitated. "If even Danny and Hannah aren't solid, what hope is there for the rest of us?"

I had to admit that she had a point. But, naturally, I only admitted as much in my own mind.

"Anyway, Lucy - you've said almost nothing about yourself, and what you've been doing."

"There's not much to tell that I haven't told you already, by phone. I worked in a couple of offices, and in a souvenir shop, selling postcards and sticks of rock, and cheap gifts with kids' names on."

"Oh, I totally remember those name gifts." Deborah smiled. "My aunt bought the kids some name plates, for their bedrooms, except that she bought *Tony* and *Emma*. Toby wasn't bothered, but Gem threw a tantrum. Kev sorted it, in the end, by adding a "G" in marker pen. It looked ridiculous, but she was happy, so I didn't object." She paused. "How about your novel? Is it really finished?"

"First draft, yes," I replied. "But don't tell anyone, okay?"

"Are there real people in it?"

"It's a novel, Deb. I won't say there aren't aspects inspired by real life, but it's fiction. Please don't say anything, because I'm not even sure if I want to do anything with the thing."

Deborah nodded. "I won't say a word, but I totally want to read it, once you've edited it, and you feel ready."

"If and when I reach that stage, you'll be the first to know. And, if I only ever let one person see it, it will be you - although probably, I'll also show Charlotte, because she knew I was writing it."

The subject of my book couldn't be continued, for which I was thankful - because Gemma returned with baby Selina.

Closely followed by Matthew. Finally. And, of course, whatever else was going on, I was thrilled to see him.

Still, after the initial elation and hugs: "Matt, what's going on with Danny and Hannah? And where *is* he?"

"I can give you the address, if you want to go over there," he said. "If you think you'll have more success than the rest of us."

"I certainly intend to try. But can you fill me in on some of this first? What happened? Why did Hannah kick Danny out, and why is Josh with Hannah's mum?"

"You know, we've all missed you so much, Luce. You *are* going to stay, aren't you? You could get your own place here - maybe share with Charlotte or something. It's so obvious this is where you're meant to be."

"We'll talk about that later, okay? Now, the deal with Danny and Hannah...?"

***

I stepped out into the sunny afternoon. Was heading in the direction of Charlotte's car.

"Lucy?" A familiar voice.

"Phil."

He indicated for me to follow him, around the side of the flats, where we sat on a bench, opposite the newsagent's, chemist, and chip shop. "I didn't expect to see you here," he admitted. "You look amazing, by the way."

"Thanks."

"So, you've seen Hannah? Is she all right?"

"Yes, I'm hoping so. I brought Danny to see her."

Phil frowned. "Is that such a good idea? You do know about him and his ex, and everything that happened? I'm going in there - check she's safe."

I grabbed his arm. "Please, Phil. I'm asking you to leave it. Melanie's gone, over a week ago. Danny isn't interested in her, not really. He knows he messed up, but all he wants now is his wife and kid."

"You do realise your brother's probably back on drugs? You, of all people, know the implications of that."

"He isn't on drugs. He told me that, and I believe him. And, as you pointed out, I ought to know something about that." Phil looked unconvinced. "Look, I'm not saying he hasn't been on a bender, with the drink, and I know Mel...Anyway, it doesn't matter, because Mel's gone, and she isn't coming back. And Danny and Hannah need to talk."

"She's been a complete mess, since he walked out."

"Since she *threw* him out. But, yes - I know. She was in bed, when we arrived. And I can't believe she let your mum take Josh. Hardly something Hannah would do - at least, not the Hannah I remember. You know as well as I do, Danny and Hannah belong together. Danny, Hannah, and their son."

Phil nodded. "All right. We'll give it a few minutes. But then, I'm going in. She *is* my sister."

"Thank you."

"She *was* becoming obsessed with Josh - increasingly overprotective. Mum always thought she'd improve, as he got older." He hesitated. "Sarah's not much better with Caleb, but then, she has other issues and..." But my expression begged him not to continue.

He took my right hand, noting the emerald ring. Deb had noticed too, and probably Matt, but they hadn't mentioned it. Phil didn't say anything either, but the gesture had been enough.

I'd primarily kept it in a locked drawer, for precisely six months. Worn it on a chain around my neck, on a couple of occasions. On the six month anniversary, I'd started to wear it - but on my right hand, not left. Not an engagement ring.

"How are you, Luce? And I mean, really."

"I'm okay. Look, Phil - I spoke to James. About Sarah."

"And he told you there's nothing between them?"

"Yes. I take it you don't believe that?"

"I don't think James is seriously interested in Sarah. But something *did* happen, and she likes him. She isn't interested in me any more, so it makes sense. We've got Caleb, but there aren't likely to be any more children."

"Get real," I said. "This is Sarah we're talking about. She always used to say she wanted six to eight, and it wouldn't surprise me."

"Six to eight kids? Yeah, well - let's hope she gets them, but it won't be with me. She won't let me near her. And it's reached the stage...Look at me, Lucy - please."

I met his gaze. "Maybe you should check on Hannah, as you said."

"No, you were right. Danny and Hannah will be fine. We both know that. It's always been you, Luce. I couldn't compete with your alternating obsessions with James McIntyre and Kev Tanner. But things have changed now. Our letters, and the phone calls - we really connected. Tell me if I'm wrong, and I'll leave it alone, but I've still got feelings for you, and I think you feel the same."

"You're wrong," I said, but without conviction.

"Really?"

And I returned his kiss, with sufficient passion to be its own response.

"Okay, no - you're not wrong. But this isn't happening - you and me. Not now. You're married to my sister, and you have a son. Whether Charlotte decides to stay or not, I'm going back to

Bournemouth. Maybe I'll rent a flat there - buy, even. I'm twenty-seven, and I've never lived on my own."

"I'll come with you."

"Not happening, Phil. It's the easy way: jumping from one relationship to another. People do it all the time, and occasionally, maybe they do end up happier. Mostly, not. And people get hurt and discarded, in the process. You've got a better chance of happiness with Sarah than me - and Sarah's the one you married, and mother of your child."

"Luce..."

"Charlotte's waiting." I stood. "I'll probably be leaving in a day or two, but I'm hoping this time, I'll stay in touch more - with everyone. Come back, now and again. Once I'm in my own flat, you should come to stay, with Sarah and Caleb. I hardly know my nephew, and that isn't right."

"You think that will end well: Sarah and me, and our little boy, coming to stay with you?"

"Sure," I said, even though we both knew it wouldn't be happening. "'Bye, Phil. Give Danny and Hannah my love."

In case I didn't see them again, before I left? Was that what I'd meant?

I'd ask Deborah to keep in touch with James and Claudia. She and Claudia both had baby girls, and Deb had emphasized how much she liked James's wife. I was concerned about James - and Deborah too, in different ways. And I hoped they could support each other, when I wasn't around.

I wondered whether it would be another three years. Why home didn't feel like home any more. I would be back, when necessary. For as long as necessary.

But you can't turn back time, and I had a future to think about. My future. Twenty-seven wasn't old. I needed to be somewhere I could breathe, and work towards making my own dreams come true.

Yeah, my writing. I would focus upon that. Living by the sea, and writing novels and poetry.

"You took your time," said Charlotte. "I know you were talking to Phil. I saw you wander off with him."

"Yes, that's right. I was talking to Phil." Responding to my friend's words, whilst ignoring her tone.

"And?"

"And nothing. We talked for a few minutes, that's all. I wanted to speak to him, before I left. Probably tonight."

"Tonight? I don't know if I want to go back so soon. Or at all, to be honest."

"That's okay, but I do. To Abigail's initially, and after that, I hope to get my own place. It's about time."

"You haven't seen your mum and Jessica yet."

"I know. I'll pop in there, on my way. I'll probably see if Matt or Danny can drive me. Ideally, both of them will come, and possibly Sarah. It would be great to spend some time with them."

"I could come along, too. Then again, not sure I trust myself around Matt, right now. I'm on the rebound from Tara."

"Yeah, and you've always fancied Matt." I giggled. Then, more seriously: "You haven't heard from my cousin at all?"

"Not a word, since she walked out. I guess she's with Amanda, and I wish them both well, but she could have said something - given a forwarding address or phone number. She definitely hasn't...?"

"No, nothing. Uncle Mike knew more, but he wasn't saying. Charlotte, you know - you need to give Horace a chance. Your mum deserves some happiness, too. And you know you'll always come first."

"Yeah, I know. But, honestly, Luce: Horace? I *ask* you. Surely she could've found a guy with a less embarrassing name?"

"I doubt if he got to choose his own name, Charlie. That would have been down to his parents."

"He could have changed it by Deed Poll - and, if you ask me, he lives up to his name. But yeah, I'll give him a chance. You can, too. I take it you're having tea with us tonight, before you up and leave again? In which case, you get to meet Horrid - sorry, *Horace*."

And, with that, my friend started up the engine.

Milton Keynes UK
Ingram Content Group UK Ltd.
UKHW010802080923
428296UK00001B/89